THE LOST MINE MURDERS

A JOHN GRANVILLE & EMILY TURNER HISTORICAL MYSTERY

SHARON ROWSE

THREE CEDARS PRESS

The Lost Mine Murders
A John Granville & Emily Turner Historical Mystery
By Sharon Rowse

Published by Three Cedars Press
www.threecedarspress.com

ISBN: 978-1-988037-15-8

ALSO BY SHARON ROWSE

The John Granville & Emily Turner Historical Mystery Series: (in order)

The Silk Train Murder

The Lost Mine Murders

The Missing Heir Murders

The Terminal City Murders

The Cannery Row Murders

The Hidden City Murders

The Barbara O'Grady Series: (in order)

Death of a Secret

Death of a Threat

Death of a Promise

Death of a Shadow

Death of a Lie

Death of a Dream

Want to know out more? Or be the first to find out when Sharon's next book is coming out?

Check out her website: www.sharonrowse.com

For my parents – with love

1

SATURDAY, DECEMBER 30, 1899

John Lansdowne Granville eyed the grimy old man standing in the middle of their newly decorated office. His feet were defiantly planted and rain dripped from the brim of his hat. Between his dark scowl and surly attitude, Marty Cole wasn't exactly their ideal client. Especially given the fellow's questionable reputation when it came to fair dealing.

Granville glanced over at his partner, Sam Scott, and the big man gave him a wry grin and rolled his eyes. Business was slow as the new year loomed, and they needed to build their new firm's reputation somehow. But this particular case didn't sit well with either of them.

"So why hire us?" Granville asked their would-be client.

"You're detectives, ain't you?" Cole ran a rheumy eye over them. "You look like you c'n take care of yourselves. And rumor has it you know a thing or two about mining.

He coughed, a deep hacking sound, then stared at Granville. "And since you're gentry, I figure you won't try to cheat me."

Which showed how little the fellow knew about the English nobility. "Where exactly is this mine?" Granville asked.

"Out past Pitt Lake. I figure it'll take us two, three days to get there. More if the snow's drifted."

From Vancouver, at this time of year? Granville didn't know the Pitt Lake area, but he suspected it would take a longer than Cole was telling them.

It might be raining in town, but the nearby mountain ranges had been buried deep for weeks. And their Klondike experience had taught both him and Scott never to underestimate winter snow in the mountains.

"Why not wait till spring?" Scott asked. He stood with one shoulder leaning against the wall, deceptively casual.

Cole shook his head. "I want to get that claim staked and registered before anybody else happens on it. No-one'll be getting in ahead of us, not this time of year." He chuckled wetly and spat.

Granville stepped back as the stream of tobacco juice barely missed his feet. He'd met Cole's like before, prospectors who'd spent years chasing rumors of gold—and finding it, wouldn't breathe a word to a soul before the mine was safely registered. So why was he telling them all of this now? What did the fellow really want?

"And what role would you see us playing?" Granville asked.

"You know something about locating mines. Plus you're witnesses, ain't you? And protection, in case anybody gets ideas. Specially since I'll be bringing the gold out."

"This time of year? How do you figure on doing that? Everything's frozen solid. You'll get nothing out of the ground or the streams now," Scott said.

"Do I look fresh off the train to you?" Cole said. "I'm not planning on digging it out. There's a cache, ain't there?"

Granville and Scott exchanged glances. A cache? That was unusual. So who had mined it? And if there was enough gold already out of the ground, why hadn't Cole already staked his claim? Something was wrong here.

But the unwritten rules of the miner, learned the hard way on the frozen creeks of the Klondike—don't ask, don't tell—kept them from asking outright.

"How do you plan to bring the gold out?" Granville asked the old miner instead.

"Don't plan on taking much this time—just what a couple of pack mules can carry."

So how much gold had already been mined? Granville's eyes met Scott's, and his friend shrugged.

"Assuming we were foolish enough to sign on for this adventure of yours, what would it be worth to us?" Granville said, still trying to get a read on their would-be client. "We'd expect adequate compensation for the hazards, of course."

"Course." Cole rubbed gnarled hands together.

Granville noted the fellow had lost the fingertips on his right hand to frostbite. He obviously knew the dangers of undertaking a winter expedition, but gold hunger could trap even the wariest.

"You and your partner here will be entitled to as much gold as you can carry out between you," Cole said. "But only on the first trip."

"The cache is that large?"

Cole nodded, but there was a furtive look in the old man's eyes that Granville didn't like.

It sounded too good to be legitimate, especially given the lies and half-truths the old man was trying to slide by them. Under truly bad conditions, they might be able to bring out almost nothing. He'd known miners lucky to carry each other out.

Before he could speak, Cole smiled, showing long, yellowed teeth. "Too smart to miss the problems in my offer, are ya? And not greedy enough to think you can overcome them. That's good, that's good."

He looked from Granville to Scott and back. "So I'm also offering five percent of the profit of that mine, for as long as I mine it."

"What if you sell it?" Scott said, frowning at the old miner.

"Said you were smart, didn't I? If I sell, you get five percent of the sale."

Cole had sweetened it too much. He was too seasoned a miner to offer more than he had to. And, rumor had it, too cheap to spend a nickel he didn't have to. He had to be desperate to make such an offer.

"If this mine of yours is as rich as you say it is, that's a lot of money," Granville said. "Why are you willing to pay us so much?"

"Because without your help I might be lucky to get the gold out at all."

"Why is that?" Scott asked.

"Storms c'n be pretty bad up there," Cole said, but his eyes shifted away from theirs.

Granville didn't think it was weather the old miner was worried about. "Is someone after this map of yours?"

"Hope not."

Which meant they were. Granville scanned Cole's weathered face, but the old man's expression gave nothing away.

"If we're so important, maybe we should get more of the profits," Scott said.

"You want to stay on, help me work it?" Cole asked.

Granville caught Scott's eyes, and raised an eyebrow. Scott's grimace had him grinning. They'd both had a bellyful of groveling in the dirt and the cold. Gold fever had been frozen out of them long ago. "No thanks."

"Then you get five percent. It's good pay for a week's work."

Too good. "If we find this mythical mine of yours. If not, I assume we get nothing?" Granville asked, curious to see how far the old man would go.

"See, I said you warn't stupid," Cole said.

At least the old miner was honest about that. "Then why come to us with this job?" Granville asked. "You must have known we wouldn't be foolish enough to take it on."

"It's just a week, Granville. And we have the time," Scott broke in.

Where had that come from?

"I'LL NEED a moment to discuss this with my partner," Granville said as he ushered their would-be client back into the waiting room his fiancée Emily Turner had decorated for them. Walls papered in a soft cream with a faint blue stripe, a gently faded oriental carpet and upholstered mahogany chairs spoke of the success they hadn't yet achieved.

Closing the door, he looked over at Scott. "You really think we should take this on? Even if the mine is real, it may be impossible to find."

Scott's face took on a closed look. "We know something about looking for mines, and we've nothin' better to do until we get word from Denver. If we do find it, that kind of money would give us a solid start. And it might come in handy in finding little Sarah. So why not?"

His partner's voice had a reckless edge and a hint of desperation to it that Granville didn't like. They'd never talked about the fruitless search the two of them had made through the back alleys of Denver a few weeks before. They'd been searching for Scott's baby niece—abandoned by her unscrupulous father nearly three years before—and their inability to find her had hit both of them hard.

That failure and their fear for the child hung heavily between them. And hope for new information on the little girl's whereabouts diminished with each passing day.

"We haven't got a stellar record for actually finding mines," Granville said. "And Cole is lying to us. He's worried about protection from more than the weather."

"We're both decent shots," Scott said. "And this beats the boring jobs we've been offered. I'm willing to risk a week on a gamble like this one. We've nothing to lose."

"Nothing except our lives," Granville said with a grin that covered his concern at the fatalistic note in Scott's voice.

He'd known anxiety over little Sarah's fate was taking a toll on Scott. But he'd had no idea it was this bad. Perhaps searching for Cole's lost mine would provide a distraction for his friend.

"But we'll do it, right?" Scott asked.

"Yes. We'll take the job," Granville said, making a split-second decision. There was nothing either of them could do for little Sarah without more information, anyway. And at least this job would give Scott something else to think about.

"But only if this map of Cole's is good," he added.

"Alright then," Scott said with a wide grin, and opened the office door.

FIVE MINUTES LATER, the three of them were poring over Cole's map. The fellow had put up an argument against sharing it, but when Granville stood fast, he'd caved in.

Nearly illegible in places, the hand-drawn map was rain spattered and frayed around the edges and along the folds. It was dated 1889, or maybe it was 1896—the last digits were smudged. It was signed, too, but the ink had run and the scribbled signature was nothing but a blur.

Fading blue lines showed what Cole said was Pitt Lake and a long funnel-shaped valley with a stream meandering through it some distance beyond. Gold deposits were marked along the stream at the narrow end of the valley for what looked to be a good fifty yards.

The main landmarks on the map were a couple of steep mountains, the valley itself with the lake and the river beyond it and a formation to the west of the valley.

Scott peered at the yellowed paper. "Is that a hill?"

"It's a triangular rock, ya fool," snapped the old man. "Anyone can see that."

"How do we know this map is authentic?" Granville asked.

"It's real," their new client said.

"We'll need more than that. How did you get it?"

"James, my late—partner," Cole said.

It was a very slight hesitation, but Granville and Scott exchanged wary glances. "Is James his first name or the last?" Granville asked.

"Last."

"How'd he die?" Scott threw at him.

"Gut shot. Near dead from blood loss when I found him."

"But he still had the map?" Granville asked.

"Yeah."

"And no-one knew he had it?" Granville said.

Cole looked at him like he was an idiot. "Folks knew, or maybe just suspected. Why d'you think he was shot?"

"Then how come the map wasn't stolen when this partner of yours was killed?" Scott asked.

"Poor shot from a distance," Cole said. "He told me he crawled away, and they couldn't find him."

"The killer couldn't follow the trail left by a badly wounded man who was bleeding heavily?" Granville said.

"I got to him first," Cole said, sliding a glance at Granville.

"I see," Granville said neutrally. All those years of playing poker were serving him well with this client. "So whoever shot your partner knows you have the map now?"

Cole shrugged. "Maybe, maybe not. They didn't see me, and I covered my trail."

Right. Granville didn't believe the old man for a moment. But this was clearly all they'd get out of him for now. "What makes you so sure the find is worthwhile?"

The old man looked from Granville to Scott, then reached into his pocket and pulled out a grimy, creased leather bag. Mutely he spilled a plum-sized nugget into his palm and held it out to them. Pure gold, with rounded edges and white quartz veins.

"Holy Christopher!" Scott exclaimed, bending closer. "How long have you been carrying this without cashing it in?"

"There were two. The other was even larger. That one I cashed to pay expenses."

"James gave them to you?" Granville asked, extending his hand.

The old man closed his own hand protectively for a moment, then dropped the nugget into his palm, nodding as he did so. "Yeah. He'd—no kin."

Cole's words didn't match his tone. Granville studied the old miner's expressionless face for a moment, then looked at the nugget, hefting it in his palm. There was no doubt it was genuine—soft, nearly pure gold.

If there truly was a mine this rich, even five percent of it would be worth a fortune. For a moment, a vista of all the things he could do with that much money unrolled before him, and he felt gold madness grip him once again. Then sanity prevailed.

Cole was too eager to give away a fortune. Just how deep did his lies go?

Whatever he was keeping from them, Granville suspected it would be a problem before they were done. They'd do better to stay in town and wait for a lead from the police in Denver.

Beside him, Scott reached to take the nugget, and Granville reluctantly let it go.

"So you'll you hire on?" Cole demanded.

About to say no, Granville glanced at his friend's tense expression—and the way his hand gripped that nugget—and changed his mind. For Scott's sake, it was worth the risk.

"Yes, we'll do it," he said. "When do we start?"

"If you have your own gear, then we just need to buy grub," Cole said. "We c'n leave tomorrow."

"I'm afraid not. I have a prior engagement," said Granville, with a flash of inner amusement as he thought about the upcoming New Year's ball, and about Emily. "I'll be ready to leave Tuesday morning."

2

MONDAY, JANUARY 1, 1900

"The Honorable John Granville and Miss Emily Turner," intoned the butler hired for the occasion. As they entered the crowded, high-ceilinged ballroom, Emily hid a delighted grin. Less than two weeks ago, she'd been locked in her room in disgrace, yet here she was at the Howe's "Turn of the Century" ball, on the arm of her intriguing pretend-fiancé.

Unlike her older sisters, she hadn't even planned a new dress for tonight, but after Granville announced their engagement, Mama had given her the gown for Christmas. In keeping with the occasion, her dress was pale green silk, with sheer lace sleeves and an elegant train that shimmered as she moved. She'd checked, pirouetting in front of the old cheval glass in the parlor when no one was looking.

The silk was from China, and came in on one of the *Empress* ships. It hadn't been made up, of course. Mama had to pay Madame Christina an outrageous amount for the three rushed fittings it had taken to finish it in time. Emily had always hated dress fittings—standing so still, being poked and prodded at—but this time it might have been worth it.

"What is *she* doing with *him*?" Emily could imagine the whispers behind the ladies' fans. Thank goodness their engagement wasn't real. She'd have felt like a sideshow act.

Mama kept giving her little looks to make sure she hadn't tripped over her train or something equally dire. Papa looked so proud, yet two weeks ago he'd forbidden her even to speak to Granville. Until he'd found out about his noble birth, that is. She shot a glance at Granville.

"Enjoying yourself?" he asked.

"Immensely," she said, surveying the room.

It was packed with the cream of Vancouver society, dressed in their finest, while maids in crisp black and white circulated with trays of champagne. Her eyes followed the whirl of colors on the dance floor.

"Usually I hate balls, but tonight feels different. Maybe it is because we are bidding goodbye to the century. And the music is superb, don't you think?" Emily said.

I'm babbling, she thought, but couldn't seem to stop herself. "I've heard there will be an amazing buffet. I'm particularly looking forward to trying the lobster patties and the cranberry fool."

"In the meantime, would you care to dance?" Granville asked. His tone was smooth but there was laughter glimmering in his eyes.

She flushed, and smiled back at him. "I'd love to. But you don't have to stay with me," she said in an undertone. "There are so many people here you haven't yet met. And we are only pretending to be engaged, after all. Until I finish my typewriting course and can earn my own living."

"Or until your father forgets you're in disgrace for helping me free Scott from a charge of murder," he said, whirling her into a waltz.

He bent his head down, lowered his voice. "But I'm enjoying your company."

"Thank you," she said, then was silent while he swirled her through a graceful turn. "We haven't had the chance to talk since you got back from Denver. Is there news of little Sarah?"

"Not yet. We're hoping one of the connections we made there will give us a lead."

She shivered despite the heat of the dance. "That poor child. Has Lizzie the papers for her?"

"Not even a record of her birth. And only the late unlamented Jackson's word that he left the baby in care in Denver." He was silent for a moment while he neatly avoided another couple and executed a truly masterly turn. "I'm beginning to fear he sold the child."

"But that's horrible! Do you think you'll ever find her?"

"I promised Lizzie we'd bring her daughter back."

The arms that held her so lightly through the dance tightened a little and his jaw firmed. Granville would keep his word, no matter what it cost him.

Just as he'd done when he cleared his friend Scott of murder. Emily gripped his arm a little tighter, sought a lighter topic. "And how are things with your business? Have you any new clients?"

He grinned.

"You do," she said. "Tell me."

But when she'd heard about their new client and his lost mine, her enthusiasm dimmed. She'd heard the stories of men losing their lives in those mountains. "You do know it's dangerous?"

A grin was her only answer.

The dance came to an end and he escorted her off the floor.

One of the maids stopped and proffered her tray. Emily gave the girl a quick smile as they each accepted a glass of champagne.

Granville raised his glass to her in a silent toast.

Emily could feel her cheeks heating, and hoped he'd blame it on the dancing. "This affair must seem awfully dull to you," she said quickly, "after all the grand balls you attended in London."

"Actually, I avoided most of them, and spent the better part of the ones I did attend in the card rooms."

"Truly?"

"Yes. The grander the ball, the more formal it is, and the more rules there are. Too much posturing for my taste."

"I know. It's fun to dress up, but none of this is real." She waved a gloved hand at the throng.

"You don't enjoy the dancing?"

Most men didn't dance as well as he did. "Yes, but I'd much rather have spent the evening skating, then stopped for hot chocolate."

"Then we must plan such an evening."

She flushed a little, but met his eyes. "You needn't pretend..." she began.

"Emily!" came her father's voice from behind her.

"...To agree if you don't," she finished quickly. Granville's eyes were glinting, the scoundrel. Removing her hand from his arm, she turned to face her father.

"Hello, Papa."

He gave her the slightly baffled look that said he thought he'd missed something. "Hello, puss. Are you enjoying your chat with your fiancé?"

"Enormously," she said. Beside her, she thought Granville choked on his champagne. Serve him right.

"And what are you discussing so earnestly?"

"We were talking about whether today is really the dawn of a new century," Granville said smoothly.

Here we go, Emily thought.

"Indeed it is, and it will be Vancouver's century," Mr. Turner said with the air of a true enthusiast. "We've electric streetcars and lighting, steam trains running clear across the continent. More settlers are arriving every day and real estate is booming. Who knows what might be ahead of us."

The same blond maid stopped beside them and held out her tray. Granville and Mr. Turner each accepted a glass of champagne. Emily still hadn't finished hers.

Turner raised his glass in a toast. "To progress," he said. Then catching the eye of an acquaintance, he gave them a nod and strode off. Emily and Granville exchanged glances.

"He's right, you know," Granville said softly. "Here we stand amongst the signs of progress," and with a wave he indicated the glittering crowd, brightly lit by the electricity that had so inspired Mr. Turner. "And the irony is, tomorrow I'll be tramping into a wilderness that hasn't changed in thousands of years."

"While I will be mastering the typewriting machines Papa says are changing the face of business," said Emily, watching his expressive face. "But then, that's why you're taking this job, isn't it? You appear entirely the polished sophisticate, but it's the wilderness that appeals to you, is it not?"

Granville looked into her eyes for a long moment, but before he could answer their hostess came bustling up.

"I must introduce you to the Seymours," she said, and the moment was lost.

3

TUESDAY, JANUARY 2, 1900

As he folded a pair of sturdy wool trousers into his knapsack, Granville thought about Emily's comment. Much as he'd hated alternately freezing and roasting with few comforts and less food while searching for Klondike gold, something about the vastness of the primitive landscape had fascinated him.

And here he was choosing to venture into another wilderness, with only the amenities he could carry on his back. From a tailed frock coat to a Mackinaw in one day.

He checked that both water bottle and whiskey flask were full. Shouldering the heavy canvas knapsack, he took a last look around the narrow, twin-bunked room he shared with Trent Davis, their assistant and would-be apprentice. He was glad he'd insisted the boy stay in town and keep the office open.

The lad meant well, but they were going into difficult country. With his enthusiastic, no-holds-barred approach to life, Trent would probably get himself killed. Though the boy probably had better wilderness skills than he'd had, arriving in Alaska with the social polish of a gentleman and little else.

He shook his head at the memory of eighteen months of lessons learned the hard way.

At least they wouldn't have to trek in a thousand pounds of supplies this time.

Pulling open the door, Granville came face to face with Trent. "What are you doing here?"

"I want to help look for the lost mine."

He glanced at his watch, flipped it closed. "Walk with me, but lower your voice. The shops on Water Street can barely keep up with the demand to outfit Klondike hopefuls, even now. One mention of a local mine and half of them will be following us instead."

"There're rumors anyway. People have been looking for that mine for years."

Granville settled his pack, turned towards Burrard. "Tell me."

"'Bout ten years ago, an old Indian named Slumach was hanged for killing another Indian. Later, people talked about how he used to come into town and pay for things with gold nuggets. Rumor was he drew a map to his mine before he died. A lot of folks looked for it, but no one found the mine. Or the map."

"Anyone know where the nuggets came from?"

"Nope. Old Slumach had a trap line, spent a lot of time in those mountains behind Pitt Lake. But my Pa talked to a geologist once, and the man said it was the wrong country for gold. Wrong kind of rocks, or something."

Granville nodded to an acquaintance on the far side of the street. The streets were still fairly empty—too much celebrating the night before. Which meant they wouldn't be overheard.

"Gold can be a funny thing," he said. "Sometimes it washes downstream for miles, sometimes it hides just under the surface. One stream bed can be rich with nuggets, while another just a few yards further down the mountain has nothing. Unless you look in exactly the right place, you don't find the gold."

"And you think your new client knows where the right place is?"

Granville shrugged. "He has a map."

"Slumach's map? Let me come with you!" The boy's eyes were shining. "I'm strong, and I work hard. Please, Granville?"

"Chasing gold this time of year is dangerous work. Ever been in the mountains behind Pitt Lake?" Granville asked, expecting to hear a no.

Trent gave him an odd look and a cocky grin. "Sure. Pa and I used to hunt there every year."

"In fall, perhaps. Mountains can be deadly in winter."

"It was winter. We was trapping weasel, and they sell for more after the fur turns white. It's a big area, but I know parts of it pretty good."

Granville gave him a considering look. In the month since they'd met, good food had filled out some of the hollows in Trent's face and he was starting to take on some bulk to match his height. His knowledge of the region could be useful—otherwise they'd be at the mercy of their client's knowledge.

Still, it was a risky undertaking—probably best to leave the boy behind. "We need you to wait on word from Denver."

Trent's face fell, but he nodded. "You'd best take the interurban tram to New Westminster, rent horses there. Central Livery on Begbie are honest and they've good stock."

Mentally saluting Trent for accepting his disappointment like a man, Granville picked up the olive branch he had offered. "On Begbie? Thanks."

"When d'you plan to be back?"

"No more than a week. We'll take enough grub for longer, though."

If there was one thing he'd learned on the creeks of the Klondike it was the danger of packing in too little food. The cold and the lack of amenities he could deal with, but he'd had enough of starving.

Trent was looking at the rifle strapped to one side of the pack. "You planning on hunting for fresh meat?"

"That's my intent."

"I'm a good hunter."

"Trent..."

"And I hate to miss an adventure. I could help. Really."

For a moment Granville wavered. He remembered being Trent's age and feeling exactly the same way when his older brothers forbade him to join the Hunt. "You're not good enough yet, John," William had drawled.

William was the Baron now, with a growing brood of his own. He hoped the years had taught his eldest brother to have more empathy in dealing with youngsters, but suspected they hadn't. He felt a flash of pity for his nephews.

In that moment, he nearly said yes to Trent's beseeching look. Then his gaze traveled to the shadows still evident under the boy's eyes and he thought better of his impulse. "No. It's too dangerous."

"I've faced danger in those mountains before."

There was something in that simple statement that stopped him. Granville looked hard at the youngster matching pace with him, saw the changes that presaged the man to come. The boy was growing up. He deserved the chance to prove himself.

"Right," he said. "You can come, but I'll need your word of honor you won't take foolish risks."

"You have it," Trent said, but the gleam in his eye almost made Granville regret his words.

TEN O'CLOCK FOUND TRENT, Scott and Granville still at the interurban depot on Carroll, anxious to be underway. Cole was late.

"Finally," Granville said to Scott half an hour later as they boarded the cream and olive car.

Scott grinned at him. "This isn't London, y'know," the big man said. "More than one train a day's a luxury. Few years ago, you'd be waiting until tomorrow."

Scott was definitely in better spirits today. He'd made the right decision in agreeing to this mad venture, after all. Despite Cole's lies. "I'm surprised Trent suggested taking the tram, then."

"You'd lose more time riding," Scott said. "This way, we cover nearly fifteen miles of very rough ground in less than an hour, courtesy of electricity, so stop griping. And you even had time for a second cup of coffee."

"You call that coffee?"

Scott's grin widened.

Settling into padded leather seats, watching the gray, dripping forest fly by the windows, Granville had to admit Scott had a point. They'd be out in the damp and the cold soon enough.

Things went smoothly when they reached the terminus in New Westminster. Central Livery, just two doors down from the train station, was as clean and efficient as Trent had promised. Proprietor Pat Devoy quickly found four mounts for them, plus two mules for their packs. Running an expert eye over the animals' proportions, Granville was pleased to approve.

Each of the horses had good lines, strong teeth, and the thick coats that said they'd survive the weather. Even the mules looked healthy and surprisingly obedient, for mules. "We'll need them for a week, maybe longer," Granville said, with a nod of approval.

"Good enough. We need five dollars down per mount, two for the mules, and we'll settle up on your return," Devoy told him.

They'd been riding for more than an hour when the tiny hairs on the back of Granville's neck prickled. His hand went to the revolver that rode low on his hip, and he turned to look back.

It was drizzling lightly, and the flat light made it difficult to see any distance. They'd kept a steady pace along the flat lands bordering the Fraser and left the township well behind. He watched for a long moment, but nothing moved except a tug pulling a log boom down the river.

Scott and Trent both saw him reach for his gun and sat alert. Cole's eyes were watchful but not worried.

Granville nodded to them, tightened the reins and fell back.

Once the others had moved out of earshot, he listened hard, his eyes scanning the riverbanks and the woods beyond them.

Nothing.

No sound, no movement to explain the feeling of being watched. After a bit, he urged his mount forward and caught up with the others, though the uneasy feeling persisted.

Another hour's hard riding saw them reach the merging point of two rivers. Granville reined in and stared at the water stretched wide and flat before him.

The Fraser was a muddy brown, slow moving and dotted here and there with chunks of ice that must have broken off somewhere further upstream. The second river flowed a deep blue-green, its faster current spreading into the brown of the Fraser in drifting patterns.

"That's the Pitt," Trent said, pointing to the blue water. "We follow it north and east."

His eyes followed the river upstream. The land was marshy, the banks low, covered in long grass and brambles and edged with poplars and firs. The curve of the river and the height of the trees screened any hint of the mountains they were heading for. "Which bank?"

"The south. North bank's steeper," Trent said. "We'll have to cross the Pitt on the railroad bridge and the horses won't like it, but it's easier going later."

Granville turned to his client. "Does the map indicate the best way to the mine?"

Cole smiled, showing long yellow teeth. "Nope. Just shows where the color is, nothin' about getting there."

"Figures," Scott said, rolling his eyes at Granville.

Trent looked interested. "Can I see the map?"

Cole examined him up and down. "Can I trust him with it?"

"Yes," Granville said and Scott nodded.

Cole brought out the map, unfolded it. "Hold it careful," he said, handing it to Trent.

"Course," said Trent absently, his attention already on the yellowed paper with its faded ink lines. "This Pitt Lake?"

"Yup," said Cole.

Trent frowned.

Granville moved to look over Trent's shoulder. "What is it?"

"If it's where I think it is, it won't be easy to get in there. In summer it would take us a day, maybe two. This time of year, with the snow that'll have filled the valleys and covered over the trails, it'll take three at least, and that's just going in."

Granville grimaced, but he'd expected as much. "We have provisions for that long."

"And we can't take the horses."

"What?" Scott asked, riding up on Trent's other side.

Trent pointed to the section of the map bordering the mine's location. "It's too steep to ride with the ice that'll be on these trails. And see these hatch marks?"

"Yes."

"Ice fields. The horses can't cross them.""

"Can we leave them somewhere on the trail?" Scott asked.

"This time of year?" Trent shook his head.

Granville looked at Cole. "Is this true?"

"Maybe, maybe not. Prob'ly not worth risking it, though."

"And you couldn't have said something before we hired the horses?" In his annoyance, Granville's Oxford accent was more pronounced than usual.

Cole smirked. "We needed them to get to the lake."

"And what do you propose we do with them then?"

"Wal, we could leave them with the traders. Or the Indians."

"There's a Katzie village at the mouth of the lake, and a trading post a mile or so east, place called Port Hammond." Trent said.

What other little surprises did their client have in store for them? "Can we make either today, before the light fails?" Granville asked.

Trent nodded.

"Since it's closer, I propose we head for this Katzie village."

"No, we'll stop the night in Port Hammond. Have to camp, but at least we'll get a hot meal." Cole's tone was definite.

"Might I ask why?" Granville said.

"Why is my business. I'm payin' the bills."

Cole was up to something, but the more they learned about the man before they reached the wilderness, the better. "Port Hammond it is, then."

4

WEDNESDAY, JANUARY 3, 1900

Granville woke abruptly, disoriented. The scent of wet canvas, fresh mountain air and dirty socks was so familiar he half expected to pull back the tent flap and see the tumbled boulders and deep trenches of Stikine Creek. Then he remembered setting up the tents just beyond the cluster of wooden bungalows that constituted Port Hammond.

The town boasted a general store —where he and Scott had purchased snowshoes—a tavern, a livery stable and a Chinese laundry, strung along a main street built of rough logs. On the far end of the street, a red lantern hanging outside a double size cabin indicated the local brothel. All the necessities, he'd thought dryly.

Their client had handed his mount over to Scott and headed straight for the red light, answering the question of why he'd chosen to overnight here.

A snuffling sound had him turning his head to see Trent's tousled head. Their assistant had buried his face in a pillow he'd made of his shirt and sweater, and seemed to be having some difficulty breathing. Granville grinned, and tossed a wool glove at the boy.

Trent woke with a start and reared up, aiming his shotgun. The sound of a round being chambered echoed in the stillness.

The grin faded from Granville's lips. He kept underestimating the boy's survival skills. He held up his hands. "Easy there, Trent."

"Sorry." The boy lowered the shotgun. "Something hit me."

"You have excellent reflexes," he said, holding up the offending glove. "I won't make that mistake again."

Trent gave him an insulted look. "Out here I'm an adult."

Granville nodded in recognition. "Let's get some food into us, then break camp."

Trent grinned at him. "I get to cook, right?"

"Why do I think I'm going to regret that decision?

TWO HOURS later they were picking their way along the rocky, uneven lakeshore. Mist clung thickly to the water, limiting visibility to a few feet. Granville pulled the brim of his hat lower against the moisture that dripped from the branches of the huge cedar and pine trees.

Gradually a snowcapped range emerged, dark and intimidating against the bleak greenish gray of the lake and the white-gray sky. He nudged Trent. "I'd expected something similar to Mount Seymour, but these are mountains."

"Told you. Folks round here call 'em death traps. Supposed to be as bad as anything on the continent."

Granville looked again at the forbidding crags. "Why?"

"It's not just that they're steep. They're unpredictable—fog, blizzards, even ice storms coming off the glaciers. And that's in fall; this time of year it's even worse."

"Perhaps this year the weather will cooperate."

Cole, who'd obviously been listening, snorted loudly. "Only thing you can count on in those mountains is that it'll be worse than you expected."

Granville glanced over at their client. He seemed tense this morning, jumping at every sound, and deep lines bracketed his mouth. Had something happened in Port Hammond?

He'd known all along that Cole was hiding something, but it had seemed less important in mostly-civilized Vancouver. His hand fell to his gun, and he cast a wary eye around him. Picking their way along the lakeshore, they were easy targets. He'd have to keep a closer eye on the old man.

Granville turned back to Trent. "If it's so bad in winter, why did you and your father trap here?"

"The worse the weather, the better the pelts. The better the pelts, the more money we made."

"Hmmm. And yet you turned to a life of crime."

Trent flushed and glared at him. "I wish you wouldn't keep bringing that up."

Scott rode up on the other side of Trent. Leaning over, he said in a loud whisper, "The man has a strange sense of humor, but he has some tales he'd rather were not told. Ask him sometime about his dealings with Gipson, up in the Klondike."

Trent looked at Granville, eyes wide but a smile twitching at the corner of his mouth. "This is the Gipson we dealt with before Christmas? The one kept trying to kill you?"

"Yup. The one just got himself out of a jail term," Scott added.

"More like bought himself out of it," Granville said.

Trent's smile widened. "So, what did he do to you?"

"None of your business." He looked at Scott across the boy's head. "Thanks, partner."

"Don't mention it. Always happy to clear up any misunderstandings."

"You have dealings with Gipson?" the old miner's voice cut across their banter, hard-edged and suspicious.

"Not willingly. Why?"

"He's as crooked as they come."

"On that we agree."

Scott had been watching their client with narrowed eyes.

"Mayhap he's the reason we're going to be freezing our tail feathers off braving those mountains in January?"

The old miner just spat a chaw of tobacco into a nearby clump of reeds and quickened his pace.

Granville nodded to himself. Was George Gipson another piece of this puzzle? He didn't want any part of a scheme involving that weasel, but he was happy to be part of an enterprise that foiled the fellow's plans. With an inward smile, he whistled a few notes.

Trent gave him an odd look. "Pop goes the weasel?" he said. "Why ever are you whistling a nursery rhyme?"

Scott, knowing Granville's favorite term for Gipson, gave a bellow of laughter. "You think that's it?" he asked.

"I certainly hope so."

Trent was looking from one to the other. "I don't think it's fair you're keeping secrets."

Granville winked at him.

As they climbed, bare rock gave way to a cushioning layer of pine needles. It was warmer here—the trees sheltered them from the wind, though the treetops bent and swayed as the wind moaned through them. There was little undergrowth to hinder their passage, but huge roots ran everywhere, and the occasional deadfall probably sheltered the white weasels Trent talked about hunting.

Granville was awed by the size of the huge trunks surrounding them. This was virgin forest, and there was the same weight of age and long history here that he'd found in the Alaskan coastal forests. Oddly, it reminded him of parts of London, where whole districts dated back five hundred years or more.

He smiled at the thought—if England's history was in her buildings, Canada's seemed to be in her untouched land. There wasn't a structure in Vancouver built more than thirty years ago, yet these trees could easily be five hundred or more years old.

Trent's voice broke into his thoughts. "If you don't like weasels, how do you feel about cougars?" he asked, pointing upwards and to the left.

He scanned the clump of brush Trent indicated. At first, he

didn't see anything, then he caught the twitch of a whisker, the gleam of a golden eye. The big cat crouched motionless, blending into the browns and gray tones around it.

"Think he's hungry enough we look like prey?"

"Doubt it. But this late in the season, the mules might look like dinner," Trent said, raising his rifle as he spoke. He sighted, then shot.

"Ya missed him," Cole said.

"Nope. Just aimed to scare him. He's not good eating anyway."

"Fool boy," Cole muttered.

His words were followed by a sharp whine and a dull crack. Rifle!

All four pulled their weapons and hit the ground, tensed for the next shot.

Nothing moved. The only sounds were their harsh breathing and the sighing of the wind through the trees.

"Anyone hit?" Granville asked after a long, tense moment.

"My hat," Cole said, holding up that battered object, which now had a neat hole through the crown. "Damn hunters. If I hadn't bent to spit, would've been my head."

It was too near a miss to be accidental. Especially when Trent's shot had told them someone was here.

"Think they're after that cougar?" Scott asked, his face neutral but his eyes measuring their client.

Cole shrugged, but he was pale under the weathering and the grime. "Prob'ly. Might as well move into denser forest anyways. Harder to get hit by a stray shot there."

Cole set a fast pace, clearly familiar with the area.

There were no further shots, but Granville was uneasy, alert to every sound. He tapped Scott's shoulder. "You think Cole's trying to leave something behind?" he asked softly.

"Yup."

"Think it'll work?"

Scott patted his rifle. "I think I'll sleep with this beside me."

5

THURSDAY, JANUARY 4, 1900

Batting a cedar branch out of his way, Granville shifted the heavy pack on his back as he bent his body into the hill. The faint track they'd followed was lost under the snow, and icy patches made the footing treacherous. He drew in a breath and watched it puff out in little clouds.

It was cold, a damp cold that seemed to have settled in his bones, still stiff from sleeping with nothing between him and the snow but the canvas of the tent and his bedroll. They'd been forced to camp when the light failed in the late afternoon, and had been underway since first light.

He glanced behind to see Trent toiling up the slope, leading the two mules. Scott and Cole were ahead, the old miner keeping to a fast pace despite the deepening snow. For all his years, he seemed fit as a mountain goat, and as at home here.

Granville was keeping an eye on him. There was a nervous alertness about their client he didn't think was entirely due to their environment.

There'd been no repeat of yesterday's shooting, and they hadn't caught sight of anyone since. Still, he was uneasy. Scott was, also. The alert angle of the big man's head signaled his watchfulness.

Cole stopped at a fairly level spot and raised his arm to signal a break.

Good. That would give him a chance to check the map, see how far they'd come. He could see Scott rummaging in his pack for hazelnuts and dried fruit.

A soft whoosh of displaced air from behind alerted him and he swung, gun drawn.

And found himself staring into the beady black eyes of a small white and gray bird. Tufted head aslant, it was perched on a branch no more than two feet from him, eyeing him closely.

Another landed a foot from the first.

A quick glance showed him a half dozen birds forming a rough circle around the four of them.

Scott was putting up his rifle with a sheepish look and Trent was laughing.

He gave the boy a glare. "It's not that funny."

"Your face, Granville, your face. If you could just see it," Trent gasped out.

"What are they, anyway?"

"Whiskey Jacks. Seem to know when there's grub to be had," Cole said.

"Were they following us?"

"Yup."

Perhaps the birds explained the uneasy feeling of being watched he'd had all morning. "They expect us to feed them?"

"Sure. Here, take this." Trent handed Granville a half slice of dried apple. "Stretch out your arm with the apple on your palm and don't move."

Granville just looked at him.

Trent grinned widely. "Try it."

With a shrug, he did. For a moment nothing happened, then a Whiskey Jack appeared on his hand, tiny black claws gripping delicately. For a long moment man and bird eyed each other, then the small bird picked up the apple in one claw and was gone.

Granville looked up, met the boy's dancing eyes, and smiled back at him.

"Let's eat," he said. Inside he was reliving that moment of connection with the wild thing that had perched so confidently on his hand a moment ago.

He'd never felt anything like it.

They ate quickly, then scattered a few crumbs for the birds. He sauntered over to where Cole stood scanning the path they'd just climbed. "See something?"

Cole jumped. "Nope. Nothin' at all."

So what was Cole expecting to see? Or should that be whom? "I'd like to have a look at the map."

Grimacing, Cole reached inside his layers of wool and pulled out the waxed oilcloth pouch he'd hung around his neck. He unfolded the map with care, bent over it.

A stubby, black nailed finger traced a path to just over halfway around the west side of the lake. "We're 'bout here."

Granville and Scott exchanged glances.

"That's all?" Granville said.

The arduous progress they'd made took up less than three inches on the map. "How long do you think it'll take us to get there?"

"We can maybe camp there tonight," Trent said from where he'd been peering over Granville's shoulder.

"Prob'ly. Less'n we run into an ice storm or somethin'," Cole said.

Or something. Granville cast a quick glance down the trail behind them. Nothing moved, but he couldn't shake the uneasy feeling of unseen eyes, evaluating every move they made.

Emily stood one tiptoe in front of the bureau mirror and tugged at her long skirt, straightened the front of her white shirtwaist. There!

She was ready, and as neat as she was ever going to be. Tucking a stray strand back into the tight bun at her nape she took a deep breath. It was time for her third day of learning stenographic skills. She just hoped it wouldn't be as bad as the first two.

"Emily? Oh, there you are, dear. And don't you look—efficient." Her mother's eyes softened and she reached out to tuck that stray curl of hair back into place again.

"I don't know why you want to study business so much, dear, especially now you're engaged to Mr. Granville, but you certainly look the part." She stepped back and looked her youngest daughter up and down, nodding briskly. "Yes, very nice. I'm sure you'll be the top of your class."

Emily gave her a smile that she hoped looked genuine and nodded.

She doubted she could say anything without revealing the anxiety clenched in her stomach. And she needed to leave before her too astute mother noticed.

On Tuesday, setting off for her first day at the Pitman Business College, Emily would have been thrilled with her mother's belief in her. Today she had the memory of those awful moments when half a dozen of the little metal bars of the typewriter had stuck together while her fingers jammed between the keys.

She hadn't been prepared for it to be so difficult.

Watching the typewriter in her father's office, his fingers flying, the clackety-clack of the keys so rhythmic as to be almost musical, Emily had expected to do that herself before long. Now she wasn't so sure.

For one thing, the layout of the keyboard made no sense. When she looked at a word and tried to reproduce it on the typewriting machine, her brain seemed to scramble. What her mind wanted and what her fingers produced had no relation to each other.

And her fingers still ached from striking each key with enough pressure to send the type bar flying against the ribbon, which transferred the ink to the paper.

She wasn't giving up, though. If men could learn to typewrite, so could she.

"You have your fare?" her mother asked.

Perhaps she had picked up on some of her worries. It wasn't like her mother to hover so.

"Yes, I'll be off now," Emily said, buttoning up her frieze jacket and holding up the coin with her brightest smile.

Two hours later Emily was too frustrated even to pretend to smile.

She sat in the midst of a sea of desks, each with a large black typewriting machine in the center of it. From all around her came the cheerful rattle of keys. Most of the students were men, all in dark business suits, but there was a scattering of women dressed exactly as she was. None of them seemed to have any difficulty in coaxing words out of the stupid machines.

She gritted her teeth.

"Is something wrong?"

Emily jumped. She hadn't realized that Miss Richards had come up behind her.

Evelyn Richards owned the school, together with her father Frank, and Emily admired her calm efficiency. She hated to admit that she couldn't get the infernal machine to work properly.

"Ah, I see," Miss Richards said as she bent closer. Was that a hint of laughter in her voice? Her deft fingers untangled the type bars, which plopped back into their rightful positions. "Start by typing more slowly. And keep your back very straight."

"But…" Emily began, looking at the flying fingers all around her.

"Learning to typewrite is like any skill. You have to progress at your own speed."

But Emily's speed was a breakneck pace. She'd never had to slow down before. How could typewriting be so difficult? And why wouldn't her fingers obey her?

She let out a little sigh of sheer frustration.

Miss Richards smiled. "Believe me, I know. I used to be the slowest typewriter in my class."

"Truly?"

"Truly. But I persevered, and so must you."

Emily nodded.

As soon as Miss Richards moved on, she glared at the round metal circles with their black letters stark against a white background. "All right, keys," she muttered. "Let's see who will be master here."

An hour later Emily was seriously reconsidering her plans for her future. The reality of spending nine or more hours every day trapped behind a typewriting machine just like this one bore no resemblance to her dream of a meaningful life.

As if in emphasis, the keys jammed together. Again.

"Darn," she said under her breath. The highly improper exclamation helped release some of her frustration.

She was peering into the depths of the stupid contraption, having tried and failed to pry up the stuck keys, when a soft voice from behind interrupted her. "Excuse me?"

Emily half turned and smiled at the frail looking blond seated behind her. "Yes?"

"I'm sorry to interrupt you, but do you need help?"

"Yes, I'm afraid I do," she said, studying the delicate features and determined jaw of her classmate. "It seems to be permanently jammed."

The blond got up and leaned over Emily's typewriter. "I'm Laura Kent."

"Emily Turner. Forgive me, but you seem familiar. Have we met?"

"No, but I served you champagne at the Howe's ball."

Which meant they were from different social spheres. Not that anyone should care, in her opinion, but most did. She liked Laura's directness in simply telling her. "I hope you were able to enjoy some of the festivities?"

Laura's eyes widened slightly, then she smiled at Emily. "I

enjoyed the music and the seeing some of the gowns. And the fireworks at midnight were a treat."

"The supper was delicious, too. Were you able to sample some of it?"

Laura gave her a conspiratorial look. "Don't tell Mrs. Howe, but my favorite were the lobster patties."

She reached into Emily's typewriting machine and tweaked several keys. The clumped mass separated.

"Thank you. However did you do that?"

"It's a simple principal—the first keys you struck need to be separated last," Laura said.

She glanced around them, leaned a little closer to Emily and lowered her voice. "I saw you with Mr. Granville at the ball. You are engaged to him, aren't you?"

"Yes, I am," Emily said.

She expected Laura to ask why she was taking a typewriting course when she was engaged. Most businesses would not hire married women, after all. But the other girl surprised her.

"I think your fiancé might be in danger," Laura said.

"What?"

"Not here." Laura cast a nervous glance behind her, and Emily realized that several pairs of eyes were fixed on them.

"We're due for a tea-break soon. Can you meet me at the foot of the stairwell? We can talk there."

Laura gave her a quick nod and resumed her seat. The steady rhythm of keystrokes told Emily she was hard at work. And she had no difficulty keeping her keys unstuck.

Emily spent the next twenty minutes tangling and untangling her keys while she wondered about Laura and what she had to say.

EMILY HAD BEEN WAITING IMPATIENTLY for what felt like ten minutes when she saw her classmate cautiously descending the stairs.

Laura's step quickened when she saw Emily waiting for her.

"I'm glad you're willing to listen to me," Laura said in a voice just above a whisper as she reached the last stair. "I overheard several of the other students talking about your fiancé, and it sounded serious. I didn't know what to do, but I couldn't just ignore what I heard."

"What did you hear?" asked Emily, moving towards her and taking Laura's arm. Together they moved to stand looking out the narrow window onto Broadway.

"Several of the men were trying to impress Louise Markham. You know how they do."

Emily nodded. Louise was the class flirt, as blond as Laura, but with a shapely figure and an effervescent personality that mostly disguised a sharp eye and a sharper tongue. "Go on."

"Andy Riggs was saying how his father's about to become very rich as part owner in a gold mine, and someone else would do all the work."

And Granville was looking for a gold mine, but that was hardly evidence of anything, Emily thought impatiently. She made the kind of encouraging sound she'd heard her mother make when her sister Jane was babbling on.

"He was quoting his father, and he said," and here Laura's voice fell and deepened. "This time, it's the toffs'll do all the work, and us plain folk get the rewards."

She gave Emily a sidelong glance. "A lot of people still dislike Englishmen who live off their monthly remittance."

Laura was enjoying this, Emily thought. Was she just looking for a little drama in what might be a drab life, or did she really have information about Granville? "And you think this 'toff' is my fiancé?"

Laura leaned a little closer. "I know it is. Louise made some remark about you and your 'lordling'—they don't much like you, you know."

Emily did know. Several of her classmates clearly resented what they perceived to be her privileged position. If only they knew.

"So Andy Riggs gave her a little smile and told her not to worry.

'See how uppity she is when that fancy fiancé of hers doesn't come back from his little trip,' he said." Laura touched Emily's arm lightly. "I'm sorry. But I thought you needed to know."

Emily's mind was darting here and there, trying to judge how seriously she should take this purported threat, and what she could do about it. "Were there any details?"

Laura shook her head. "No. They stopped talking because we had to get back to class."

"And how did you happen to overhear all this?"

Laura flushed and looked down, brushing a tiny speck off of her navy skirt. "I was part of the group."

Emily admired her honesty, especially when it meant Laura was probably one of those who didn't much like Emily. It also made it more likely she was telling the truth. "Thank you for telling me. Was there anything else about my fiancé?"

"No, I'm afraid not. But if I do find out anything else, I'll tell you right away."

Emily wondered if Laura's emphasis came from guilt or a liking for being part of an unfolding drama. She'd have to find out, but she rather hoped it was the latter.

It made it less likely that Granville was truly in danger.

6

FRIDAY, JANUARY 5, 1900

"There!"

Granville squinted into the driving snow, trying to see where their client was pointing. They'd woken that morning to find a thick layer of snow covering their small tents, all but obliterating the landscape.

Seven hours of hard slogging, made somewhat easier by their snowshoes, had brought them to the top of this sharp ridge. He estimated they were some twenty miles northeast of the lake, looking down into yet another snowbound, v-shaped valley.

With a muttered curse, he adjusted the heavy pack on his shoulders. "How do you expect to find the cache in this weather?" he hollered against the wind.

Cole shrugged. "Don't see that's your business."

"It is if the rest of us freeze in the process," Granville said under his breath, feeling a warning twinge in the toes he'd once nearly frostbitten.

Scott's meaty hand came down on his shoulder. "Think the old geezer's still sane?" his partner muttered in his ear. "This is pretty bad."

"I was wondering that myself. He seems to be recognizing something."

"Damned if I know how."

Scanning the steep peaks rising on every side of him, Granville had to agree. "At least we've lost whoever was tracking us."

"You still think there's someone following us?"

"Yes. You?"

"Yeah."

Granville nodded. "And I think this storm's about to get worse. We'll need to find shelter."

"Looks like we're about to get out of the wind at least." Scott waved towards Cole, who had started descending into the valley far below them.

"Nope. Wind's worse down there. Whistles off the glacier and straight up the valley." Trent had come up behind them, obviously in time to hear Scott's last words.

"Wonderful."

The light was already fading by the time they made their way to the floor of the valley, but the mist had lifted. There might be a stream under the snow, but then again there might not.

Was this the destination they had been pushing towards?

Picturing the map in his mind's eye, Granville traced the steep sides of the valley, the stand of three pines to the right. He looked for the rough triangle the mapmaker had drawn beside the stream… And his eyes found a huge, roughly triangular boulder, covered in snow.

Maybe the old man wasn't so crazy after all.

Nudging Scott, he pointed out the snow-covered shape, and raised snow-crusted eyebrows.

Scott's eyes swept the landscape. He looked back at Granville. "Pay dirt."

"We'll see."

Trent came up behind them again. "What d'you see?"

Granville pointed out the mound. Trent's eyes followed the

pointing finger, and a grin split his face. "That's the mark on the map. We found gold."

"If the map is real," Granville said. His time in the Klondike had beaten the assumptions out of him.

As they watched, Cole reached the triangular boulder and crouched on the near side of it, brushing away snow. He bent closer, examining something. Standing again, he waved them on.

They set up the tents against the cliff, then rigged a spare piece of canvas in a rough lean-to against the near side of the rock. Lighting a small fire in its shelter, they picked up their shovels.

The ground they were digging into had been dug before but was still frozen hard. After nearly an hour of digging with only the flickering fire to cut the darkness, Granville's shovel hit something with a dull thunk.

His eyes met Scott's, and he knew without asking what his partner was thinking. Months of digging into frozen creeks and they'd found just enough dust to buy flour and lard. How ironic if they finally struck gold here.

Even if it was someone else's buried cache.

"Give it to me." Their client was at his elbow, almost dancing from foot to foot in his impatience.

"Trent, keep watch," Granville said, with a jerk of his head towards the front of the lean-to.

"Awww," said Trent, but did as he was bid.

Granville and Scott cleared enough dirt to see the edge of a grime-crusted flour sack. Each taking an edge, they gave a mighty heave and pulled it out. More lay stacked underneath.

Gold, Granville thought as he watched their client untie the first sack. The fire flickered richly off the large lumps that partly filled it.

He swallowed hard, and Scott's hand clenched on his shoulder. A claim yielding nuggets that size was as rich as any he'd ever heard of. And he and Scott held a five percent share of it.

He watched as Cole clutched the nuggets in gnarled fingers, his eyes gleaming avariciously.

At least they did if they made it out alive.

It was five minutes past twelve when Emily and her friend Clara Miles joined Tim O'Hearn at a small table in the back of Stroh's Tea Shop. Emily leaned her dripping umbrella beside the window and tucked her wet feet under the chair.

The restaurant was warm and bright after the damp grayness outside. She didn't recognize anyone at the nearby tables. In any case, the cheerful din of news and gossip shared meant their conversation would stay private. Good.

Despite her deep unease about Granville's safety, Emily smiled to see O'Hearn's eyes light up when they rested on Clara. Though Clara showed no outward sign of attraction to the young reporter, she'd gone to a great deal of effort to ensure that her new hat perfectly matched her outfit.

Emily looked from one to the other. They suited each other, and Clara was practically glowing. She hated to have to damp that glow with her news.

As soon as their tea, scones and sandwiches has been served, Emily took a deep breath and began. "Thank you for meeting me. I'm very worried about Mr. Granville and I need your help."

"What? Why?" O'Hearn asked, leaning forward.

Clara put her gloved hand over Emily's, squeezed gently in support and comfort.

"Before I tell you, you'll have to swear you'll not mention a word to anyone. Or write it," she said, looking directly at O'Hearn.

The reporter grimaced, then nodded. "What is it?" he asked.

"My fiancé is out searching for a mine. And I've been told someone is planning to ambush and kill him and his party," Emily said. It was hard to put into words the fear that had kept her awake all night.

Laura hadn't come back with more information, so Emily had

only her word that someone wanted Granville dead. “I don’t know whether to believe it or not,” she finished.

Clara’s blue eyes widened and O’Hearn’s hazel ones narrowed. “Searching for a mine?” he said. “Where? Not out beyond Pitt Meadow?”

“How did you know?” Emily asked.

“There’ve been rumors about that mine for years. Folk ‘round the area call it the Lost Mine, and a few prospectors have already lost their lives looking for it. Supposedly an old Katzie Indian named Slumach had a fabulously rich mine back in those mountains, but he was hanged in New Westminster for murder a few years back without disclosing his secret. And you say Granville’s gone looking for it?”

Emily nodded.

“This time of year? They’ll freeze to death,” O’Hearn said.

“He and Mr. Scott both spent time in the Yukon,” Emily told him. “I think they’re used to worse cold.”

O’Hearn didn’t look any happier. “Those mountains have a bad reputation amongst the old-timers. They call them killers.”

Emily felt the cold knot in her stomach get bigger at his words. “The mountains may not get the chance.”

“Who is planning the ambush?” Clara asked.

“I don’t know all the details, but the father of one of my classmates is supposed to be part of it,” she said. “Laura, another of my classmates told me about it.”

“Oh, yes. Your typewriting classes,” said Clara. “But how could she know?”

Emily flashed her friend a look. Did Clara resent her new studies? She’d never said what she thought of Emily’s desire to be a typewriter, which was unlike her.

“She heard the son boasting about it,” Emily said. “He didn’t give details—mostly he was showing off.”

“But you think it might be a serious threat to Granville?” O’Hearn had his notebook out.

"Yes. Yes, I'm afraid I do." And the more Emily talked about it, the more certain she was, and the more worried she became.

"If you tell me the name, I'll look through our archives, see if I can learn anything about the father and his associates," O'Hearn said.

"Andy Riggs was the one talking about it."

"But I know him," said Clara. "Or at least I know his father."

"You do? How?" Emily asked.

"Mr. Riggs and his eldest sons own the livery where we stable our horses," Clara said.

O'Hearn looked at her, his forehead creased. "Riggs? I've heard something about him recently. I'll look into it right away." He drained the last of his tea and put the cup down with a snap.

"Please hurry," Emily said as he put a few coins on the table and with an oddly formal half bow took his leave.

"And you'll go back to class and wait to hear from him?" Clara asked after he'd gone, raising her brows in mock surprise.

"Of course not. Since Mr. Riggs already knows you as a customer, you and I are going to rent horses."

"But I don't like to ride," Clara said.

EMILY STARED AT MR. RIGGS. All around her were the stompings and janglings of a busy livery stable. Men were saddling horses, harnessing buggies and negotiating rates. The mingled smells of hay and horse manure reminded her of trips to the country.

Emily, Clara and the proprietor stood in what seemed a small oasis of calm as he refused to rent them the horses she had requested.

"Sorry, Miss," he said, his eyes darting to her bare ring finger as he spoke, as if confirming her unmarried status. Her spinster status in his mind, she thought in annoyance.

"If your father'll sign for you, we'd be happy to provide our finest mounts. But legally, I can't rent to you." As you should know, his look seemed to say.

Behind the obsequious tone was an arrogance that reminded her of his son.

"I see," Emily said. "Would my fiancé be able to rent horses for me?"

"Of course. As long as he accompanied you ladies on your ride."

"Naturally. I'll speak with him on his return, then." Emily considered the man before her for a moment, then took a risk she knew Granville would be upset with her for.

But she couldn't picture this man being a threat to her, and she needed to *know*. "Perhaps you know him? Mr. John Granville?"

His face didn't change, but one hand jerked slightly, then tightened on the bridle he was holding.

"I'm not perfectly certain if it is this stable he usually deals with?" Emily said, smiling a blithely as she knew how.

"No, don't believe I've ever met the man. He new to town?"

Emily nodded, fascinated by the contrast between the empty face and the clenching and unclenching hand. "Yes, he is."

Riggs's eyes went past her. "Have him come see me then, we can arrange something. Now, if that's all…?" he said and began to edge them towards the door.

With a quick glance at the man who had just entered, Emily inclined her head in a passable imitation of Mama's most regal nod. "Good day," she said and swept out, gesturing Clara to follow her.

Unfortunately, Emily tripped on the lintel, entirely spoiling the effect of her exit.

"I don't trust that man," Clara said as they reached the board sidewalk outside the livery stable. "He has mean eyes."

Emily paused in the act of sweeping her skirts out of the mud and looked at her friend in surprise. Clara seldom took a dislike to anyone, but she was right about the man's eyes.

"He knows something," Emily said. "He obviously recognized Mr. Granville's name, but he wouldn't admit it."

Clara glanced at her. "I have an idea, but I'll need to talk to Mr. O'Hearn first."

Despite her growing concern about Granville, Emily couldn't resist teasing her friend. "Again?"

Clara smiled at her. "Indeed. I think we need a man's opinion before we do anything else."

"Mr. Riggs would certainly agree with you. And of course, this would have nothing to do with your desire to see Mr. O'Hearn again?"

"Naturally not. But since it was Mr. Gipson who came in, I think we need to share the information."

"That was Mr. Gipson?"

"Indeed it was," Clara said.

Emily considered the implication of this. "My father still thinks Mr. Gipson was wrongly accused, you know."

"My father thinks him guilty, but rather admires his smoothness."

"Hmmph. I'd call him slimy, not smooth," Emily said, but picturing the elegant suit and manicured hands of the man she'd just seen, she reluctantly admitted to herself that she could see why Clara's papa held the opinion he did.

"Shall we see if we can find Mr. O'Hearn at the newsroom?"

Emily was too busy calculating how she would get word to Granville to wonder about Clara's new decisiveness.

THE *DAILY WORLD* newsroom seemed even more crowded and noisy than usual. Brash voices and shouts of laughter echoed over the relentless clatter of typewriter keyboards. Every desk was filled, and a group of men stood over an old stove in the far corner, deep in conversation. Emily didn't see a single woman anywhere.

As they neared Tim O'Hearn's desk, Emily watched Clara's face. The reporter obviously did mean more to her friend than she had originally guessed. She wondered for a moment if her face was that easy to read when Granville was around, and rather hoped it wasn't.

O'Hearn looked up, saw Clara and beamed. Then he scrambled to his feet. "You'll never guess what I've uncovered."

Clara's dimples showed. "Mr. Riggs is in partnership with Mr. Gipson."

"How the blazes did you know that? I just found out myself because I checked the land titles and articles of incorporation, and that's da—darned tedious reading, let me tell you."

"We have our ways," Clara said in an airy tone.

Emily smiled at the baffled look on O'Hearn's face.

"Tell us about the articles of incorporation," Clara said. "Are these for the livery? Whatever made you think to look for them?"

He gazed into Clara's wide blue eyes, then looked down at the papers strewn across his desk with a visible effort. "Yes, they're for the livery. And it seemed the place to start—it's always interesting to know where the financing comes from."

"How did Mr. Gipson end up a partner in the stables?" Emily asked. "It seems an odd fit."

O'Hearn laughed. "He isn't exactly a partner," he said. "Word is that Riggs is rather fond of the cards, and lost pretty heavily to Gipson. Now Gipson holds the mortgage."

"Hmmm," said Clara. "So Mr. Riggs would have an incentive to participate in any business Mr. Gipson wanted him to."

"Exactly."

"We don't yet know that he did so," Emily said. "But if he did, how did he know there really is gold? And what are they planning?"

"You'd make a good reporter," said O'Hearn with a broad grin, tipping his cap to her. "I'll see what else I can find out."

"Thank you. If you need to reach me, we're on the telephone. It's 3079. Just tell them you're calling about my classes."

"Right." O'Hearn scribbled down the number.

Emily and Clara linked arms and strolled out. Clara's hand tightened on her arm. "Are you all right?"

"Yes, of course," Emily said.

"You'll call me if you hear anything about Mr. Granville?"

"Yes, I will. Or when I hear he's returned." And let that be soon, Emily thought. Please, let it be soon.

But it wasn't enough to sit and hope.

As she rode home on the streetcar, Emily mentally composed the note she would send to Granville. Caught up in her thoughts, she rode past her stop, and had to hurry back the extra two blocks to her family's home.

Dashing up the stairs to change for dinner, Emily stopped dead and stared at the dark shape lurking outside her room. "Bertie? Whatever are you doing here?"

"A telegram comes for Master Granville."

Emily's heart began to race. "For Mr. Granville? Where is it?"

Silently their houseboy handed her a folded yellow paper. Emily quickly opened it and scanned the terse message. "Have lead. Come at once. Harris."

Harris was the detective Granville had met in Denver, so this was about little Sarah. Had they found her?

She took a deep breath to steady herself. "I must get word to Mr. Granville as soon as possible. Bertie, Trent said you know a way?"

Bertie nodded, his long pigtail bobbing against the gray tunic he wore. "The cousin of my cousin is ancestor hunter. He leave soon for Hope, but for me he stop in Port Hammond."

"And Katzie, just in case."

"Yes."

Despite the urgency she felt, she was intrigued his words. "What is an ancestor hunter?"

"He look for the bones of Chinese who die while working on the iron road. The—remains?" Bertie stumbled over the 'R's.

Bertie's cousin was searching for the bodies of the men who had died building the railroad. Emily felt a shiver at the thought, but kept her voice steady. "Yes, remains is correct. But why?"

"To send home. Bones then given proper burial in the home of ancestors."

It seemed to Emily a gruesome thing to do, but obviously it was important to Bertie. She inclined her head, which could be taken as agreement or homage to the dead, then asked, "Can your cousin take the message tomorrow?"

"I ask."

"Thank you, Bertie. I'll write two copies of a note for Mr. Granville now, and give them to you after dinner.

Bertie bowed. Emily smiled her thanks then raced back down-stairs to search for paper, ink and a working pen.

7

SUNDAY, JANUARY 7, 1900

Granville's day started early, leading the heavily laden mules down the steep slope. His pack was heavy with gold, as was Scott's. It was an odd feeling to carry such a fortune. He'd known men's lives destroyed by half of what they'd brought out.

When he'd seen the glittering hoard in the firelight, little Sarah's rescue had been his first thought, the opportunity to really build a new life in this new land his second. Their fledgling business had possibilities, but no new enterprise succeeds without capital. Gentry or not, he'd seen enough fail to know that.

More snow had fallen overnight, and the limbs of every tree they passed hung low and heavy. The dry powder packed easily, crunching underfoot. Every now and then a fir would drop its burden of snow with a whump, leaving fine particles drifting and sparkling in the crisp air.

Knowing how much gold they carried, his every sense was tuned high.

The light was already failing and his shoulders screaming from the weight of the gold when the back of his neck began to prickle. Granville scanned the wall of trunks stretching off in every direction. The underbrush was too thin to hide much.

Nothing moved except the boughs overhead as the wind sighed through them. Even the whiskey jacks that had been following them earlier had vanished. He sniffed the air. Only the clean freshness of cedar and snow.

Quickening his pace, he moved into step with Scott and touched his arm. Gesturing towards the trees ahead, he raised an eyebrow.

His partner's eyes met his, then scanned the forest around them. Scott nodded once, his hand falling to his rifle. His partner was as uneasy as he was, and Scott's woodcraft skills were better developed than his own.

Glancing over his shoulder at Trent, Granville was relieved to see the boy was also alert, rifle at hand and eyes scanning the area ahead of them. Whatever was out there, the boy sensed it too.

Granville's eyes sought out their client. Cole looked tense, and his eyes darted back and forth.

They pressed on, moving as quickly as the deep snow, their heavy packs and the mules would allow. The track ahead widened and the trees grew further apart, with denser undergrowth and clear patches between.

Granville didn't like the look of it. Too much potential for ambushes.

He slowed his pace, fell into step with Trent, who was still leading the mules. "Is there another route when we get to the lake?"

Trent didn't take his eyes off the trail ahead. "No. Or at least, not one that makes sense. It's too steep, and if someone's following us, we'd be targets."

"I've a feeling we may be targets in any case."

Trent slung his rifle forward, a look of determination on his face. "There's four of us, armed."

"We can't shoot what we can't see."

"Then maybe they can't see us, either."

The boy could be right, though Granville doubted either of them believed it. It depended on how wily an attacker was, and how familiar with the terrain. "Wonder who Cole's told about his map?"

"You think it's the map they're after?"

"I think any hint of gold brings out the worst in my fellow man." Granville's eyes sought out their client. He and Trent were too far ahead of the other two. Before he could shout a warning, he heard a high whining sound above the sound of the wind, then a second.

"Get down," he yelled, pulling Trent down with him.

Ahead of him he saw the old miner stagger, then fall, with Scott right behind him.

Were they hit?

BRUSHING snow out of his eyes, Granville squinted towards where he'd last seen Scott and Cole.

Two forms lay dark and still against the white snow.

No!

He hadn't saved Scott from hanging just to see him killed by some petty thief.

"Anyone hit?" Trent asked, raising his head to look.

"Stay down," Granville snarled, pushing his head back down. "No point you getting shot too."

"Too?" Trent said. "You mean...?" His head was rising again as he spoke.

"Down, I said."

As if to emphasize his words, another bullet whirred just over their heads and vanished into the cedar boughs behind them.

A part of Granville's mind seemed to be standing to one side, watching calmly. He drew his revolver, took aim, fired. "I hope whiskey jacks know how to duck."

"Is Mr. Scott okay?"

Granville had seen no sign of movement from either man. "Just stay down. I'm going to find out."

Trent gave him a quick look, but said nothing.

Keeping close to the little cover available, Granville started towards the two still figures. He inched his way forward, braced for the whine of another bullet.

It didn't come.

What were they waiting for?

Glancing back, he saw Trent calmly aim his rifle and fire. Good thing they'd brought the boy along, after all. He kept crawling.

As he got closer, he saw Scott's head move slightly. Brown eyes met his. One closed in a wink.

A slight dip kept Scott and Cole out of his sight for a moment. When he could see them again, Scott was moving, taking advantage of the cover Trent had provided to drag their client behind a large boulder.

Granville released a breath he didn't know he'd been holding. If his partner was injured, it wasn't badly.

A bullet whined by and he ducked. That one had been too close.

An answering shot from Trent followed by a yelp had him grinning fiercely. "Good for you, boy," he said, resuming his slow progress towards Scott and Cole.

When he got close enough, he could see Scott was holding his red bandanna against their client's shoulder. Granville hoped the old man had been winged rather than something more serious.

Then it dawned on him that Scott didn't own a red bandana, just the large white one he used as a handkerchief. "Not good," he muttered, moving faster.

"How is he?" he asked when he was within whispering distance.

Scott just shook his head.

Taking in their client's pallor, Granville could see that. He reached for a wrist. There was a pulse, but it was thready. Shock. "Can you stop the bleeding?"

"Not so far," Scott said, pressing even harder against the old miner's shoulder. "The bullet may have nicked something."

An artery? Granville hoped not. If that was arterial blood, Cole was a goner. "Were they aiming for him?"

"Think so," Scott said. "I'm bigger'n he is, and he's the one got hit, so it's a good bet."

"The map?"

"It figures, doesn't it?"

Granville couldn't argue with that. It did figure. "Problem is, what do they do now? They can't get to the map without going through the three of us. Do you think they know about the gold?"

"Two heavily laden pack mules coming down where two lightly laden ones went up have to tell them something."

"Assuming they've been behind us all along. We'll be better off if they don't know about the gold. If they know, they'll never give up."

Scott nodded, his hand still pressed firmly against the old man's wound. "Yeah."

Two shots from above quickly followed by one from Trent suggested their attackers were growing bolder. "Can you tell how many there are?"

"Muzzle flashes from at least three locations," Scott said.

Which meant the bastards had them pinned, because they had the higher ground. In a fair fight, he'd be willing to bet on the three of them against any three villains, but...

"Make that four," Scott said as another bullet whined past.

"Damn." Out-numbered and out-maneuvered.

"Doesn't look good. Can you take over here?"

They switched places, Granville pressing the soaked pad against their client's shoulder while Scott unslung his rifle. A gurgling sound had him looking down. Cole was staring at him.

"I'm—still your client," he said in a voice so weak Granville had to lean closer to hear him.

"You are."

A bullet ricocheted off the boulder that sheltered them and missed him by less than a foot. Scott returned fire, then ducked and ran to take cover behind another boulder with a better angle.

Cole was still trying to talk. "Want to hire you—Five percent," he began, then stopped on a gasp.

The man's wits were wandering, Granville thought with pity. "You already did that."

"No—no, another ass—assignment. The map—the gold. You have to find…"

"We found the gold. Yesterday."

Cole somehow found the strength to glare at him. "I'm a goner—not an idiot." He gasped, choked a little. "The map—I'm hiring you—to find the rightful heir."

"You want us to find your heir?"

That earned him another glare. "Not my—heir. Rightful heir. Hire you and your—partner. For another five—percent of the mine. D'you—agree?"

He'd known their client was hiding something. Who had he stolen the map from, anyway?

But Cole was dying.

"You want to hire Scott and myself to find the rightful heir to your map. And you'll pay us another five percent of the mine if we do. Right?"

"Yes." It was a sigh. Then Cole seemed to gather his strength. Meeting Granville's eyes, he said clearly. "Swear you'll do this. Swear—on your honor—as a gentleman."

Granville hesitated, caught. If he swore such an oath, then he would follow through, no matter how difficult or dangerous the task became. He trusted their client even less than before. But the man had no time left.

"Swear," Cole said.

He needed more information before he committed to what could well be an impossible task. "Who is the heir?"

"James's daughter—Mary."

A woman? "How did James die?"

"My—fault. Please. Mary. She needs—the money. Swear."

A woman in need? How could he deny that request?

But Cole could have killed his former partner for the map and the gold. How could he be sure he wasn't lying now?

He met the old man's eyes. Saw the truth and the plea in them. "I swear."

"On—honor."

"I swear on my honor to find the rightful heir to the map. What was James's name? Mary's last name?" A gurgling breath was his only answer.

Cole's face had gone gray and his breathing was shallow gasps. Granville took the gnarled fingers in his own. "I need a name," he said urgently.

Blue-tinged lips tried to frame a word, then the hand fell limp. The light died out of the old man's eyes.

"Damn. Now we have to find a nameless woman," Granville said, closing the staring eyes. "Rest in peace, old-timer."

Scott fired off a shot, turned. "He's gone?" he asked, just loud enough for Granville to hear.

"Yes."

"Then let's get out of here. What'd he say to you, anyway?"

"You could say we have ongoing employment."

"Uh huh. That like the time you agreed to us digging the top part of Rabbit Creek, 'stead of the segment we were already working?"

A bullet whined overhead and both men ducked down behind the sheltering rocks. "Probably. But I think we should have this discussion later, don't you?"

Scott rolled his eyes, fired again, then glanced at their former client. "Do we leave him here?"

"He lied to us, and he killed his partner. Still, in the end he tried to do the right thing. And he was our client."

"Can't just leave clients lying about."

Granville ignored that. "We'll need somewhere to hide the body and the gold."

"You thinking a false trail?"

Granville nodded.

Reaching over, he removed the map pouch from around the dead man's neck and slipped it over his own head and down inside his flannel shirt. "I'll talk with Trent about hiding spots, you think of a distraction for these bounders. Cover me?"

"Done. Left."

Granville broke from behind the boulder, firing towards the shooters on the right. Behind him he could hear Scott firing at the shooters on the left and Trent, bless him, shooting at everything that moved.

Head down, body low to the ground, Granville sprinted back to where he'd left the boy. "We're getting out of here."

"About time," Trent said. "Is Scott all right?"

"Yes, but Cole's dead."

"Thought that fall looked pretty limp. So what's next?"

Trent didn't waste any time on sympathy for their departed client, Granville noted, once again aware of how different life had been for this boy than it had for him.

At Trent's age, he'd never seen violent death except on the hunting fields, and he'd hated watching the fox being torn to bits. The first death by gunshot he'd seen had been Edward, and that had sent him all the way to the Klondike goldfields. Three years later, the memory of his friend's death was still raw.

"We need a place to hide the body and the gold, and a distraction for our friends up the hill," Granville said. "Right now they have the advantage. We need to change that."

"Without gettin' shot."

"Exactly."

"Good idea," Trent said. "I've got a plan."

8

As the shadows thickened under the trees, Granville led the heavily laden mules back along their original route. Trent and Scott provided covering fire until he was out of sight. Angling away from the path, he began to climb, knowing the mules would protest. Loudly. Which they did.

Grimacing, he made his way further along the steep mountain-side. The occasional whine of a bullet told him he'd successfully drawn off their ambushers. Giving the other two time to hide the body. And the gold.

When he finally reached the cave Trent had described, Granville dumped the bags of rocks the mules had carried behind some scree along a back wall. Stretching out his aching shoulder muscles with a weary groan, he released the mules. They would make their own way down, and perhaps serve as further distraction.

Then he changed direction to race down a narrow almost-trail that would circle back to their rendezvous point.

An hour later it was clear there were a few holes in their plan. "Ambushed again," Scott said.

The three of them were crouched behind a low rock outcrop,

their pursuers well hidden on the treed slope above them. All of their exit routes were cut off.

"The mules didn't fool them long enough," Granville said.

"You think they know we found gold?" Trent asked.

"They certainly know about the map, and they'd have to be blind not to see the load the mules were carrying. Which makes them more dangerous."

"Why?"

Scott's eyes met Granville's over the boy's head.

"A gold map's no guarantee there's gold at the end of it. If we found gold, it means our map's real," Scott said.

"But the gold was already dug—we don't know for sure there's a mine there," Trent said.

"Yeah, but they don't know that."

"Together, the gold and the map are easily worth more than all three of our lives," Granville said. "If the fellows shooting at us are greedy enough, they'll keep the gold for themselves, and just forget to tell whoever hired them."

"I'll draw them off." Scott made as if to stand.

Granville held him down with one hand on his shoulder. "You're going nowhere."

"Even in this light, you're too big to miss," Trent said.

"I think that was rather the point," Granville said.

"Oh."

"You got a better idea?" Scott asked Granville.

Granville pulled out the etched sliver flask he'd carried with him since he left London and offered it to Scott. The big man grinned, saluted Granville with the flask and took a swig.

A line appeared between Trent's brows as he looked from one to the other. He started to say something, stopped, looked at Granville again. Finally he said, "Maybe there's a way out of this."

"Tell us."

"There's a ravine not far from here that most people avoid, and it'll get us out without them knowing. If we wait 'til full dark, we should be safe."

"I know I'll regret asking," said Granville. "But why do they avoid it?"

"The Katzie think it's haunted," Trent said, "and the rest of 'em think it's too steep to be safe."

"Hmmm. And is it?"

"I made it down once," Trent said.

Granville narrowed his eyes. "What aren't you telling me?"

"Well, I'd run out of bullets and a cougar was after me. But I'm sure I can find it again."

Granville turned to Scott, whose shoulders were shaking silently. "And what are you laughing at?"

"I'm not sure which is worse, being shot or using the lad's escape route."

"Well, if the escape route doesn't work, I'm sure they'd be happy to shoot us."

"Uh huh."

Trent was looking back and forth from one to the other. "Shouldn't you be more worried?"

"No point," said Granville, passing him the flask. "Have a drink. Waiting for dark is going to seem like forever."

Another shot came from above them. He returned fire.

"I'm down to my last box of cartridges," Trent said softly from his left.

Granville had been afraid of that. "How far is the entrance of this ravine of yours?"

"Not very far," Trent said. "But if we go now they'll see us."

"We'll have to make the bullets last, then," Granville said. "Try to space them out. It shouldn't be long now."

As the darkness thickened around them, he braced himself for a rush from above—it was what he'd have done—but nothing happened.

Maybe their pursuers thought they had them trapped, and were content to wait for dawn.

Maybe they hoped to freeze them out.

Finally it was too dark to see. The crackle of a branch underfoot had Granville bracing for a shot, then Trent's voice came softly. "It's me. Put your hand on my shoulder and I'll lead us down. Watch your step, it's steep."

"Right. Scott?"

"Behind you." A familiar hand came down on his shoulder, and Granville placed his own hand on Trent's shoulder.

It was cold, and as dark as the Yukon in the dead of winter. There was no light to reflect off the snow and every tree root seemed to grab at his feet. The damn slope was too steep to be going down blind.

Not that they had any choice.

Granville's foot slipped and he froze, tightening his hand on Trent's shoulder so that the boy stopped, too. He couldn't afford to knock loose anything that might make a noise and alert their unknown assailants. Still less could he afford to fall on a treacherous slope he couldn't even see.

Foot by excruciating foot, the three descended.

Granville couldn't fathom how Trent was managing to find a path for them, when even following in Trent's wake was challenging. Behind him, he felt Scott stumble more than once. Each time he tensed.

Scott was big enough that falling he'd take out the other two like bowling pins. Granville's lips twitched at the mental picture, while his left foot sought and found the next foothold. Mostly the snow had crusted enough to hold their weight.

Then his foot broke through and found ice. He started to slide.

Scott's hand grabbed his shoulder like the pincers of some huge crab.

Heart banging in his chest, Granville found his feet. Had their pursuers heard?

It was a long moment before he could hear anything over the rushing of blood in his ears. Then all was still except the slight shush of snow as Trent put another careful foot down, a soft whump as another branch lost its weight of snow.

From somewhere not too far away came a sharp crack and he stiffened.

"Ice," came Trent's voice on a quiet breath and Granville nodded, releasing the breath he'd been holding. A branch somewhere had frozen and exploded.

Another explosion had Granville instinctively ducking, then laughing at himself.

He ignored the third explosion until Scott suddenly threw himself forward, knocking Granville and Trent to the ground. They slid downwards in one out of control mass, slamming into the trunk of a mammoth cedar.

It took a moment to find his scattered wits. "Scott, what…?" Granville began, only to find a huge hand over his mouth.

"Rifle shot," came Scott's voice harsh in his ear.

Granville replayed the last few minutes. The first two cracks had been ice, or at least he thought they had, but the last had been different. Scott was right. "How did they know where we were?"

"Somebody has sharp ears."

"Wonderful," Granville said, then realized that he was lying half atop Trent, and the boy didn't seem to be moving. His breath stopped. "Trent?"

He reached out and shook the boy's shoulder. "Trent?"

No response.

Granville suddenly felt cold in a whole new way. "Scott, I think Trent's been hit," he said quietly to his friend, who was still sprawled half on top of him.

Scott's voice sounded strained. "Can't have been. That last shot —got me."

"What? How bad?"

"Bad enough. I'm bleeding some, and my arm's gone numb."

"Can you move?"

"I can try."

Granville felt Scott gather himself, muttering curses, then the weight lifted off him and he sensed Scott sprawled just a little uphill of him. "Let's get that bleeding stopped."

"Look to the boy."

Whether Trent was knocked out or had broken his neck, nothing Granville could do would help. "I'll see to you first."

"I'll be fine."

"That's my intention." Something in Granville's voice must have gotten through to Scott, or he was more injured than Granville wanted to think, because he stopped protesting.

Carefully Granville moved uphill towards where Scott's voice had come from. "Where's the wound?" he asked.

"Left shoulder." Scott sounded short of breath.

"Lucky shot."

"For them, maybe."

If Scott was joking, surely he couldn't be too badly off? Reaching out, Granville found Scott's shoulder then eased down, letting out a soft curse when he felt the warm stickiness soaking down his arm.

"I'm going to stop the bleeding," he said in a low voice, hoping he could stop do so.

As he spoke, there was a crack and another shot whined overhead. Their pursuers were getting closer.

Granville unbuttoned the layers of clothing Scott was wearing, working as quickly as he could, but hampered by the pervasive darkness and the need for silence. As his hands worked, his mind slid to Trent and the cold knot in his stomach grew.

He forced himself to concentrate on stopping Scott's bleeding. With an effort of will, he mentally ran through the contents of his pack. What could he use for bandages?

Granville's fingers found icy cold skin, and a clean entry wound, bleeding freely. He let out a quiet sigh of relief.

The bullet would need to come out, but it had missed anything vital. If he could stop the bleeding, Scott would be fine, unless he succumbed to infection or cold.

Or another bullet.

"I gather it's isn't a major wound," came Scott's voice in a harsh whisper.

"You'll live."

"Feels like I've been kicked by one of our donkeys. And I'm freezing."

"Right. I'll just get a nurse to bind you up."

Scott snorted and Granville started to shrug out of his pack.

"Here," came Trent's voice and two folded bandanas were thrust into his hand.

Granville felt a weight roll off his shoulders. "Thanks. Glad you've rejoined us. You okay?"

"My head hurts but I'm fine."

"Dizzy?"

"Uh—no."

"Truth."

"Well, maybe a little."

Sounded like the boy was concussed. He'd have to keep a close eye on him the rest of the night.

Another crack, closer yet, and another bullet sung by, a little to the left of where they lay. Assuming they made it through the rest of the night.

Cursing under his breath, Granville packed one of the squares Trent had handed him tightly against the wound in Scott's shoulder, wrapping the other of it around him to keep the pressure on. It was an awkward business while trying to keep low to the ground, but at last it was done and Scott buttoned up again.

"We need to get out of here," he said in an undertone as he sat back. "Trent?"

"Nowhere to go but down," Trent said. "Follow me. And just hope they keep missing."

It wasn't a great option. Still, as long as their pursuers were shooting blind…

"But the moon'll be up soon," the boy finished.

Great.

Before he could say anything, there was another crack, closer yet, then a deep rumble that he seemed to feel through his body as much as hear. What was that?

Then he realized. The slope was steeper here, the snow deeper, and the idiots had set off an avalanche. Granville froze.

Behind him he could hear Trent's harsh intake of breath. How close was it?

From somewhere above came a loud yell suddenly choked off. Too close. He had to get them out of here.

The only survival trick he'd ever heard was to try to swim your way through an avalanche as it engulfed you. With his shoulder wound, that wasn't an option for Scott. Granville had to get him clear of the avalanche's path.

The roar made by the falling snow seemed to be coming from below as well as above. Granville had a feeling none of them were going to make it out alive.

But he had to try.

Grabbing Scott's arm and draping it over his shoulder, he half-ran up the steep slope, drawing on a strength he hadn't known he possessed. "Come on, Trent," he yelled.

When they were halfway up the side of the ravine, the sound died. It was eerily quiet. Granville held his breath, listening hard.

Nothing.

The avalanche had missed them. Before he could do more than draw in a relieved breath, there was a loud 'crack'. What the hell?

"The fool is signaling to his buddies," came Scott's voice in his ear. "Now, if we're really lucky, it won't set off..."

His words were cut-off by another deep rumble.

"Guess we weren't that lucky," muttered Granville as he half supported, half dragged his wounded partner upwards as quickly as he could. But not quickly enough.

Between one breath and another, the snow was on them.

9

Granville drew in a deep breath, relieved to find he could do so. His body was aching and all but buried, yet somehow he wasn't crushed.

He drew another breath, then slowly sat up, expecting to feel the throbbing sharpness of broken bones. Nothing.

Moving in what felt like slow motion, he reached up and wiped the snow from his face, noting with detached interest that while his wool cap appeared to be gone, he still had both his mitts.

The world came back into focus, and with it, fear. Scott. Trent. Where were they?

The last thing he remembered, he'd been dragging Scott towards higher ground, with Trent beside him. Looking at the featureless white around him, Granville felt despair wash over him. They could be anywhere.

A groan from somewhere to his right had him digging through the snow.

His eyes saw nothing. His hands met nothing but cold snow. He heard only the shushing of the wind through the cedar trees.

The trees.

If the trees had forced the avalanche to break around them, maybe it had left pockets of safety in which one or both of them might still live. His eyes scanned the slopes. No motion, no color anywhere, only moon-silvered white and the still black trunks.

He spared a moment to wonder where their pursuers were, if any of them were still alive, but there was no time to care.

If Trent and Scott had been buried by the heavy snow, he had little time to find them. Assuming they were still alive.

How long had he been out? He held his breath, listened hard.

Another groan, fainter. Just ahead of him. Granville waited with everything in him for the next faint sound.

Was that breathing?

Someone else was alive out here.

His eyes darted from one patch of shadow to another, listening hard. It came again.

A breath.

Another.

"Scott?" he called. "Trent?"

A movement. There, in the shadow of that tree. Granville stumbled toward the motion, hoping it wasn't a squirrel or one of the ambushers, carried down by the snow.

"Trent? Scott?"

Ducking under a low hanging branch, he found himself in a small cavern of snow, staring into Scott's pain-glazed eyes.

The big man was upside down, his legs extending upward out of sight, his head facing downhill. Blood stained the snow beneath his shoulder. "Scott?"

Scott blinked a few times, as though clearing his vision. An attempt at a smile quirked the big man's lips. "Good—to see you," he managed. "Can't—move."

Granville bit back a curse.

"Let's get you out of there," he said in an undertone. "Hang on."

He reached out, quickly felt Scott's limbs. Scott's legs were caught under a thick tangle of branches uphill from where he lay.

He was truly lucky they weren't broken—a little more pressure, a slightly different angle, and they would have been.

Granville didn't share that thought with Scott.

His friend had enough problems, blood loss and hypothermia being the most immediate. He needed to get Scott turned around, stop the bleeding and get him warm.

Somehow.

His mind flipped to Trent, then he blanked the thought. First he had to see to Scott.

"Hang on, this might hurt," he said, as he levered Scott's legs free of the branches that were pinning him.

Scott groaned. "Might—hurt," he said in a thin voice. "Always—the comedian..."

"Save your strength," Granville said. As gently as possible, he levered Scott's legs downhill, pulled his torso around so he faced uphill. Scott's face went whiter than the snow he lay against, but the spread of blood from his shoulder seemed to stop.

Yanking off the wool scarf he wore, Granville wrapped it twice around Scott's shoulder and pulled tight. The big man groaned again, then his eyes rolled up in his head.

"Probably a good thing," Granville muttered to himself as he pulled the scarf even tighter and tied it off. "Now, how am I going to get you warm?"

"I've got a blanket. Would that help?" said a voice from behind him.

Granville turned. "Trent?"

The snow-covered figure grimaced. "Doesn't sound much like me, does it? Think I swallowed some snow."

"Are you all right?"

"Fetched up under a tree. Luckily without cracking my skull this time. But one of my arms isn't working too well."

"Thank God!"

"Yeah, well, we've still got to get out of here. Even with the moon up it'll be hard."

"Any sign of our pursuers?"

"Nope. They might of got swept away worse than we did. Where they were? Fewer trees."

"Ah."

"Is Mr. Scott going to be all right? He doesn't look so good."

"If we can get him out of here, he'll be fine," Granville said, hoping it was true. "Think you can help me get him upright without jostling your bad arm?"

"I can try." Trent moved to take Scott's good side, while Granville took the injured side.

Scott slowly revived and helped as much as he could. Between them, they got him standing without any of them passing out. Looking at the steep expanse of white stretching below them in the moonlight, Granville groaned inwardly.

How exactly were they going to get themselves out of here?

FIVE SLOW AND painful hours later, they reached the head of the lake. With the help of the moonlight, Trent had found a shorter route. Somehow Scott managed to help, half-stumbling, half dragged between them.

Granville didn't want to think about what the effort had cost his friend. Scott's pale, sweaty face and the glazed look in his eyes told their own story. But they had to get him out before he bled or froze to death. He was too big and the terrain too steep to drag him.

Scott knew it, too. He clung to consciousness with a tenacity that Granville had seen before in men fighting to survive.

At least there was no further sign of their pursuers.

Granville glanced at his companions. Trent looked beyond exhausted. Scott was paler than ever. As he watched, the big man's eyes rolled up in his head.

Granville made a frantic grab for him, managing to get a shoulder under his side, enough to keep him from crashing to the rocky path.

"Is he all right?" Trent's worried voice came from Scott's other side, where he was braced against Scott's right shoulder.

Granville's hand went to the pulse at Scott's neck. To his relief, it was even and fairly strong. By the look of the bandage Scott's wound had bled again, but the blood was already drying.

He eased him down. "Pain and blood loss. He needs a doctor. Is there one in Port Hammond?"

"No. Closest is New Westminster."

"Scott won't make it that far."

"The Katzie medicine man is rumored to be skilled at healing."

"Rumored?" Granville hated to trust his friend's life to a rumor, but at the moment he had little choice. "Never mind. We'll take him to Katzie."

Trent looked at their sagging burden. "And how are we going to do that?"

"Ever built a travois?"

Trent looked from Scott's big frame to the steep path they'd be taking along the lake. "Sure. But they don't work too well on this kind of slope."

"Got a better idea?"

Trent shook his head. Without further comment, he helped Granville lower their burden to the path. Then he melted into the woods.

Granville listened to the whistle of the wind, checked Scott's pulse again. Too fast, but at least it was regular. He pulled Scott's coat more closely around him, then tucked the blanket from his pack tightly around his friend.

Taking out his knife, Granville headed for the trees, breaking his way through thigh high snow. The snow wasn't as deep under the trees, which made it easier.

Choosing long, sturdy branches with thick clusters of needles, he made short work of cutting them free with his knife. Dragging several of the thick branches behind him, he tramped back to where he'd left Scott.

His friend was still unconscious, but Trent was with him, along with a quantity of branches. Trent was rummaging in his pack. Granville noted with approval that he'd already found the rope they'd need.

The lad had arranged the greenery in a rough triangle and was binding the branches tightly together at the corners. Granville left him to it and went to check on Scott.

His partner's pulse was still steady, but his lips had a blue tinge and he was shivering lightly. The sooner they got him down and warm, the better. Granville brushed snow off Scott's face, wrapped the blanket more tightly around him.

Scott's eyes flickered, then opened. Glazed with pain, they fastened on Granville with something like desperation. "Granville…?"

"I'm here."

"Sarah. Must find—little—Sarah."

Was Scott's mind wandering? "When we get back to town, there may be word from Denver about her."

"You—find her. Promise."

"I already promised Lizzie I'd find her daughter, remember?"

For a mad moment Granville felt like laughing. What was it about this mountain and men wanting him to make promises?

The sudden realization that Scott thought he was dying sobered him instantly. "I'll find little Sarah, and you're going to help me. You're going to be fine, Scott."

No answer. Scott was unconscious again.

"I'm done," Trent said from where he crouched by the travois.

Granville walked over, checked the structure, finding it sound. "Good work, Trent."

The boy flushed slightly. "Thanks."

"Can you give me a hand here?"

Trent nodded and helped him set the travois beside Scott's prone body, the wide part near his head, the narrow part at his heels. Between them they half lifted, half dragged Scott onto the travois and tied him firmly in place.

Then Granville attached lengths of rope to the two corners of the wide end and shrugged into his pack. Trent mirrored his actions, then each of them took a length of rope and hoisted the travois so only the narrow end rested on the snow.

With a quick grin at Granville, Trent put his back into it, and they began to drag their makeshift sled with its unconscious burden down the uneven lakeshore.

10

MONDAY, JANUARY 8, 1900

Monday morning found Emily back in typewriting class, seated neatly in front of her machine and nearly frantic with worry. She'd heard nothing from Granville, nothing from O'Hearn, and between church and afternoon visiting yesterday, she'd not been able to get away from her family even long enough to make a telephone call.

All around her was the clacking of typewriter keys, and the low hum of voices as some of the students repeated the words to themselves as they typed. Emily raised her hands into position. She typed a word or two, then dropped them again.

It was no use. She couldn't concentrate.

"Miss Turner."

Emily jumped, looked up to find Miss Richards standing over her. She hadn't heard her teacher approach.

"You're meant to be doing the fingering exercise. Is there some problem?"

"No. No, I'm sorry, I didn't sleep well last night, and am having difficulty concentrating."

"I'm afraid that is no excuse," Miss Richards said. "When you join the world of work, as your presence in this course says you are intent on doing, there will be no acceptable excuses for inattention to your work. The efficiency of an office will depend on you—you must be effective and alert at all times."

"Yes, I'm sorry," mumbled Emily. She could feel herself flushing.

For the next half hour she typed, "The quick brown fox jumped over the lazy dog," over and over again, forcing herself to focus. She could feel Miss Richards's sharp glances, but she didn't look up.

When it was finally time for the break, Laura came up behind her. "Emily, are you all right?" she said in a low voice. "Come outside, I must speak with you. And bring your coat. The wind has come up, and there's snow in it."

Quickly Emily fetched her thick wool jacket and followed Laura.

Once they were standing in the lea of the building with their backs to the sharp wind, Laura turned to face Emily. A few heavily laden carts clattered by on the street behind her and one of the horses neighed a protest, but Laura ignored them. She looked worried, Emily thought, and braced herself.

"Emily, I overheard Liz Andrews, Julie Parker and Andy Riggs gossiping before class."

"What did they say?"

"I'm sorry to have to tell you, but—they said Mr. Granville has been shot."

She couldn't get her breath. "Shot! Are you sure?"

Laura nodded and pressed her arm. "Oh Emily. You haven't heard anything?"

"No. How—how bad is it?"

"From what I could hear he is still alive, but that's all I know. I'm so, so sorry." She gripped Emily's arm tighter.

"I must know more."

"I'll find out for you. They won't talk to you."

"They'll have to talk to me, whether they like me or not."

"It's your father's money they don't like. They resent your being here because they think you don't need to find work. But they think I'm like them." There was disdain in Laura's voice. "I'll—I'll flirt with Andy. Get him to talk. He's soft on me, anyway. It shouldn't be hard."

"You're sure you want to do this? It may be dangerous."

Laura gave her a sharp smile. "I'm sure."

"Be careful," Emily said as she watched her unexpected champion depart. She found it impossible to concentrate the rest of the morning.

Even Emily's growing knowledge of shorthand deserted her. Everything she took down was indecipherable when she went to type it back. She'd never been so glad of anything as when Miss Richards called the lunch break and she saw Laura signaling to meet her in the cloakroom.

"What did you learn?" Emily asked her.

"It sounds as if the injuries were minor."

Unlike her sister Jane, Emily wasn't a fainter, but she had to steady herself with a hand against the wall. She closed her eyes, breathed a silent prayer.

"But they say your fiancé has a map to a cursed gold mine, and that the map was stolen from a murdered man," Laura said.

Who had been murdered, and when? "Did they mention a Mr. Gipson?"

"They didn't mention any names. Why?"

"Never mind," Emily said. "Go on."

"They say Mr. Granville can't escape the curse."

"What curse?"

"Apparently all who touch the map die a horrible death by unseen hands," Laura said in a shaky voice.

"Meaning they'll be attacked at night," Emily said. "Those who go around talking about people dying from curses usually attack after dark."

"But—don't you believe in curses?"

Emily shook her head. "No, and I don't believe in hauntings, either. But thank you for telling me, Laura. Can you make my excuses to Miss Richards? Say I'm feeling unwell and have gone home."

"You've been so distracted she'll believe that easily," Laura said. "Yes, of course I'll tell her."

"Thank you," Emily said absently, reaching for her coat. At least it was a minor injury Granville had suffered. She'd force herself to believe he would be fine, but she hated the helplessness she was feeling.

What she really wanted was to get a horse and ride into the mountains to save him, though she had to smile at the image. She enjoyed riding through a snowfall in Stanley Park, but she didn't have the knowledge or the skills to survive in the snow-covered mountains beyond town.

Shaking her head at her own foolishness, Emily resolved to do the only thing she could—to see what she could find out about the map and the conspiracy against Granville. It might be reckless, but at least she'd be doing something.

And once he was safely back, perhaps that information would help him. And he would be back safely. She refused to consider any other possibility.

Bundling into her coat and bonnet, she hurried down the narrow back stairs to avoid Miss Richards. Pushing through the heavy door, she paused for a moment, irresolute, then pulled her coat closer against the sharp wind and turned away from her route home.

THE LIVERY STABLE was quieter than the last time Emily had been here. A few horses nickered back and forth. From somewhere came the steady thump of shod hooves kicking a stall.

"Quiet, there," a voice yelled, and the noise stopped.

Bits of hay drifted through the air, and the midday sun glittered off cobwebs thickly draped between the high rafters. Emily brushed at the back of her neck. She hated the very thought of spiders.

Catching Mr. Riggs' eye on her, she hurriedly dropped her hand.

"Don't know why you're here again, Missy. I can't help you," he was saying with a heavy frown. Small brown eyes darted from Emily to Clara and back.

"Oh, I know," said Emily, with a confidence she didn't feel. She was glad she'd stopped to collect Clara—even with her company, this felt risky. "However since your son has been somewhat indiscreet about the plot against my fiancé, I thought you might like to clarify a few details."

The man's scowl deepened. "Young idiot don't know what he's talking about. You'd best go, the both of you. A livery stable is no place for a lady."

And he turned his back on them, busying himself with a stack of papers that looked ready to topple onto the scarred wooden table. "He'll regret he ever heard of that map, though," he added under his breath.

Emily shivered at the venom in the man's voice. Suddenly she wanted to be as far away from the livery stable as possible. "Thank you for your time. Come along, Clara."

"Well, that was useful," Clara said when they were safely outside. "Can we go shopping now?"

"I know it was a waste of time," Emily said. "But he might have been startled into telling us something. Anything I can learn about the conspiracy might help Granville."

Clara patted her arm. "So what do we do next?"

She must have sounded more desperate than she'd realized. "Thank you, Clara." Snapping open her watchcase, Emily glanced at the time. "We still have more than an hour before dinner. Time enough to visit Mr. Gipson."

"Since he's a released felon, I'm sure no one will think anything of our going to see him," said Clara in her sweetest tone.

"He's pretending to be just a businessman. It won't be too bad."

And indeed it wasn't.

Mr. Gipson's offices were in a much pleasanter part of town than the livery stable, and bore no resemblance to what Emily would have expected of a criminal. The dark oak paneling topped with soberly striped wallpaper and heavy furniture reminded her of her father's office. They were received by a very polite clerk, and asked to wait until Mr. Gipson could see them.

Impatient, Emily distracted herself by watching the clerk's fingers fly over his typewriting machine. He seemed to be having no difficulties with keys sticking together or having his fingers stuck between the keys. And he had to be typing more than sixty words per minute.

Before she could ask him how long he had been a typewriter, which would probably have thoroughly embarrassed Clara, a slim, silver-haired gentleman dressed in impeccable black appeared at the door.

"Please come in, ladies," he said.

This was the fraud who was Granville's mortal enemy? Emily looked past the sartorial splendor to take in the narrowing of his eyes as he assessed them. Did he know who she was?

Something about the way he watched her said he did.

"Why, thank you, Mr. Gipson," she said as she and Clara preceded him into his office.

Here the resemblance to her father's substantial office was even stronger. Everything from the heavy wood furniture down to the thick carpets spoke of a successful man. He knew it too, Emily thought, seating herself and watching as Gipson gracefully rounded his desk and sank back in his large leather chair.

He brought his hands together, index fingers tapping against his chin. "Now, how may I be of service?"

"Mr. Riggs suggested we should talk with you," she said.

"Indeed? Now why would he make such a suggestion, I wonder?"

Had he looked just a little startled? Perhaps she could shake him further. "You are in business together, are you not?"

"In a manner of speaking. But how may I help you?"

He'd recovered himself far too quickly. Emily decided to play the role of a rather naïve young lady. "I'm engaged to Mr. Granville," she said, and managed to blush. "Do you know him?"

"I had the pleasure of meeting him in the Klondike, where we both spent some time."

Pleasure indeed. Granville had told her some of what this man had done, including that he'd tried on at least one occasion to kill him, and would have succeeded if not for Mr. Scott.

"Mr. Granville is out of town at the moment, on business, you know, but before he left he told me a little bit about the mine with the curse on it," Emily said. "Mr. Riggs is the father of a friend of mine, and he said you might be able to tell me more about the mine? I think it so romantic the mine was discovered by a lady, and that she died before seeing a penny from it."

Pausing for breath, Emily noted out of the corner of her eye that Clara was staring at her in fascination. She hoped her friend wouldn't give her away.

Mr. Gipson also stared at her for a moment, then burst out laughing. "Bravo. A very inventive story, and one that almost convinces me your Mr. Granville is looking for something he's not. But I'm afraid it really won't work.

You see, I know Granville to be searching for a mine discovered by a murderous Indian who was hanged some ten years ago. Hardly a romantic story, and not something a young lady should be bothering her head with. Surely you have a trousseau to prepare?"

Emily gave him her company smile, the one that showed no teeth and didn't reach her eyes. She ignored the question, which Gipson hadn't meant anyway. "You're quite mistaken."

"Oh, I think not."

"Then you can tell me nothing of this mine?"

"I'm afraid not."

"Nor the conspiracy against my fiancé's life?" Emily focused on

Gipson's face, ignoring Clara's little gasp, but the man's expression didn't even flicker at her words.

"Again, I'm afraid I can't help you."

"I see. Then thank you for your time."

"I'm always happy to assist so attractive a young lady," he said with a little bow.

Snake!

"Goodbye, Mr. Gipson," she said in a tone even her mother could not have found fault with as she turned to the door.

At least she'd learned that Mr. Gipson knew where Granville had gone. And O'Hearn had been right about Slumach's lost mine. But who was really behind the ambush on Granville's party?

"Do you think Mr. O'Hearn would be interested in going to New Westminster to find out more about that mine?" she asked Clara as they walked back towards the streetcar stop.

"Not unless he can publish a story on it. Emily, are you trying to get yourself killed?"

"Not at all," she said.

A large puddle in the middle of the sidewalk forced them onto the muddy road for a short stretch. Emily waited for a carriage and two carts to pass, then took Clara's arm. "Watch your step," she said, steering Clara around a steaming pile of manure at the edge of the street.

It was a good thing she'd never told Clara the full story of the enmity between Granville and Gipson. "Besides, I'm not worth Mr. Gipson's trouble. I clearly know nothing at all."

Clara sputtered for a moment, then glared at Emily. "You have lost your senses. And I thought Mr. Granville wanted to keep the mine a secret?"

Emily smoothed her gloves and adjusted the angle of her bonnet. "He does, though it hardly seems to be much of a secret, does it? But I don't see why Mr. O'Hearn would have to report on it now."

"Because his editor is concerned that he isn't filing enough stories, and he may be in danger of being fired," Clara said. "He can't afford the time away from his real work."

"Even though he broke the story behind the murder of Mr. Jackson last month?"

"Especially because of that. The other reporters are watching him more closely than ever, and he is under pressure to produce another story of that caliber. Do you think this could be it?"

"Until I talk with Mr. Granville, I don't know what to think. But how do you know all this?"

Clara flushed lightly. "Tim—Mr. O'Hearn has telephoned me once or twice. When he knew I'd be free to talk to him."

Emily smiled. "I see."

"So what do we do now?" Clara asked quickly.

"Bertie's cousin leaves tonight. I'll be sending a message to Mr. Granville about the ambush and about Mr. Riggs and Mr. Gipson. I only hope he gets it in time."

Clara nodded. She knew all about Bertie's cousin and his macabre errand.

"I'll need you to help me keep gathering information for him. I just hope it will be useful." And that Granville would still be alive to hear it.

She couldn't bring herself to voice her fear that he might even now be dead or grievously injured.

GRANVILLE WATCHED as the Katzie shaman probed the wound in Scott's shoulder with quick strokes of a long, narrow blade. Within moments, he had the bullet out. The man seemed to know what he was about, but when he began to pack Scott's wound with long grayish green strands of lichen, Granville stiffened, ready to protest.

Trent, still too pale, put out a hand and touched Granville's shoulder. "They all use that here—says it helps the healing. Works, too."

Granville gave the wiry strands a skeptical look. "You're sure of that?"

"Uh huh. You don't want to risk rot, do you?"

No. He'd seen what gangrene looked and smelled like as it ate away at a frostbitten foot, then began to devour healthy flesh. Granville shuddered. Scott wouldn't last a week.

Medicine in this remote part of the world seemed nearly as advanced as in London, but there was no effective way to combat gangrene once it took hold. If the dry grayish threads were an effective deterrent, then he didn't care what they looked like.

The rich smell of something cooking had Granville's stomach rumbling. He sniffed the air appreciatively. It had been far too long since any of them had eaten. "What smells so good?"

Trent smiled. "Salmon chowder."

"At this time of year?"

"Dried salmon. And it'll taste nearly as good as it smells, as long as you don't ask what else is in it. But don't you think you'd best get your arm seen to, before you think about food?"

"My arm?" Just how hard was the blow to the head the boy had received, anyway?

Trent pointed, and Granville looked down. The stain of dark blood on his jacket surprised him. "It must be Scott's," he said.

"I don't think so. It's spreading."

Granville looked back at his arm. Sure enough, the edges of the bloodstain had widened slightly. As he watched, they widened again.

"Well, damn," he said, suddenly aware of a throbbing pain, sharper than the bruising from the avalanche…

11

Granville opened his eyes to find dark eyes watching him out of a broad, smooth face. The man looked vaguely familiar, but who? And where?

He blinked twice, willing his mind to clear. He didn't feel threatened, but he did feel decidedly odd. Where was he? He drew in a deep breath, relieved to find he could do so.

Another face moved into his field of vision. This one he recognized.

"Granville, are you all right?" Trent asked.

"What happened?"

"You passed out. The shaman here says it's from blood loss. And the bullet was still lodged in your arm. I'm amazed you didn't feel it."

Granville felt like someone had wrapped his brain in wool as he tried to process what Trent was saying.

He recognized the first face now. It was the same Indian who had seen to Scott's wounds. He remembered he'd been impressed by the man's confidence and air of wisdom, despite the fact that he seemed barely into middle age.

At least he'd been impressed until the man had started shoving dried plants into Scott's arm. Granville's fuzzy mind focused on that thought.

What had the shaman put into his own wound? And had Trent said they'd pulled out a bullet? Surely that couldn't be right. When had he been shot and how bad was it?

He tried to scan his body for pain, but everything hurt too much to distinguish any particular pain. There was that aching that seemed to be a new pain, but aside from the infernal muzziness, he was fine.

He just needed to sit up and...

"GRANVILLE. HEY, GRANVILLE."

Trent's voice seemed to be coming from a long way off, but the urgency in it had Granville forcing his eyes open. "Wha...?"

He lifted his head and a cup was held to his lips. Obediently he took a long swallow, and then began to sputter. It was the most bitter, wrong-tasting liquid he'd ever had the misfortune to swallow. And after his time in the Klondike, that was saying something.

"Are you trying to poison me? What is that infernal stuff?"

"I told you, you've lost some blood. The shaman says this will build your blood. Or something like that."

Granville swallowed, trying to get the bitterness out of his mouth. "He told you this potion of his would build my blood, and you just fed it to me?"

"Well, I think he said it would fix your blood."

"You think? How do you know he isn't trying to poison me?"

"This shaman is one of the good guys," Trent protested. "He treated me once, that time I took on a mountain lion and lost."

"You took on a—never mind. I don't want to know. Did he dose you with one of these potions of his?"

"Yeah."

"Then how could you feed it to me?"

"I'm still here, aren't I?" Trent said. "And by rights, I shouldn't be. Pa had to drag me more than ten miles with my shoulder laid open, bleeding all the way. We were lucky the blood didn't pull another lion."

At least it wasn't poison. And the shaman did seem to know what he was doing. But he wasn't staying for another dose of that medicine. Granville closed his eyes, trying to find the energy to get himself back on his feet.

He drew in a deep breath, noting the sharp, clean scent of the cedar branches he lay on. He couldn't remember the last time he felt so weak. Gritting his teeth, he began to lever himself off the soft mat of branches.

Trent's hand against his shoulder stopped him. Granville was chagrined to realize that it took very little pressure to keep him lying there. "How deep was the bullet?"

"I was clawed, not shot," Trent said.

He chuckled, then winced to hear how weak he sounded. From the look on the boy's face, Trent thought his mind was wandering. "I mean the bullet they dug out of me," he said. "Isn't that what you told me earlier? So how deep was it?"

"Granville, that was four hours ago."

"You mean I've been out all that time?"

Trent nodded.

And the boy hadn't mentioned Scott. Granville pictured Scott's drained face, heard again his shaky words, his certainty he was dying, and felt a clench of fear. "How is Scott?"

"He's fine, sleeping. He lost even more blood than you did."

Trent waved to a blanket-covered lump some ten feet from where he himself lay. "See for yourself. That's him."

Scott's face was turned away from them, but he could see the steady rise and fall of the blankets. Relief made his tone sharper than he'd intended. "So you've been dosing him with that potion of yours too?"

Trent didn't seem to take it amiss. "No, the shaman says he needs to sleep."

"You didn't let me sleep."

"He said you need the potion more."

"Great," muttered Granville. "Are you going to tell me where I got shot or not?"

"You sure get demanding when you're laid up," Trent said with a grin. "It was lodged against the bone. The bullet must have been nearly spent, cause it should have broken the bone. Bruised it some, though."

Granville tried to picture it. "How is that even possible?"

Trent shrugged, "The shooter was uphill, the bullet probably ricocheted, maybe even a couple of times."

A jumble of images flashed through Granville's mind—the whine of a bullet, the rumble of the avalanche, the moment of stark terror as the world had turned white, then upside down. He drew in a deep breath, forced his tired mind to make sense of what he was remembering.

Then his mind focused and his hand went to his neck. The map!

There was no sign of the oilcloth pouch that had hung there. If the avalanche had been torn it off, they'd never find it. Despite the headache that pounded behind his eyes, he tried to visualize the lines and words in faded ink that marked a debt of honor and perhaps a woman's salvation.

Before he could comprehend the enormity of the loss Trent's hand touched his shoulder.

Granville looked up to see Trent tapping his own chest. "I have it," he said. "We had to get your shirt off to get at your wound, but I made sure no-one saw it."

Granville blinked twice, trying to get Trent to come into focus. He could feel himself fading, and it was an effort to comprehend what the boy was saying. He blinked again, stared at Trent's chest, and suddenly understood.

A moment of overwhelming relief was followed by a wave of dizziness. Then the blackness closed in on him.

12

WEDNESDAY, JANUARY 10, 1900

Emily stared out the streetcar window as thick forest gave way to rain drenched fields and thought about Granville. How badly wounded was he? Would he have received the note she'd sent him?

Would it help?

She could only pray it would. All she could do now was keep gathering information, hope it would help him when he returned.

To keep from thinking about him injured, perhaps dying, and the helpless feeling it gave her, she focused on the empty fields, dotted here and there with stumps that must have been too big to remove. She busied her mind trying to imagine clearing this land. How had they done it?—logged thick forests with no more than axes, saws and horses to pull out the stumps, clearing acre after acre of land, built farms?

Her father said the land here was rich—a former river delta, so things grew easily. But that meant the trees must have grown easily, too, with deep, strong roots. What made someone want to farm such land, to see a dense forest and think of clearing it to grow food to feed the cities?

"What are you looking at, Emily?" Clara asked

"Do you ever wonder where our food comes from, Clara?"

Clara looked at Emily, then out the window. "You think too much, Emily," she said.

Disembarking in New Westminster some half hour later, Emily looked around her for a confused moment. Columbia Street was still lined with graceful buildings of wood and brick and stone, but some of them looked temporary, and she didn't recognize anything.

"Which way are we going?" Clara asked.

"I'm not sure. I was fourteen when I was last here, and the fire two Septembers ago burned down so many of the landmarks. I saw the photos, and they were awful, but after all this time they are still repairing the damage. I had no idea how devastating that fire really was."

Clara looked at the bustling downtown around her. "I don't see even any hint of damage."

"No, because most of these buildings are newly built. If you look, though, some of them are still temporary." Emily looked towards the end of the street, finally recognizing something. "The train station is original, and I think Queen's Hotel, but everything else is new."

"It really is impressive," Clara said. Then, practical as always, "So how do we know where to go?"

"The streets are the same," Emily said, recognizing the signs for Columbia and Begbie Streets with a feeling of relief. "So the *Columbian* building should be to the right and two blocks down."

"Good," said Clara. "And if we're finished in time, we can shop. I've seen several intriguing windows."

Mentally rolling her eyes at Clara's predictability, Emily nodded, and took her arm. "Then let's be on our way."

Once they reached the newspaper building they were quickly directed to the basement, where oversized volumes of the paper, bound in dark blue buckram, were kept in serried ranks.

Mr. O'Hearn had told them Slumach was hanged ten years before, so Emily began with newspapers from 1890. She chose

October through December and handed Clara the previous volume.

At any other time, she would have been fascinated by stories on the growth of the city, but her fear for Granville kept her focused. Not so Clara.

"Emily, look at the prices on silks," her friend said. "They had a sale at Globe House."

"Clara, please try to focus on finding the article," Emily said. "Otherwise you might not have time to shop before the last tram."

Clara nodded, but Emily could see her eyes widen as she scanned the pages. If she'd been a man, she'd have laid a wager that Clara was reading every advertisement. She'd have won, too, she thought with a silent sigh as her own eyes scanned each page.

After half an hour of searching, her eyes were blurring and she'd sneezed twice from the dust.

"Emily, look at this."

The excitement in Clara's voice raised Emily's hopes as she turned to see what her friend had found.

"Do you believe these styles?" Clara asked, stabbing at an illustration of an evening dress with a pronounced bustle. "How very dowdy. And so uncomfortable. I am glad fashion has changed, I'd hate to have to appear in something like this."

"Clara..." Emily began. Then her eye caught a word halfway down the page. Slumach. She leaned over to read the article, peering at the time-blurred type.

"Emily! I'm trying to read this!"

"Clara, this is the story I've been searching for. Can you look at another month?"

"You mean I found it? How exciting! What a good thing I came with you."

Speechless, Emily glanced at Clara. The twinkle in her friend's eyes reassured her. "Indeed."

Clara smiled, not the least impressed by Emily's tone, and passed her the volume. "Now you sound like your fiancé. Here you are."

"Thank you," said Emily, already scanning the article titled Shot Dead. "Listen to this, Clara. Apparently this Slumach was accused of shooting another Indian named Louis Bee. And the shooting took place near the Pitt River. That's where Granville has gone."

"When was this?"

"September 9th, 1890. Ten years ago."

"Did they arrest him?"

"No, he escaped before the law arrived. When this was written, they hadn't found him." Emily flipped pages until she found another article. "There was a coroner's inquest two days later that returned a verdict of willful murder against Slumach, but they still hadn't found him."

"What about the gold mine?"

"No mention of it," Emily said as she flipped more pages. "They still haven't found him—and he's an old man. Sixty!"

By the time she found the article where Slumach, starving and ill, had surrendered himself to his nephew, Peter Pierre, Clara had lost interest and was back to looking at ads. Emily read on. "I don't believe it!"

"What?"

"They nursed the man back to health, then took him for trial, found him guilty of murder and hanged him. And the hanging is described as "very ably managed." Can you imagine?"

Clara shuddered. "I'd rather not. I don't see why you have to read those awful details," she complained.

"I find it most unfair that from the first article, the reporter clearly judged Slumach guilty of murdering Bee. And how could they save someone's life in order to hang him?"

"But if he killed a man?"

"I just wonder how fair his trial was." Emily did note that for the last week of Slumach's life, he'd shared his cell with a medicine man named Pierre, presumably the nephew they'd mentioned earlier, so at least he'd had family with him. That thought led to another.

If there were a gold mine, perhaps Slumach would have told his nephew about it. And if Peter Pierre was still alive, he might be willing to talk about Slumach's gold mine, which was surely the mine Granville was seeking? The mine that could cost him his life. She shivered.

Closing her notebook, Emily returned the volume to the shelf. "We can go, Clara," she said.

"I'll just finish this article."

Emily checked the pendant watch she wore. "We still have an hour to shop if we leave now."

Clara closed the book with a bang. "I'm finished."

As they ascended the staircase from the basement, the helpful young man they had first spoken to came over with a smile. "Did you ladies find what you were searching for?"

"Yes, thank you," Emily said.

"And what were you looking for, if I might be so bold?"

"We were looking for stories on Slumach's gold mine," Clara said.

Emily shot her a look. She hadn't intended to tell anyone, even thought she'd found no mention of the mine.

The young man was nodding. He had a nice face, and he seemed to genuinely want to help them. "I've looked up those stories myself," he was saying with a grin. "The good stuff never made it into the paper, though."

"The good stuff?" Emily asked.

"Yes indeed. In the years before the murder, Slumach often showed up in town with a sack full of gold nuggets. Used those nuggets to pay for his whiskey, and he did like his whiskey. Liked women too, begging your pardon, ma'am, but it's said that each year a young woman went back into the bush with him and was never seen again."

"Do you know anyone yourself who knew any of the young women?" Emily asked.

"Well no, not personally, but everyone knows it."

"What about the gold? Do you know anyone who actually saw it?"

"Well sure. My uncle Red was the bartender at the Royal Saloon where old Slumach used to drink. He handled those nuggets himself. The gold is there, alright."

"And did anyone you know ever see a map?" Clara asked.

"No, but he had to have a way to get back to his gold, didn't he? Stands to reason."

Emily gave him her best smile. "It does indeed. Thank you so much for your help. Come along, Clara."

Standing on the wide plank sidewalk, Clara turned to Emily, her face bright with excitement. "I can certainly see why Mr. Gipson is interested in Slumach's map."

Emily nodded, and taking Clara's elbow, drew them both back to escape a spray of water as a carriage passed by too quickly. The sun had vanished again, and it was growing chilly. Getting wet as well could mean a winter cold.

"Yes, but it is still just gossip," Emily said. "Nothing in the newspaper reports suggests there was any gold at all."

"Perhaps they didn't want to start a panic."

"Perhaps." And if Gipson thought Granville had the map to Slumach's gold, he would probably stop at nothing to lay his hands on it, Emily thought, her throat tightening.

"Where are you, Granville?" she said under her breath. "Please be safe."

13

Granville woke abruptly and took careful stock. Every muscle in his body ached, but the headache was gone, and his mind was clear.

He turned his head cautiously from side to side.

No pain.

He looked from the cedar planks above his head to the blankets that covered him. He was warm and dry. He was also out of the snow, and the roughness of the blankets above and beneath him felt good. He could smell smoke and cedar and bear grease and hear the crackle of a fire. The sound of many voices rising and falling came from somewhere beyond him.

Where was he?

Drawing in a breath, Granville levered himself to a sitting position, wincing as a particularly sharp pain stabbed down his arm.

He sat at one end of a long wooden building. Rough bunks mounded with blankets lined the walls and flames flickered in a huge fire pit in the center. The air was thick with wood smoke and the smells of cooking. His stomach rumbled.

The mingled scents took him back to winter camps on the streams of the Klondike, warm with the fires he and Scott had used to melt the permafrost and dig out yard after yard of the gold-rich beds of old streams. Fire and furs had been their only defence against a cold that could freeze a man's beard solid with his own sweat in less than a minute. That same cold made bathing a luxury.

He grinned at the memory, his eyes searching his new surroundings.

Katzie. He remembered now. They were safe.

And this was the first chance he'd had to think about what had happened. And why. From the moment Cole had been killed, all he'd thought about was getting them out alive.

He put a hand against his chest, relieved to feel the outline of the map packet through his thick shirt. Whoever had tracked and then ambushed them knew about the map, had probably been on their trail since Port Hammond.

Had Cole spoken too freely? The image of the brothel in Port Hammond flashed across his vision. Well, it wasn't the first time he and Scott had come up against would be claim-jumpers, and likely wouldn't be the last. Especially now they were part owners in what promised to be a very rich mine.

But where was Scott? Granville's gaze sharpened, searched. And found his friend two bunks over. Scott's face was drawn and pale but his eyes were alert.

Meeting Granville's gaze, he smiled. "Glad to see you're awake, pardner," he said in a thin voice unlike his usual booming tone.

"Where's Trent?"

"No idea. Haven't seen him since I woke."

Which wasn't that long ago, from the look of him. Still, very little could keep his massive friend down for long. Unless his wound was infected, Granville thought in sudden alarm.

With a stifled grunt, he got his feet under him and heaved. Head swimming, he put a hand against one of the massive cedar beams.

"Steady there," came Scott's voice. "Maybe you should wait 'till that medicine man comes back."

And risk being dosed with that foul concoction again? Not if he had anything to say about it. "I'll be fine."

Scott shook his head. "You're even stubborner than I thought, and that's saying something. But thanks for getting me down, partner."

"Don't mention it," Granville said.

"And what are you doing up?" Trent asked from behind him.

Trent's sudden appearance startled Granville into losing his train of thought and nearly his balance. "Why would I not be up? And who made you my physician?"

"Don't mind him. He gets testy when he's injured," said Scott.

Trent grinned. "I'd noticed. Does that mean you don't?"

"I'm the soul of meekness," Scott said.

Granville snorted.

"Ignore him," Scott continued with a grin, though his voice was growing weaker.

"Trent, I need a word," Granville said, putting a hand on Trent's shoulder. "Somewhere out of earshot."

"I need to talk to you, too," Trent said.

"Awww," said Scott. "You're spoiling my fun." But his eyes closed as they walked away.

Granville directed Trent far enough away that Scott couldn't hear them, assuming he was still conscious. "How is Scott? Has gangrene set in?"

Trent looked confused. "I told you he's fine. You were just talking to him."

"He seems infernally weak. Even a short conversation exhausted him."

"He lost a lot of blood. The shaman says he's doing good."

"You're positive there's no rot?"

"Uh huh."

"Fine. What did you want to talk to me about?"

"A couple things. The first is—this." And Trent thrust a carefully folded and sealed note at Granville.

Breaking the seal, Granville was stunned to see Emily's wide-spaced handwriting. "How did this get here?"

"A cousin of Bertie's brought it."

"How did he know to find us here?"

"I told Miss Emily to try here or Port Hammond. He'll have left another note waiting for you in Port Hammond."

Granville's eyes dropped back to the note. There was news from Harris in Denver, and it sounded urgent. He skimmed the rest and his heart seized. Emily had talked to Gipson? And to someone named Riggs, trying to find out who wanted to kill him?

Was she daft? She'd put herself in danger asking questions, and he was very much afraid she wouldn't stop there. He needed to get back to Vancouver.

He turned to Trent. "I must talk with this messenger."

"Too late. He's gone on."

"On where?"

"Further up the Fraser. He won't be back this way for a couple of months. Why?"

"I need to know if he told anyone in Port Hammond who sent him."

"I doubt it. I told you, he's Bertie's cousin—they don't much like Chinamen in Port Hammond. He'd have asked for you, then come here."

Which didn't decrease the danger Emily might be in, if anyone had read that note.

WORRYING about Emily wasn't going to help her. Granville had to heal, and get back to Vancouver. Now.

"What was the other thing you wanted to tell me?" he asked Trent.

"Oh, about Mr. Arbuthnot. He's English, like you, and he's making a study of the Indians. Maybe he can tell you more about the shaman's medicine—he's the one who told me what to call him. Wait, I'll get him."

Before Granville could say a word, Trent had dashed off.

Moments later he was back with a stout, middle-aged man with the full beard and sober dress of a Victorian gentleman. His high-buttoned black lounge suit was a tad dated for a London drawing room, but in the middle of a Katzie village it looked ludicrous.

"This is Mr. Arbuthnot," Trent said. "He has a farm near Langley but he spends time with the Indian tribes when he can."

The gentleman advanced on Granville and held out a hand. "Happy to make your acquaintance," he said. "I too have been sharing the Katzie hospitality. I gather from our young friend here that you have a few questions as to the nature of the medicine practiced by the *olia*."

"The *olia*?"

Mr. Arbuthnot smiled forgivingly. "The Katzie word for a shaman. I don't profess to be an expert, but I have been making a fairly intensive study of the ethnography of the local tribes, particularly the languages, along the same lines as the chap called Hill-Tout. I don't suppose you met him last time you were here? No? Splendid chap, and knows his dialects. They are all related, the dialects you know, stretching over several hundred miles and right across to Vancouver Island. All Coast Salish, but the dialectic inflections of the various tribes show remarkably few differences. Quite fascinating, really."

"And the shaman?"

Arbuthnot gave a little laugh. "Oh, yes, forgive me. Favorite topic, you know. The shaman, yes—actually the *olia* is the middle of three levels of shamans within the Coast Salish structure, but he's the one who does the actual healing. The top level, the *sqelam* is more concerned with the pathology, and making the spells to cast out the evil influences that may be affecting health."

He gave another little laugh. "Not much use with a bullet, though, is it?"

"I was curious about the plant he used in my partner's wound, just before he bound it," Granville said before Arbuthnot could go off on another tangent.

He'd met his like before—amateur scientists with an unfailing enthusiasm for their discoveries. Their contribution to scientific knowledge was often enormous, but he knew from experience that once fully launched on the subject of their hobbies, they were difficult to divert. "What did you call it, Trent?"

"Lichen."

"Lichen, eh?" said Arbuthnot. "Long strands of gray-green stuff?"

Trent nodded.

"Hmmm—related to Spanish moss, I believe. I've seen it used to great effect in the prevention of infection in an open wound. Very useful stuff, though I know our good Dr. McKecknie is rather skeptical of its use."

"Does it prevent gangrene?" Granville asked.

Arbuthnot looked thoughtful. "That I don't know, but I have heard of few instances of rot among the tribes, so perhaps it does."

It wasn't the definitive answer he'd hoped for, but at least the shaman's ministrations were unlikely to cause Scott harm. "And are you staying here?"

"I am indeed. I have a small tent pitched outside, and plan to be here for another week or more."

It might serve. Scott couldn't be moved for at least another few days. He should be safe enough from their attackers here, surrounded by so many people, but wounds turned bad so easily. If Arbuthnot was willing to keep an eye on things... When he broached the matter, Arbuthnot beamed.

"Delighted to help. I can converse with the *olia*, and, you know, follow the course of his treatment. I know a little of medicine myself, have to living so far from town. Not that we are too isolated in Langley, there's a small community of us, but no doctor. Depending on the weather it can take most of a day to fetch him, so we need to be somewhat self-reliant."

Granville nodded without comment, afraid of setting the man off again. "Let me introduce you to Scott," he said. "And I deeply appreciate your willingness to take this on."

"Not at all, my dear chap. Not at all."

14

Port Hammond didn't look any more promising in thin sunlight. In daylight, the few buildings were faded and barely standing and the road more potholes than surface. The only thing Granville could find in its favor was that no one was shooting at them. Yet.

Trent was still protesting. "I don't see why we had to come back here."

Granville silenced him with a look, and made his way to the weathered general store cum post office. It was in slightly better shape than the rest of the town, probably because it also served as the town's meeting place.

He asked for his mail and was handed another copy of Emily's note, along with an unfriendly stare. The seal on the note was intact, but the edges were suspiciously frayed.

Had they identified the sender? He could only hope not.

It was bad enough that Gipson and this Riggs knew of Emily's suspicions—he'd rather no one else did.

He glanced around. Two old men and a boy a little younger than Trent were leaning against the battered counter. Well, since they already knew who he was, he might as well ask them a few questions.

For all the good it did him.

None of them seemed to remember Cole's last visit, or anyone he might have talked to. The shopkeeper, plump but narrow-eyed, was little better.

Faced with this façade of ignorance, Granville held onto his fraying patience—they had little time and he needed answers. At the door, he turned back. "I hear rumors about a lost mine in the area. Any truth to that story?"

The locals glanced at each other.

"That's a pretty old story," the white-bearded one finally said. "Why ask now?"

"My late client seemed uncommonly interested in the tale. And since he's dead, I can't very well ask him."

This prompted another exchange of glances. "He's dead?" the second old man asked. "Cole?"

"I'm afraid so."

"That why you're so interested in who he talked to here?"

"That's why."

Four pairs of eyes were staring at him. "What makes you think we'd know something?"

"That's privileged, I'm afraid," Granville said, watching with amusement as the statement produced the exchange of glances he'd anticipated. "You'll understand I can't say anything further."

"Well, if you're chasin' a killer, I can see where you'd need information," the storekeeper said. "Have you talked to the police in New Westminster yet?"

He'd wondered who had jurisdiction. And wasn't it interesting that they'd jumped straight to the conclusion that Cole had been murdered. "I'll be reporting the death on my way back to town."

He noticed the youth edging towards the door while the shop owner engaged his attention. From the corner of his eye, he saw Trent sliding into the boy's wake. Good for him.

Granville kept his own attention firmly fixed on his portly interrogator, who was nodding. "Then your best bet is to talk to

Joe over at the saloon. He'll be opening a couple hours from now."

"Thanks, I'll do that," he said, and went to fetch the horses. He'd just finished saddling the mare when Trent returned.

"He headed for the telegraph office, sent a wire to Vancouver," the boy said, out of breath and clearly pleased with himself.

"Good work. How did you find out?"

"Stood in line behind him. Couldn't read it, though."

"We'll find out in Vancouver. Let's go."

"Aren't we going to wait and talk to the bar owner?"

"No. He isn't likely to tell us anything anyway. We'll do better in town."

"You hope," muttered Trent.

Granville just smiled.

SALLY'S DINER WAS HOT, crowded and smelled wonderful. Both Granville and Trent had been so hungry they'd headed here the minute they got off the streetcar from New Westminster. Watching Trent shovel an enormous piece of steak into his mouth, oblivious to the crowded booths and buzz of conversation around him, Granville couldn't quite decide whether to be grateful he was no longer that age, or a little envious of Trent's single minded focus.

His own thoughts were torn between the need to take the next train to Denver to search for little Sarah and the need to stay in Vancouver and ensure Emily's safety. Emily would be at her type-writing class tomorrow, so this evening was likely his best chance to talk with her. Unless Trent decided he needed a third steak, that is.

Trent looked up to find Granville's eyes on him. "What?" he said, putting down his fork. "You can't tell me you weren't hungry."

"No, I definitely was," he said, emphasizing the past tense. "But I'd forgotten how much a boy your age can eat. It's truly amazing."

"I'm not a boy," Trent said. "And I can pay for my share, if that's what's worrying you."

Granville waved that off. "Hardly. With the work you've done the last few days, I should be paying you extra."

"Good idea. Especially now with the gold, and the extra work in finding the missing heiress."

"And just how did you know about that?"

Trent forked up another piece of steak, chewed thoughtfully, then grinned at him. "You talk in your sleep."

"I have it on good authority I do not."

"When you've a bullet in you, you do."

This was not good news. "Did anyone else hear me?"

Trent gave him an injured look. "Course not. Think I'd let you go blathering on about private matters if someone could overhear you?"

"What did I say?"

"You seemed to be assuring the old man you would find the girl, the map's true heir. On your honor, you said. She's pretty, too."

He noted that Trent sounded impressed by his vow. He kept discovering new depth to the lad. Then his last words sunk in. "Who is pretty?"

"Mary."

Granville felt a surge of excitement. "You know her?"

"Nah. But there's a picture. And part of a letter."

Why was he only hearing about this now? "Where are they?"

"Tucked in behind the map. I held onto the package while the shaman fixed your arm, remember?"

And he was quick thinking too. "How do you know her name is Mary?"

"Name's written on the back."

Right. "I'll check it out later."

"Why not now?"

"I take it you want to make it easier for our pursuers?"

"Sorry." Trent looked around him. "You don't think any of them are here, do you?"

"Since we don't know who 'they' are, I can't answer that with any validity. We haven't been shot at yet today, though." Granville leaned forward, lowered his voice. "Whoever they are, keep in mind they want the gold very badly. And they suspect you know where it is."

"We all do."

"And we're all in danger."

"Huh. So, are we going after them tonight?"

He smiled at the boy's eagerness. "No, I plan to visit Emily this evening."

"But why…" Trent began, then looked at Granville. A knowing grin slid across his face. "Oh, I see. You missed her."

"It is simply a courtesy expected of an engaged man," he said, but Trent was right. Underneath his worry for her safety, he had missed Emily. She was refreshing.

"Uh huh," said Trent with a grin and a sideways look. "Well, I'll go to the kitchen and catch up with Bertie."

"We'll need to shower first. And I need a shave," he said, fingering his seven-day growth of beard.

"We will?"

EMILY SAT IN THEIR HOT, over-decorated parlor, sipping her mother's second best Assam tea and wishing she were out for a brisk walk somewhere. When Granville's name was announced, her teacup clattered in her hand and she had to place it carefully on a side table.

It took every ounce of the training her mother had drummed into her to sit quietly as he was ushered into the parlor, impeccably dressed and looking as if he'd never left town, much less been shot at.

Luckily the ritual of greeting gave her time to recover.

'"Granville. Good to see you," her father boomed at him. "You've been out of town?"

"Yes, a small matter of business," Granville said.

"I trust it went well?"

"Very well, indeed."

How could he respond so blandly when she knew he'd been ambushed and nearly killed? And where were Trent and Mr. Scott?

She searched his face. Surely he wouldn't look so calm if either of them had been injured?

"Emily? Are you going to greet your fiancé, dear?" her mother said.

What to say? She couldn't blurt out what she wanted to know. "Good evening, Mr. Granville."

"Good evening, Emily. You are well?"

"Very well. And yourself?" She met his eyes, a question and the fear she'd felt in hers.

He smiled at her, but he looked tired. "Also well, though my partner suffered a minor injury."

"Mr. Scott? Will he be all right?"

"Indeed. I left him near Port Hammond, where he is recovering."

It must have been serious then. Emily's eyes ran quickly over Granville's tall frame, pausing on a slight bulge on his right arm that marred the fit of his black coat. A bandage?

"Emily? Dear?"

Emily realized she was staring again, and felt her cheeks heat. If she weren't careful, Mama would forbid her to see Granville until her manners improved, which would be a disaster. "I hope he'll recover quickly."

He inclined his head. "As do I."

"Will you have a cup of tea, Mr. Granville?" Mama asked.

"Thank you, no, I must go. I only returned to town today, but wanted to pay my respects and inquire how Emily's typewriting classes are progressing."

All eyes focused on her. Her father looked unhappy to hear her training acknowledged, since he preferred to ignore it entirely.

"They are going well, thank you. I do look forward to meeting Clara for lunch most days, though."

"Indeed," Granville said. "And do you still meet at Stroh's teashop?"

She gave him a relieved smile. He had understood. "Yes. It's a favorite of ours."

"Then I hope you enjoy your lunch. And that your lessons continue to go well."

As her father saw him out, Emily drew in a ragged breath. At least she knew he was alive and unhurt, or mostly unhurt.

"Emily? Are you all right? You look pale."

"I'm fine, Mama. Just a little tired."

Her mother gave her a sharp look, then her lips relaxed and she smiled. "Then go on up to bed, my dear."

Emily stood up before her mother changed her mind, bending to give that lady's softly powdered cheek a kiss.

With a little luck she could use the telephone in the hall without anyone overhearing. She only hoped Clara was free for lunch tomorrow, because she intended to meet Granville regardless, and that was sure to cause a scandal.

Behind her she could hear Miriam's sharp voice saying, "Well, she does give herself airs, and all because she is engaged. Personally, I don't believe he will ever marry her. After all, what can a gentleman like that see in Emily? She has no manners."

Emily grinned as she heard her mother hushing Miriam.

Miriam was right, Granville wouldn't marry her. But not for the reasons her sister thought. Though the truth, if she ever heard it, would undoubtedly upset Miriam even more.

15

THURSDAY, JANUARY 11, 1900

As Granville strolled into the teashop accompanied by Trent, he was struck by the mingled scents of vanilla and honey. It smelled of home.

He nodded affably to several of the matrons he'd met at the Morton's New Year's Ball, then his gaze settled on Emily.

Her green dress matched her eyes and brought out red lights in her hair, and her gestures added life to some point she was making. Clara's blue eyes and curly blond locks were what society considered beauty, but it was to Emily's bright smile his eyes returned.

"Good afternoon, ladies. Emily, thank you for your message," he said as he slid into the chair opposite hers, taking care not to put too much stress on the fancifully designed and fragile-looking wrought iron.

She was smiling at him. "So you did get it. I'm relieved."

"But in sending it, you may have put yourself in danger. And then talking to Riggs and Gipson—Emily, what were you thinking of?"

"I heard you'd been shot."

"It was nothing. And it's hardly a reason to put yourself in danger."

"So you were injured."

Her tone was accusing. He held back a grin. "I'm here now."

"But you were shot?"

"In the arm," Trent broke in, leaning towards Emily. "And Mr. Scott too. That's why he's still at Katzie. And we were caught in an avalanche."

Emily went pale and Granville gave Trent a look. The boy just crossed his arms and settled back in his chair. "She has the right to know," he said.

"Thank you, Trent," Emily said. "And I had to send that message. You needed to know about little Sarah. And you needed to know about the plot against you."

"Getting yourself killed would not help me. They've already killed our client."

Emily went even paler and Clara covered her mouth with a white-gloved hand. "Oh, no."

"I'm afraid so. How did you learn of the plot?"

"I overheard several of my classmates talking. One of them was Mr. Riggs' son."

"When was this?"

"Last Friday."

Three days after they'd camped in Port Hammond. Cole must indeed have talked. "That explains Riggs. But why Gipson?"

"He's involved with Riggs. Besides, Clara was with me."

"Gipson is dangerous. You can't meet with him again." And he'd warn Gipson what would happen if he ever touched her.

A tiny frown appeared between her brows. "But what if…"

"Emily, we're engaged. He'll know he can get at me through you. You make far too tempting a target for him."

A faint color showed in her cheeks. "But…"

"Emily, please. I'm asking this of you."

She sat back in her seat, her eyes fixed on him. She seemed to consider for a moment, then gave a small nod. "Yes. All right."

"Will you swear it?"

She smiled at that, and her eyes warmed. "Most men would not believe a woman had enough sense of honor to swear. Yes, I swear."

"Thank you. And you won't meet again with Riggs, or anyone else you feel may be involved."

She met his eyes, hesitated.

"Emily, someone has killed my client. They also tried very hard to kill the three of us. I can't leave town to search for Sarah until I know you won't give them a reason to go after you."

Emily breathed out a little sigh, then nodded. "I swear."

That fear laid to rest, Granville turned his mind to the problem of Gipson's possible involvement. "What exactly did Gipson tell you?"

"Very little. Mostly he dropped broad hints about lost gold mines.

Granville turned that information over in his head. It seemed likely Gipson knew about the map, though it would be like him to mislead Emily, if only to cause confusion. He had no difficulty envisioning the man involved in a plot to kill him, though. He turned to Trent. "Is there a record kept of telegrams sent and received?"

"You're thinking of the one the boy sent from Port Hammond?"

"Yes."

"The railway keeps carbons of every incoming and outgoing message," Emily said. "I'm sure Papa could obtain a copy for you, if you explained about the attack."

She was as quick as ever. "Thank you, Emily. And perhaps the operator might remember who collected that particular message."

"Even if he does, how likely is he to tell us?" Trent said.

"Maybe the telegraph operator would talk to a reporter," Clara said.

Granville was surprised to hear Clara's soft voice.

Emily looked less surprised. "Like Mr. O'Hearn?" she said.

Clara nodded, a faint color dusting her porcelain cheeks. She might look like a china doll, but she was no fool. Not that Emily would have a fool for a friend.

"Thank you. I'll talk to O'Hearn," Granville said.

He smiled at Emily. "Shouldn't you be in class?" He pointed to the large clock over the door, black hands standing at two.

"I am officially ill today."

"I'm sorry to hear it."

Emily smiled. "I was ill yesterday, also, because I was looking into lost mines."

"Oh?"

"Mr. Gipson implied that your map leads to the lost mine of an Indian named Slumach. Clara and I went to New Westminster to research the original newspaper stories from when Mr. Slumach was caught, tried and hung."

"Go on."

"He surrendered to his nephew, a man named Peter Pierre, who apparently spent the week prior to the hanging with Mr. Slumach. The nephew might know something that would help, though the articles didn't mention the gold or the map. But rumors of nugget-sized gold and a map to a lost mine somewhere near Pitt Lake seem so numerous that almost everyone takes them for fact."

Granville's mind raced. If he could find this Pierre, perhaps the man could tell them something that would assist them in finding Mary.

"But you still haven't told us what happened to you," Emily said.

In a few succinct phrases Granville described their journey, the discovery of the mine and the ambush. He downplayed the severity of his injury, but Emily's eyes flashed to his arm and her lips tightened.

He had the feeling she was seeing the bandage beneath his tight jacket. Though she said nothing, there was no mistaking the concern in her eyes. It was time for a change of subject. He told them about his search for the map's rightful owner.

"But how will you find her?" Emily asked. "With nothing but the name Mary and a last name that may not be hers."

"That isn't quite all." Granville drew out a torn sheet of paper and handed it to her. Clara craned to see over her shoulder.

"What is it?"

"A fragment of a letter that may be either from or to the map's owner. And it mentions Mary."

Emily considered the spiky handwriting. "It's a man's hand, and he seems to be talking about mining. Where is Cripple Creek?"

"I've never heard of it, unfortunately."

"It's too bad there isn't more information."

Granville drew out the photo from a silk-lined inside pocket of his coat and handed it to her. "There's this, also."

She looked at the photo for a moment, then back at him. "Is this she?"

"I believe so. The name is the same, and I can think of no other reason for Cole to be carrying it with the map and letter."

Granville watched as Emily fingered the much-handled photograph. He had spent a half hour that morning studying the pale composed face, the formal hair and clothes. The sepia tones suggested brownish hair and light eyes. There was no name or date, but printed on the brown border of the card in faded gold script was the name of the studio—"A.J. Morgan." There was no address.

"She has a sweet face," Emily said.

Trent beamed.

"I suspect the photo was taken five or more years ago, judging by her dress," Granville said.

Trent's suddenly neutral expression didn't quite hide his disappointment.

Emily smiled at Granville. "I see an English gentleman's education includes fashion. In this case, you may be wrong, however. The photo may be more recent."

"Oh?"

"If she is indeed short of funds, then she may be wearing cast-off clothing. They would be a season or more out of date before being passed on."

"Emily's right," Clara said. "You can just see where the collar has been turned. This is not a young woman who has new clothes every season."

"I bow to both your knowledge," Granville said.

Emily was studying the photograph. "Perhaps I can help. May I keep the photo for today? And if we can meet here again tomorrow afternoon I'll return it then. At four?'

Granville didn't see how Emily could put herself in danger looking for a photographer, so he agreed to both suggestions. Trent and Clara also nodded their agreement, though Clara gave Emily a look he couldn't interpret. "Until tomorrow then. Trent, are you with me?"

"GRANVILLE, I've been thinking about it," Trent said as they walked past the imposing brick edifice of the Alhambra Hotel.

"About what?"

"Slumach's lost mine," Trent said. "Did I tell you Pa knew Slumach? He'd a trap line that crossed ours."

"Did your father believe the man had found a gold mine?"

Trent shook his head. "Nope. Said he never seemed to have much money, even when the traps ran well. But after Slumach died, the rumors got to Pa. We had a look for the mine a few summers back, but it's big country up there."

"Does it surprise you we found the cache where it was?"

"No. Slumach's trap line ran near there," Trent said. "Course, it ran past a lot of other likely places, too. Could've spent a whole life looking and never found it. Pa decided the mine was just rumor. Others didn't, though."

"And it seems the rumors haven't diminished over time," Granville said.

"They've got wilder. Some say a couple of people found the mine, but died before they could tell anyone. But, Granville, I'm thinking…"

"Yes?"

"Pa said Slumach was half Nanaimo Indian—that's still Salish, but they live on Vancouver Island—and also half Katzie. If he turned himself in to his nephew, I'll bet the nephew was on the Katzie side, cause they're local."

"Katzie? As in the village where we left Scott?"

Trent nodded.

"I wonder if the medicine man that treated Scott knows Pierre," Granville said thoughtfully.

"The Katzie tribe isn't that big. I'm guessing they'd know each other."

"Good thinking, Trent. We'll talk to him when we go back for Scott."

"I thought we were heading for Denver?"

Granville thought about the sense of being watched he'd had all day, decided not to mention it. "We still have to deal with the law over Cole's murder, so we'll going back to Katzie first."

Clearly this pragmatic approach didn't appeal to Trent. "And what about Mary?"

"The mine's not going anywhere. We'll find her after we rescue Scott's niece."

"But if Mary's in need, how can we just ignore her?"

He'd been trying not to think about that. "We aren't ignoring her, but sometimes it's necessary to prioritize. Little Sarah's life may be in danger, Mary's is not. And we're Mary's only hope of seeing a penny from that mine. If we're killed, do you think whoever gets the map next will care about who the rightful owner might be?"

"Oh," Trent said.

"Indeed."

16

Inside the *World* newsroom, pandemonium raged. Granville ran his eyes across a row of heads until he spotted the flash of red. Cutting between battered desks stacked with paper, he headed for Tim O'Hearn's corner.

O'Hearn looked up, his expression changing from irritation to relief when he saw who it was. "You're alive. Good." His eyes moved past him. "And Trent, too."

"I can tell you've been talking to Emily," Granville said with a grin. "She seems to have been somewhat concerned."

"Concerned is an understatement, but she had reason. I don't like what I've been hearing."

"I can't say I cared for it either. Especially when Emily brought in Gipson. Did you know Emily and Clara confronted the man?"

"Confronted Gipson? Just the two of them? If I'd known, I'd have..." O'Hearn seemed at a loss for words. "I'd have tried to talk them out of it, I guess."

"I suspect tried is the operative word. Emily can be very determined," Granville said.

"At least I could have gone with them."

"Hmmm. In any case, I've come to trade information and ask a favor."

A particularly loud demand for more typewriter ribbon from somewhere behind them had Granville looking around the crowded, noisy room. "But not here. This lacks both privacy and ambience."

O'Hearn laughed. "Nice choice of words. Sure you don't want a job as a reporter?"

"Thanks, but no. Can I buy you a drink somewhere quieter?"

"Softening me up for your request, whatever it is?"

"Absolutely. Can you take the time?"

"That depends," O'Hearn said, his eyes lighting up. "Is there a story in it for me?"

"Eventually, yes." Granville glanced around him at what he suspected were several pairs of listening ears, despite their industry and the general hubbub. "Once I've completed what I need to do."

"Then lead on."

ONCE THE THREE of them were comfortably ensconced in a nearby tavern, shots of whiskey in front of two of them—Trent had a root beer, much to his disgust—Granville filled O'Hearn in on what had been happening. With every sentence, the reporter grew more excited. Finally he whipped out his notepad and pencil, as if unable to restrain himself any longer.

"A missing heir?" O'Hearn said. "And the rightful owner was murdered by your client?"

"So it appears. You know you can't write a word of this until the heir is found and the mine secured?"

O'Hearn waved off his concerns. "I know, I know. Didn't I do you right over the Jackson affair? And what a story that made! It would've been even better if I'd done a half dozen articles building up to that trial, but I didn't breathe a word to anyone."

Granville nodded. "Which is why I'm trusting you again."

"So what can I do?"

"I need to know exactly who is trying to kill us. Can you find out who received a telegram from Port Hammond, and what it said?"

"I can try."

"If you don't want us dead before you get your story, you'll need to do better than try," Trent cut in.

He grinned. "The boy has a point, though he may be a tad heavy handed about it. We need to know who's after us if we're going to stop them."

"Then why don't you talk to Benton," O'Hearn said. "There isn't much goes on in this town that he doesn't know about, and he should still be feeling a little grateful to you after what you did for his Franny."

At the mention of the fan dancer, Trent's face lit up. "Good idea," he said. "And we should probably go to see Miss Frances first."

"Oh, so that photo of Mary hasn't lessened your appreciation for her. I was beginning to think you counted the world well lost for love," Granville said.

"I consider Miss Frances a friend," said Trent with a grave dignity that went oddly with his thin features and gangly frame. "And I'm not in love with a picture, I just appreciate Mary's beauty."

"Of course," Granville said, holding back a strong desire to laugh, but not wanting to hurt the lad's feelings.

He really shouldn't have teased him—he remembered all too well the pangs of calf love, and how real they had felt. What had been her name, anyway? Mabel? She had been the gardener's daughter and most unsuitable, but very fair. Granville smiled at the memory.

"And you needn't laugh," Trent said. "It only makes sense to find out as much as possible before confronting Mr. Benton."

"Not that any amount of information will make dealing with Benton a safe enterprise," Granville said.

The man had too much power for that. And too much to lose.

But unless it was Benton himself who ordered their death, talking with him should be safe enough.

Trent looked rather shocked. "But Mr. Benton likes you," he said. "He wouldn't order you killed."

"He'd do exactly that, if for some reason it benefited him to do so," Granville said. "We respect each other's strengths, but that means nothing at all if I should happen to stand in the way of something he wants or needs."

"But Miss Frances—you saved her brother," Trent said.

"Hmmm. And Benton was suitably grateful, which is why he might assist us now. Assuming it doesn't cost him anything."

He looked from Trent's flattened expression to O'Hearn's interested one, and raised his glass in a toast.

"Here's to dealing with underworld kingpins," he said. "It keeps life interesting."

It was late afternoon by the time Granville and Trent reached the Carlton, where Frances Scott performed. The evening performances wouldn't begin for several hours, so with a nod to the bartender, they climbed the sturdy pine steps to the second floor and the dressing rooms.

With a glance at Trent's eager face, Granville rapped once.

Frances had clearly been rehearsing for the evening show. Despite the fact that she wore only a thin robe over her glittery, revealing costume, she opened the door wide. "Granville. Trent. Come in."

It was very different from her first chilly reception of him, Granville thought as he followed her into the scented dressing room. And she was much happier to see them than he expected Benton would be.

Frances gestured them to a pair of dainty chairs and Granville sat down gingerly.

"Have you news of little Sarah?" she asked.

He couldn't face raising her hopes, then disappointing her again. "I'm sorry, no."

The eager light faded from her eyes.

"How is Lizzie doing?" Scott and Frances's youngest sister was recovering from an opium addiction, and both of them feared that only the hope of finding her young daughter was keeping her alive.

"She's eating some, and she hasn't smoked opium in nearly two weeks. But her eyes..." She drew in a shaky breath. "If only there were word of the child."

"I'll be returning to Denver in a few days. I'm hopeful we might uncover a lead."

It was the most he could bring himself to say, and perhaps would be enough to help Lizzie, at least a little. Through the ravages of the drug, the spark of who she had once been still flickered. He hoped she could continue to resist the drug's lure, but without strong incentive, he knew it unlikely. "How is she resisting the opium?"

"When the craving gets too bad, she takes a little laudanum. It helps her sleep."

"It's still opium." He knew several society ladies who were quietly addicted to their laudanum. It might be more socially acceptable than smoking opium, but he wasn't sure the effect was much different on someone as far gone as Lizzie.

"I know. But she's sunk so deep, without laudanum to take the edge off the craving, I don't know that she'd survive. And she's so frail, Granville. It frightens me how frail she is."

She shook her head and looked intently at him. "But that's not why you're here. And you look awful. What has happened?"

Granville gave her a quick summary, assuring her that her brother was recovering well.

Every trace of softness vanished from Frances' lovely face "What can I do?"

"Nothing at the moment. Scott's being cared for and recovering well."

She pushed back a lock of bright hair. "No, what can I do to help you? You're here to track those villains, aren't you? The ones that shot at both of you?"

"Yes, in part. I gather there are rumors we have the map. I wondered if you've heard anything here?"

She bit the tip of one finger as she thought. "Nothing that points towards you and Scott, but let me ask around. You're staying in town?"

"For the moment."

"Don't leave without coming to see me again, then. I might have news."

"Be careful, and don't put yourself in danger. These men are killers," Granville said.

"They tried to kill my brother," she said fiercely.

For a moment she reminded him of a falcon, hooded and jessed, but still a wild creature. "I'll stop back before I leave town, then."

"Make sure you do," Frances said.

AN HOUR LATER, on the other side of town, Robert Benton leaned back in his chair, and regarded Granville. "No sidekicks today?" he asked.

"Not today," Granville said. He'd arranged to meet Trent later. There was no need for the lad to be part of this conversation, and no benefit, either.

"And Scott?"

Wondering how much of this Benton already knew, Granville briefly explained what had happened to Scott.

"So you're looking for your attackers," Benton concluded. "Why come to me?"

"Anything happening in this town, I figure you know about it," Granville said easily.

"And why would I tell you?"

He wouldn't be the one to mention Frances. Granville shrugged, letting the reason lie unspoken between them.

Benton's eyes narrowed and his face took on a hard cast. He sipped the brandy Granville had declined, then placed the snifter back on his desk. "I've heard rumors," he said at last.

"About?"

"Lost mines. Your name has been mentioned."

"Oh?"

"Hmmm. I gather you have ownership of a certain map," Benton said. "And you've made some enemies in this town."

"Not bad for someone who's been here less than two months."

Benton returned his smile. "You have a certain—impact. You could do very well working for me, you know."

"Is that an offer?"

"Would you consider one?"

Granville shook his head, glad he was in a position to refuse. "I'd be honored, but no. Scott would never forgive me if I gave up on our business now."

"You won't reconsider? You might find it less hazardous working for me."

He'd take his chances. "I'm content with my current occupation, thanks. Besides, I don't think my fiancée's father would be too pleased with such a change."

Benton chuckled at that, then watched Granville in silence for a moment. "I know nothing more about the troubles you're having with your lost mine. I may have news of the child, however, though it's only unfounded rumors at the moment."

"Go on."

"I've heard of a ring that traffics in babies, stretching from Chicago to Denver and perhaps as far west as San Francisco," Benton said. "Though I've not been able to confirm any of it."

"What? How?"

"Adoption laws are getting tighter in some states, so there's money to be made in providing would-be parents with desirable infants."

Granville scowled, everything in him revolted at the idea of money made in such a way. "You have a contact?"

"I have a name, a lawyer by the name of Baxter, Darren Baxter, in Denver. But tread carefully. He has a reputation for deviousness."

"As do I."

Benton nodded, his expression unreadable. "You and Scott are headed for Denver?"

"Scott isn't well enough to travel, but as soon as I'm sure he and Emily are safe, I'll be on the first train south." He eyed Benton. "Anything else I should know about who might be trying to kill us?"

"I'd go carefully, if I were you."

Granville heard the warning, but decided to push anyway. "You've heard no details at all? No names of who might be involved?"

"No. I can't help you, I'm afraid."

Can't or won't? "I see," Granville said, standing. "Thank you for the information on Baxter."

17

Clara put a hand to her bonnet as a brisk wind blowing up from Burrard Inlet tilted it forward. "I think this was a mistake, Emily."

"Yes," Emily said, giving her friend a quick smile. She waved a hand at the imposing stone building that housed the *Province* newspaper. "Looking at still more newspaper stories does seem pointless. We should be looking for the photographer who took that picture."

"No, I meant buying this bonnet was a mistake," Clara said. "It matches my coat perfectly, but every time the wind blows it twists around. It's very frustrating."

"For heaven's sake, Clara, there are more important things than fashion."

"Not to me," Clara said with a serious face but a glint of laughter in her eye. "And you promised we'd look at the new dress fabrics."

"Yes, but only after you help me find the photographer."

"You mean after I help you look for the photographer."

"You don't expect us to succeed?"

"Emily, we know already that he doesn't work in Vancouver. No telephone listing, remember? And I want to see those fabrics today, before they sell out."

"I know the studio isn't in Vancouver now, but I don't know how old that photo is."

"I thought you said it was recent," Clara said.

"Oh, that was because Trent looked so upset."

"When he thought an older photo meant the girl would be too old for him? He did look smitten, didn't he? I thought it rather cute."

"Don't let him hear you say that," Emily said with a smile. "I think we need to visit the library."

"But that could take hours! Emily, if we look at fabric first, I won't need to hurry you away from the library. I'll be quick, I promise."

Nearly an hour later, they stood outside the new brick YMCA building, peering up at the heavy doors. A beaming Clara clutched a large brown parcel. Emily couldn't blame her—the maroon silk she had chosen set off her pale skin and dark hair dramatically.

"I'm sure Mr. O'Hearn will appreciate you in that color," she said. "I just hope we'll have long enough here—I hadn't realized they were only open until four."

"Are you sure this is the right place?" Clara asked. "It doesn't look like a library."

"The article I read said the Free Library had just moved here."

"As long as you're not expecting too much from a library housed in a gymnasium."

Emily laughed. "The library is in a separate room, and I understand it's very complete. Why, already they need more space. They've approached Mr. Carnegie, the American philanthropist, about funding an entire new building for it."

"Are you sure they allow entry to women?"

"It's called the Free Library, after all. Press the buzzer again, please Clara. Perhaps they just didn't hear us."

"Perhaps they have gone for the day," Clara said, but she reached out a gloved finger and did as Emily asked. Then she regarded the end of her gloved finger. "Soot," she said in a disdainful voice. "If they have a cleaning woman, she's not doing her job."

Emily was about to say that a little soot was to be expected in a city heated by coal when the door creaked open.

"WELL, now we know why there was no listing for A.J. Morgan," Clara said as they strolled back along Hastings Street, raising their voices slightly to be heard over the clip-clop of hooves on cobblestone.

"Hush Clara, I'm trying to think." How exactly did one go about finding a photographer who was no longer in business? Emily wondered.

She gave a little shiver and drew her coat more closely around her. It was getting late, and the wind was rising, damp and cold. The street lamps would light soon, and her mother would start to worry. They couldn't do anything further tonight.

"Thinking isn't going to get you to New Westminster to find out what happened to that shop. Nor is going to your typewriting class."

Clara sounded rather smug about that last, Emily thought. And what was she going to do about her typewriting class?

She had fought so hard to be allowed to take it, but now helping Granville seemed more important. Yet she did still want to be a typewriter, or at least she thought she did, she amended, remembering with a shudder that harassed looking young man in Mr. Gipson's office.

"Does that mean you'd be willing to go with me to New Westminster again?" Emily said.

Clara shot her a sideways look. "There are several shops we didn't have time to explore."

She couldn't help smiling. "So, if I go shopping with you, you'll come investigating with me?"

Clara pursed her lips slightly and nodded.

Emily burst out laughing. "Admit it, Clara, you're enjoying this every bit as much as I am."

"Only if I get to shop. And I didn't think much of that library. It smelled musty."

It had smelled a little musty, which was no easy feat when the library was only thirteen years old. But the books! Thinking of the stacks of bright bindings, Emily closed her eyes in delight and nearly tripped over a cobblestone.

"Emily, you're daydreaming," Clara said.

"I'm not, simply thinking about all those lovely books."

"Too many books."

"There's no such thing as too many books," Emily said. "They had the business directories we needed, didn't they?"

It had taken less than fifteen minutes to find the listing for A.J. Morgan in the New Westminster listings for 1895, '96 and '97, slightly longer to find that there was no current listing anywhere. "Without the library, how would we have learned anything?"

Clara ignored the question. "So what are you planning now?"

Emily thought quickly. Miss Richards would believe that she was sick again tomorrow, though it would be easier to catch up if she skipped Friday's class instead. But she didn't want to raise Miss Richard's suspicions—there were no other typewriting classes in Vancouver.

Perhaps Laura could help her catch up next week. "Why don't we take the 8:30 tram to New Westminster tomorrow morning."

"I thought we were to meet Mr. Granville for tea tomorrow?"

"Oh no. I'd forgotten."

"Why don't you tell him what we've learned and let him go to New Westminster?" Clara suggested. "It's a matter of business, after all, and you know that no businessman will answer questions put by a lady."

Her friend was right, but somehow Emily couldn't bring herself to pass over this quest to Granville. This was something she could do, she knew it was.

"It depends how a lady asks the questions," Emily said, putting up her umbrella against the light rain that was beginning to fall. “We can arrange to meet Mr. Granville on Sunday, and perhaps he’ll bring Mr. O’Hearn with him.”

Glancing ahead, she could see a familiar green and cream outline. “And if we hurry, we can catch the next streetcar home before it really starts to pour.”

18

FRIDAY, JANUARY 12, 1900

Granville woke with a groan. Every muscle ached, and his arm was on fire.

Coffee. He needed coffee.

Rolling out of the narrow bunk, he nearly tripped over a pair of carelessly dropped boots and swore. Reaching for his trousers, he looked for signs of the boy, coming fully awake with a start when he realized there were none.

No body sprawled across the other bunk, no clothes strewn across the wooden rail at the foot of the bed. No Trent, period.

So where was he? Annoyance was followed by a sharp stab of fear. Granville replayed the events of the previous evening.

After he'd talked to Benton, he'd sent a telegram to Harris in Denver, then collected Trent at the Balmoral. They'd tested the whiskey in most of the seedy bars along the docks while looking for information on their ambushers. Or rather, Granville had tested the whiskey. He'd insisted Trent stick to beer, and kept a sharp eye on the quantity the boy had imbibed.

His own youthful excesses had taught him well. Granville could remember too many occasions where he'd either drunk himself into insensibility or engaged in what started out as a prank and escalated. He'd been sent down twice from Oxford as a result, and that was only for the things they'd caught him doing.

The irony was that he'd been careful to keep an eye on Trent's drinking but paid no attention to his own. Where had they gone after they had left the Balmoral? The Drake? And then? He wasn't sure.

Ostensibly he'd been looking for any word on their attackers, but the bite and the warm burn of the whiskey had seduced him. It countered the cold that seemed to have settled in his bones, and the fire that had taken up residence in his arm.

He didn't remember the rest of the evening, didn't remember coming back here. And he had no idea where Trent was.

Granville rubbed his throbbing temples. The whiskey that seemed to distance him from his problems last night only magnified them today. So what did he do now?

He hadn't the remotest idea where to look for Trent, even less as to when he'd last seen him. Anything could have happened to him. And what of the map?

Granville put a hand to his chest, breathed a sigh of relief to feel the packet holding the map and the photo. Unless... He drew out the packet, opened it. The map and letter fragment were still there. And Emily had the photo, he did remember that.

But Trent was gone, and his head was pounding too loudly to think straight. He needed coffee, strong, black and lots of it, possibly followed by hair of the dog. Then he'd find Trent.

With another groan, he heaved to his feet. As he stood the door burst open, and Trent rushed into the room. "Granville, you'll never guess."

Granville looked at that beaming face with intense relief. "First let me get some coffee into me. It's too early for all this enthusiasm."

Trent grinned sympathetically. "It's nearly noon," he said over his shoulder as he led the way out the door.

"Now can I tell you?" Trent asked a quarter hour later, his voice nearly lost in the hubbub of voices and clatter of crockery. Sally's Diner was always busy, because the food was plentiful and cheap.

Granville drained the last of his coffee, gestured for more. "Go ahead."

Trent flashed him a grin too knowing for Granville's liking. "Head still giving you the devil, eh?"

He gave the boy a look. "If you've got something to say, say it."

Trent smiled more broadly, seemingly unfazed by his ill humor. "Pa used to get like that when he drank. He always felt better after he ate. Try it." He waved towards the stack of flapjacks and sausage on Granville's plate, awash in melted butter and maple syrup.

Trent was comparing him to his indigent father?

"Impertinent upstart," he growled, but took a tentative bite anyway. He never knew how his stomach would react after a hard night, but the sweet doughiness of the flapjacks seemed to sit just fine.

Suddenly realizing he was famished, Granville stabbed up another forkful. "So talk."

"First, here's the response to your telegram."

Granville ran his eyes over it and nodded. Harris would expect his arrival.

Trent leaned closer, lowered his voice. "And I may have a lead on the owner of the map."

Much as he appreciated Trent's discretion, he was hard pressed not to laugh at his turn to melodrama. If anyone were watching them, Trent's actions had just convinced them there was something to watch for.

Granville flicked another assessing glance around the room. No one appeared the least interested in them. He recognized a few gamblers from last night, who looked even worse than he felt, and seemed to be paying no heed to anything except the coffee they were drinking with the air of desperate men.

Another table held men who looked like they worked in the rail yards, and beyond them two brakemen, still in the gray striped coveralls and peaked caps that proclaimed their occupation, were silently working their way through mounds of flapjacks accompanied by a stack of thick sausages. None of them displayed any interest in Trent or himself.

Granville kept a wary eye on them, all the same. "Go on."

"I went into the office this morning to check the mail, like you asked, and the guy who was following us last night trailed me," Trent said. "This time I recognized him. It was the kid from Port Hammond, the one that sent the telegram."

"We were followed?" Granville cursed his lack of memory.

Trent gave him a look he couldn't read, but nodded. "You noted him right off, so we went into the Drake, then out a back door and lost him. I thought he looked familiar, but it was too dark to see clearly. When he tailed me again this morning I recognized him."

He'd seen the man? Granville prodded at the black hole in his memory, but found nothing. He cursed under his breath.

This hadn't happened to him since he'd taken ship from England for the Klondike, despite all the hard drinking he'd done there. Why now? What made last night different?

Suddenly aware that Trent was watching him closely, he gave another silent curse, and picked up the thread of the conversation. "So he followed you to the office. Then what?"

"I managed to lose him right after I got the telegram. Then I followed him."

"Good for you. So where'd he go?"

"Riggs's Livery Stable," Trent said triumphantly. "That's the one that Miss Emily told us about yesterday."

"And?"

"Riggs was mad at him for losing us, and the kid got really upset." Trent's voice hitched a little. "Seems the guys shooting at us didn't make it out, and two of them were his father and brother."

Granville could tell Trent was thinking of his own father, and wondered if the boy had any idea where the man had run. "That's hard."

"Yeah." Trent stopped, took a breath. "Anyway, the kid just wanted to shoot us."

"Understandable. I gather that's not what Riggs wanted?"

"No. Riggs wants to know what we're up to. He's passing the information to someone."

Could it be Gipson? "You get a name?" Granville asked.

"Nope, they never said. But Riggs is afraid of him."

Interesting. "What information was he after?"

"Wants to know where the map is," Trent said. "They aren't sure who has it. And Riggs said you can't question a dead man."

"We may have to do something about these idiots before one of them kills us by mistake."

"I kinda thought you might feel that way," Trent said. "So I followed him when he left Riggs's."

"And he didn't notice you?"

Trent looked offended. "He's just a boy. I've been tracking warier prey since I was eight. 'Sides, anything walking on two legs uses fewer senses than those that walk on four."

It was probably true. Granville had spent more time with the two-legged kind himself. "And?"

"And he sent a telegram back to Port Hammond." Trent pulled a second creased piece of yellow paper out of his pocket, and slid it across the table.

"How did you get this?" He scanned the words, felt his stomach clench. Scott was in danger.

"Bribed the telegraph operator. They aren't paid much, y'know."

"Good work, Trent. Finish your coffee. It's past time to lose our shadow."

Trent's eyes widened. "He's here?"

He nodded to the far corner, where the boy who'd been watching them had his face half buried in the *World*. "That him?"

"Yeah, that's the one. So how're we going to lose him?"

"I have my ways."

"You're not going to tell me?"

"Not a chance. You'll have to wait and see."

"Well, I don't call that fair. I thought we were supposed to be a team."

Granville gave him a look. "Whatever gave you that idea?"

Trent quickly raised his coffee cup, drained it. "Then what?"

"We go back to Katzie, but first we pay a quick visit to Frances."

THE MAID who answered the door at the quiet house on Beatty Street conducted them quickly to an elegant parlor. Looking about him, Granville was impressed by the lack of feathers and frills. He could imagine Benton feeling very much at home here.

"It's nice," Trent said.

Frances burst into the room before he could reply. Pointing a finger at him, she said, "I've been asking questions. Your quest for that mine has made you and Sam targets. The two of you've made someone very angry.

No surprise there. "Who?"

"I couldn't get a name. Either he's kept it hidden, or my sources are too afraid of him to say."

Neither bode well for him or Scott. "Anything else?"

"Nothing. Give it up, Granville. Before you and Sam, or Trent here, get killed.

"I wish I could, but it's too late for that," he told her. "As long as we have the map, we'll be targets."

19

Emily stepped off the streetcar in New Westminster, raising her umbrella against the persistent drizzle. She drew in a breath of fresh, river scented air. It smelled good after the soot and cigar smoke-laden air of the train carriage. Glancing up and down Columbia to get her bearings, she turned quickly to her right and set off.

Clara clutched her arm, keeping step beside her. With a bright smile, she twirled her own umbrella to an angle that framed her face at the same time it kept off the worst of the damp. "Just how are you planning to find this photographer?"

"I intend to go to the last address we found and ask. With any luck, we'll find someone who remembers him."

"That's good thinking, Emily. Your Mr. Granville will be proud."

Emily could feel her face heating up, and hoped that Clara wouldn't notice. Foolish of her. When had Clara ever not noticed people's reactions?

"Emily, you're blushing. His opinion matters to you," Clara said, a knowing look in her eyes.

Emily flushed even deeper. She hadn't even told Clara about the temporary nature of her engagement. Now she wondered if having only herself and Granville knowing the truth had made the engagement seem more real. Yes, she was determined to have a career, but her feelings for Granville seemed to keep getting stronger.

Not quite sure what to do with that thought, she brushed off Clara's insight with a little laugh. "We're engaged, aren't we?"

"But you're not sitting home embroidering your trousseau, nor bubbling over with raptures about how wonderful your fiancé is."

Clara's eyes were fixed on her face. Emily tried to school her expression to reflect nothing of her feelings. "My embroidery is dreadful, and I couldn't bubble if I tried."

"No. You're far more caught up in saving his life, even above that typewriting school you fought so hard to attend. And Emily, you're good at this investigating business. The way you're tracking down the photographer? You're as good at it as I am at finding bargains. You should be working with Mr. Granville."

"I've been thinking something similar, Clara," she confessed. "When I have completed my typewriting lessons, perhaps I can manage his office."

Clara stopped walking and turned to face Emily. "For heaven's sake Emily. What is wrong with you? I've never heard you underestimate your own abilities before. You should be a detective, not a typewriter."

"But I want to be a typewriter."

"Do you really?" Clara said. "Or do you just want to have a career, and typewriting is the only one starting to open to ladies?"

"Well..."

"Emily, do you even like your typewriting classes?"

"No!" Emily said before she thought. "Well, it is all very interesting of course..."

"Horse-feathers!" Clara said, then blushed. "Well, it is. You liked the idea of typewriting. You've been looking for every excuse to avoid the reality of it."

"Saving Granville's life is not an excuse."

"Looking for the missing heiress is not exactly saving his life, though, is it?" Clara said. "It seems to me more along the line of helping him with his detecting business."

"Yes, but..."

"But?"

"Oh, Clara, you're right," Emily burst out. "You're saying everything I've been thinking, but trying not to think."

"Why not?"

"How is it even possible? No-one will let me truly work at detecting."

"Your husband might."

Emily took a deep breath, let it out in a long sigh. It was time to tell Clara the truth. "We're not really engaged. It's only until I finish typewriting school."

Clara gave Emily a long look, nodded once and began walking, urging Emily along. "I knew there was something you weren't telling me. This calls for a cup of tea."

SHE FELT MUCH BETTER for having confided in her friend, Emily thought as she watched Clara examine several rolls of laces, comparing two delicate patterns before finally settling on a third. None of her questions were answered, and the problems were still there, but at least she was no longer trying to pretend they weren't.

"I'll take this one," Clara finally said, handing the other two back to the gentleman behind the counter. She unrolled a length of the lace she'd chosen, held it at arm's length and examined it critically, then gave a little nod. "Yes, this is the one. Three yards, please."

Turning to Emily, she asked, "What do you think?"

"It's very pretty, Clara."

"I'm thinking of using it to trim the maroon silk I bought yesterday."

"Mmm—lovely. Are you ready to go?"

Clara smiled at her. "I thought your patience was too good to last. Yes, I'm done." And to the shop clerk, "Could you wrap those, please?"

Fifteen minutes later, they were strolling along the sidewalk bordering Columbia Street. All of these handsome buildings had been damaged or destroyed by the fire and largely rebuilt.

Number 439 was now a barbershop, and the owner had never heard of an A.J. Morgan. The tobacconist on the east side was no better, nor was the hardware store on the west.

"This is hopeless," Emily said. "None of the shops are the same as they were before the fire."

"We should try the shops across the street. Perhaps one of them will remember the photographer."

Emily looked where Clara was pointing, and couldn't help but smile. It was a hat shop.

The woman showing Clara a very smart little bonnet with maroon ribbon had never heard of a photographer at that location. "I only started working here a year past," she said.

"No, the establishment we are interested in closed at least two years ago," Emily said.

Clara looked thoughtfully at Emily, then glanced back at the clerk. "You've never heard of an A.J. Morgan or his photographic studio?" she asked.

The woman shook her head. "I'm sorry, no. In fact, I think there is only one photographic studio in town. But—did you say Morgan?"

"That's right. A.J. Morgan."

"Well, how odd."

"What is odd?" Emily asked.

"Well, I do know a Morgan. Albert. But whether he is an A.J. I don't know."

"And is he a photographer?"

"No, or at least not now," the woman said. "He's a clerk. But I don't know him well—he's my mother's second cousin's son-in-law."

"And he lives in town?"

"Yes. In fact, he works right around the corner, for Butler and Resnick. The properties and accounting firm."

"Do you think he would talk to me?" Emily asked.

"I don't see why not. But you will have to wait until he finishes work. Butler's is very strict—their employees aren't allowed visitors."

"Thank you very much," Emily said. "Come along, Clara."

"Thank you for your assistance, and I'll think about the bonnet," Clara said to the clerk. "That particular shade is very effective. I shall have to bring in my material and see if it matches."

"If not, we should be able to find some trim that does match—our selection is extensive."

"Truly?" Clara said. "Oh, well in that case I will definitely be back. Thank you again."

As they stepped back into the street, the rain had cleared, but a chill wind had come up off the river. Holding her bonnet against the wind that tugged fiercely at it, Clara hurried to catch Emily's brisk pace.

Reaching her friend's side just as she turned the corner onto Columbia, Clara was too breathless to speak for several blocks. Finally she said, "Emily, slow down. What are you planning to do now? The last tram leaves at 4:30 and this Mr. Morgan does not finish work until 6:00."

"Yes, I know."

Clara looked at her. "Oh, Emily, what are you planning now? We were just told that Butler's does not allow their staff to have visitors."

"And if we are not visitors, but customers?" Emily said.

"In a properties firm? Are you mad?" Clara said. "Women cannot buy real estate."

"No, but their husbands can. Or in this case their future husbands."

"That would be their pretend future husbands?"

Emily stopped walking. "That was unkind, Clara."

Clara's cheeks turned red, but she met Emily's eyes. "I know it, and I'm sorry," she said. "But Emily, I worry about you. You insist on *doing* things."

"Wasn't it you who just said I should be a detective? Besides, why shouldn't women be able to purchase real estate? And not just in the name of our husbands, either."

Clara shook her head with a reluctant smile. "You know, your life would be so much easier if you just wanted to be the best dressed lady in town."

"But would it be this interesting?" Emily said with a little smile. "Come along, Clara, we have a former photographer to interview."

"You don't even know he's the right man," Clara said to Emily's departing back. "Oh, very well."

BEYOND THE GILT lettering on the door-window, the offices of Butler and Resnick were very orderly, with a gleaming dark-stained oak countertop and two matching desks with ledgers and neat stacks of paper on them. The walls held serried rows of photographs, presumably of the properties they had available for sale.

Emily eyed them speculatively. Could Mr. Morgan have taken these photos? If so, it might explain the otherwise odd leap from fashionable photographer to real estate and accounting clerk. Always assuming it was the same man, of course, but the photos at least gave her hope.

"May I help you?"

The voice belonged to a clerk who looked too young to be an ex-photographer now launched on a second career. He had slicked-back dark hair that wanted to wave over his ears, large brown eyes and an expression that bordered on panic as he regarded Emily.

Obviously they did not get many female clients, Emily thought as she gave him a reassuring smile.

The young man's Adam's apple bobbed, his gaze darting from her to Clara and pausing on her friend. Emily seized on his momentary distraction to examine his hands. In addition to the tell-tale ink stains on his index finger, his fingertips showed a dark staining, the kind of marks one might get from developing negatives, she thought with rising excitement.

"Good afternoon," she said, drawing his eyes back to her with a jerk. "My fiancé has asked me to collect some information on various properties he might have an interest in purchasing. But I must ask, are you the photographer for these truly excellent photos of the properties?" She gestured towards the wall.

He nodded, looking pleased. She'd been right, Emily thought. This was A.J. Morgan, and soon she would have the name of Granville's missing heiress.

"Mr. Morgan?" she asked. To her surprise, a tinge of red appeared in the clerk's cheeks and the very tips of his ears flamed.

"Ah—No, I mean—Well, some of the photos are mine. Mostly mine. Well, I helped develop them. Well, some of them."

Emily nodded. Her cousin Cyril was about this man's age, and similarly unable to get out a full sentence in mixed company. "I see. And is Mr. Morgan teaching you photography?"

"Well, yes."

"And where is Mr. Morgan?" she asked, looking behind the young man for any sign of a more mature clerk.

"I—well—he—I cannot say."

Emily blinked twice at this, but Clara spoke before her. "Cannot?" she said in a very sweet tone, and smiled at the poor young man.

"He's ill. But Mr. Resnick cannot know," the young man said quickly, lowering his voice and darting a glance to door leading to the rear offices.

"And where does Mr. Resnick think he is?" Emily asked.

"Out taking photos. He's been sick too often this winter—they're talking of firing him if he misses any more time. And he has a wife, and a baby daughter."

"It's very good of you, to protect him so," Clara said with a beaming smile. "And perhaps we can pay a visit to his wife, see if she needs any assistance."

"They aren't there."

"Not there?" Clara asked, leaning forward slightly.

The clerk flushed and hesitated. "They've gone to Vancouver, to stay with his aunt," he said at last. "I don't know where."

"Thank you for your time," Emily said, taking out a small notebook. "I'll just make a note of these properties you're offering. And I'll be sure to tell my fiancé that this is a most reputable firm, and a good place to do his real estate transactions. Come along, Clara."

When they were standing in the street once again, Clara turned to her and frowned. "Do you know how many times today you have told me to come along?"

Emily tried not to smile. "Well, I'm sorry, but I didn't want you to stay and flirt with that young man—you had confused him quite enough already."

"Flirt? Me? Why Emily, what do you take me for? And where are you going?"

"I take you for a good friend," Emily said, stopping and looking over her shoulder. "Thank you for your help in there. And I'm going back to your favorite hat shop, to ask the shop assistant whether her mother's second cousin's sister happens to live in Vancouver."

Clara hmmphed dramatically and slid her arm into Emily's. "You have no idea how fatiguing it is, being your friend," she said, giving Emily's arm a small squeeze.

20

SATURDAY, JANUARY 13, 1900

Granville and Trent rode in silence, shadows wavering ahead of them in the odd light of pre-dawn. A thick mist wound among the trees and sat heavily along the river.

"Are we going to stay at Katzie until Mr. Scott can ride?" Trent finally asked, his voice barely carrying above the soft clinking of their horse's bridles.

"Perhaps. It depends how quickly he's healing."

"I still don't see why we had to leave town so early."

"You'd rather have waited for daylight," Granville said. "And made it easy for our pursuer?"

"He's in jail," Trent said. "It was a nice trick, tying him to the robberies in the West End."

"He'd been seen there, hadn't he, wandering the residential streets, as if checking out his next target?"

"Only because he was following us, and that's where you led him. It was brilliant!"

"Thank you. It was, however, a trick, and like all tricks only good for a time," Granville said. "We needed to vanish before he was released from jail, or able to get word out to one of his gang."

"I guess that makes sense."

"Good of you to say so," Granville said, deadpan.

"You're making fun of me."

"Only a little."

"Oh, well, so long as it's only a little."

He heard the laugh in Trent's voice, and grinned. At least the boy had kept his sense of humor, even if someone was trying to kill them.

It just made him angry, but he hadn't been sure about Trent. Who was proving to be made of tougher stuff than Granville had imagined. He'd probably had to be, to survive.

"Why the sudden return to Katzie?" Trent asked. "It's about that telegram, isn't it?"

"Yes. It was veiled, but the threat was there."

"Threat?"

"Against Scott. Injured, he'd be easy pickings if they decided to kill us one by one," Granville said. "Besides, now that I have Emily's promise not to put herself in danger, we have some unfinished business in Katzie."

The sky was lightening in the east by the time they crossed the Pitt River bridge and Granville could see the tide running, creating little ripples that glittered on the wide spread of the Fraser. The Katzie village was hazed with smoke from a number of fires, under a lowering gray sky. It looked small, cold and far from welcoming.

"Where can we leave the horses?" he asked Trent.

"Follow me."

As they rounded the corner of a small wooden building, he was surprised and rather amused to see their two mules. "Too stubborn to die," he muttered.

The mule Trent had named John turned and regarded him for a moment, then brayed. Granville would swear he heard derision in the sound.

"Easy for you to say," he said to the mule. "You cost me a pretty penny at the livery."

"What's that?" Trent turned to look at him.

Granville pointed to the two mules. "Those are ours."

"I figured they'd make it down eventually—they're pretty tough. And I bet old man Devoy will be glad to get them back."

"Except they're no longer his mules. After the amount I paid him for their loss, those are now our mules."

Trent looked from the mules to Granville, his expression considering. "We going after the gold?"

"Yes. Eventually."

Trent's eyes searched Granville's face, then his nose twitched. "I smell bannock," he said. "Nothing beats the taste of fresh bannock, and I'm starved. Let's go."

"They may not be too happy to feed you."

"C'mon, you never heard of hospitality? Course they'll feed me. Us. And if we're lucky, they'll have dried salmon, too. You've never tasted anything like it—they catch a half ton of it every fall, when the salmon run up the Fraser, then dry it in the sun, to preserve it, and mmmm." He rolled his eyes and smacked his lips, an expression of such delight on his face that Granville laughed.

"Then for your sake I hope they serve us some dried salmon with the bannock."

"You'll see," Trent said as he opened the wooden door and preceded him into the longhouse.

GRANVILLE HAD a confused impression of sound and movement. Ignoring the commotion in the center, he ran his eye along the empty bunks on the far wall to where he'd last seen Scott. He spotted a still form, swathed in blankets and his breath caught in a suddenly tight throat.

Had Scott's wound gone putrid? It'd only been two days, but he'd seen men take ill and die more quickly than that. He'd also seen them linger in agony for weeks.

He made his way to where his friend lay and stooped down. A loud rattling sounded and the blankets stirred violently. He froze.

With a second raucous snore Scott flung the blanket away from his face, then turned on his side and covered his head again. With a relieved grin Granville turned back towards the center of the longhouse. That brief glimpse of Scott's fever-free face was enough to reassure him.

Trent still stood near the entrance to the longhouse. He seemed to be looking for someone. When he caught sight of Granville watching him, he rushed over.

"Mr. Moore from New Westminster wants to talk to us," Trent said. "Seems he has some questions about Mr. Cole's murder."

"And who is Mr. Moore?" Granville asked.

"I'm a detective with the New Westminster police."

The voice came from somewhere behind Trent. It was attached to a tall, gaunt-faced man with thick dark eyebrows, a shock of wiry black hair and an aggrieved expression.

"You're the one reported the death?" Moore asked him.

"I am," Granville said.

"Report says you think it was deliberate, not hunters with very poor aim," Moore said. "You sure about that?"

"Given that they managed to shoot three out of the four of us, I think we have to make that assumption," Granville said.

"Hmmm. And you don't have descriptions?

"I never saw more than dark shadows in the trees. Trent?"

"That's all I saw, too," Trent said.

One of Moore's thick eyebrows went up, and he made a note. "And you've no idea who your pursuers were?"

"None."

"Or why they were shooting at you?"

Granville shook his head, hoping that Trent wouldn't choose this moment to contribute to the conversation. "I'm afraid not. Unless they had a grudge against our client that extended to the rest of the party."

"The murdered man, Cole, was your client, then?" Moore asked.

"He was," Granville said.

"And what was it he hired you to do?"

"He hired my partner and myself to..."

"Your partner?"

Granville indicated the blanket wrapped lump that was Scott. "My partner."

Moore's eyebrows climbed. "No-one mentioned two murders."

A grin split Trent's face.

"He's injured, not dead," Granville said. "As I was saying, Cole..."

"Injured?"

"Shot. He received two bullets, I was shot once. Our assistant here," he indicated Trent, who beamed, "Received a concussion and a badly bruised arm in trying to escape the avalanche our assailants created."

"An avalanche?"

Granville gave up trying to keep the story simple, and explained the ambush.

Moore's eyebrows inched higher and his pencil flew. "So why were you hired?"

"My late client heard rumors of a lost mine, and hired us to assist him in finding it," he said.

"In January?"

"There are no other miners prospecting in January. Cole was paranoid about being followed."

"Hmmm. He may've had a point, given how he died."

Granville gave Moore a sharp look. The officer was jotting something in his notebook, his thick brows drawn slightly together. Not even a hint of a smile. "So what happens now?"

"I'll need to examine the body. Where is it?"

Granville and Trent exchanged glances. "We cached it during the attack," Granville said. "Perhaps it'd be best if we brought it here."

"I'll accompany you," Moore said.

Granville couldn't allow that, not while the body was hidden with the gold from the cache, though Moore's presence might deter any further attacks. "Of course. But first I need to see to my partner's well-being."

"I'll wait." And with a nod and another sharp look at Granville,

Moore ambled off in the direction the scent of fresh baking was coming from.

No doubt he would wait.

GRANVILLE'S EYES searched the crowd for the shaman, when he realized someone was staring at him. He turned his head slowly. Scott's gray eyes were fixed on him.

The big man was half-slumped against the rough board wall, but he was upright and his eyes were clear. Catching Granville's look, Scott levered himself upright, wavered a moment, then sauntered over and clapped him on the shoulder. "Thanks for leaving me behind."

Granville winced.

"That the shoulder got shot?"

He nodded. He'd thought the arm was healing well, but Scott's arm was nearly back to its old power, roughly similar to a swipe from a grizzly. Obviously his partner was feeling better. "You look pretty good."

"Yeah. How is Emily?"

"She's just fine."

"So how did she find out about the ambush?" Scott asked.

"Oddly enough, her classmates at the typewriting school have fathers who appear to be involved. They also have loose lips."

"Can we follow that connection?"

"She's already done so," Granville said. "And it seems Gipson may be involved—he's in partnership with one of the men."

"Him again. Too bad they can't just run him out of town."

Granville smiled. "Ah, but we are in civilization now. No frontier justice here."

"I liked the Klondike better."

In some ways, so had Granville. Life there was stripped to the essentials. You knew what mattered, when it took everything you had to survive. "That isn't what you said when we only took enough gold out of Rabbit Creek to buy food for two weeks."

"We'd have been just fine if we hadn't been at the back of beyond, with bread costing a dollar a loaf and coffee even more," Scott retorted.

"Ah, but the back of beyond was where the gold was."

"That's what I like about our new mine. It's close to civilization."

"There wasn't much civilized about that valley. We're lucky we found our way out again."

"Yeah, but that's winter," Scott said. "And this time, there's no permafrost to deal with, so we can dig in the summer, like sane people."

"Except that it isn't our mine."

Scott gave him a look that said he couldn't believe what he was hearing. "You've got the map, haven't you?" he asked. "And the rightful owner is dead? Not that I'm sure Cole was the rightful owner, but there's no one else around, so that leaves us. And a gold mine. All's we have to do is register it."

Granville realized he hadn't told Scott the details of his last conversation with their former client. "Before he died, Cole hired us to find the heir to the mine."

"What heir?"

"I don't have a name—the old man died before he could get the words out."

"That makes it easy," Scott said. "By default the map is ours. And the mine too."

"We do have a photo."

"A photo? You're foolin' with me, right?"

He grinned at Scott's tone, and shook his head. "I'm afraid not. I gave my word of honor."

Scott snorted. "I don't see why we should put all the effort into tracking down some fool doesn't deserve it more than we do."

"We're doing it for another five percent of the mine," Granville said. "We'll be entitled to ten percent of everything that comes out of the ground, and without doing any of the work."

"Ten percent sounds pretty small compared to the hundred percent we've got now. You really want to hand off ninety percent of a gold mine to some dude neither of us know?"

"I gave my word," Granville said. "And the dude is a woman."

"A woman?"

"A girl, really, judging by the photo. And one in need of money, from what Cole said."

"A girl." Scott shook his shaggy head as if to clear it.

"And a pretty girl at that."

"Ah, you're just trying to get to me," Scott said. "It's not a girl."

"Yes, I'm afraid it is."

"So where's the picture?"

"Emily has it, to help her find the photographer. There's also part of a letter. Remind me to show you later."

"Hah. If I didn't know you better, I'd think you were trying to trick me out of my share," Scott said. "So what are you really up to?"

Granville raised his right hand. "My word of honor. The map belongs to a girl named Mary, except for the ten percent that is ours."

"It really belongs to a girl?"

"Yes."

"Well, damn. It was a nice dream while it lasted," Scott said, and slumped back against the wall.

"Are you forgetting our cut?"

"No, but no young girl's going to be able to get that gold out. Probably won't even know how to register it."

"She will if we help her," Granville said.

"I thought we were out of the mining business."

"We are. Now we're in the mining exploration business," Granville said.

Scott's eyebrows drew together. "And that's different how?"

"We provide the advice, someone else does the digging."

"So who pays for the digging?"

"She will, of course, as the owner."

"I thought she was broke," Scott said.

Granville rolled his eyes. "She won't be once she gets her share of the gold Cole was carrying out."

Scott's frown gradually lifted, and a grin stretched across his face. "So once we get that cache safely in a bank, we're set."

"Precisely. Assuming we can manage not to be killed before we find the heiress and help her to register the mine."

"We've survived this long," Scott said, then shot Granville a suspicious look. "So why aren't you still in Vancouver, anyway?

"I thought you might have had visitors."

"Visitors? You mean like those polecats who were after us?"

"Exactly like them," Granville said.

"Nope, haven't seen hide nor hair of them. In this crowd, I would have noticed."

"Is it my imagination, or is it more crowded in here than it was the last time I was here?"

"There's a bunch of visitors here," Scott said. "Mostly from the Island."

Granville raised an eyebrow inquiringly.

"Vancouver Island," Scott clarified. "Bout thirty miles away, most of those miles open ocean. Anyway, they all showed up day before yesterday. I think they're planning some kind of dance."

Visions of these solemn people clad in ball gowns and tuxedos and swirling to the strains of a Viennese waltz glided through Granville's mind, and his lips quirked. "Dance?"

"Some kind of a celebration and healing ceremony, I gather," Scott told him. "Supposed to be quite something, according to Arbuthnot. Isn't something non-Indians usually get to see, but until they decide I'm well, they're not about to kick me out."

"So what does the shaman say about you?"

Scott grinned. "He tends to shake his head and mutter a lot."

"Not surprising. But what does he say about your injuries?"

Scott ignored him. "As I was saying, on the whole the shaman seems pleased with how I'm doing. So I'm ready to leave whenever you are."

GRANVILLE LOOKED CLOSELY AT SCOTT, seeing the small beads of sweat that had popped out on his upper lip, and the way he'd gradually leaned more solidly against the pillar as they'd talked. "I'm thinking about making this my base for a while."

"Why? And don't be thinking I'm not up to riding."

Remembering Scott bent forward, hauling fifty pound loads up the steep Chilkoot Trail, then going back and doing it again and again and again, all the while suffering from the remains of a persistent bout of influenza, Granville had no doubt his partner could do anything he set his mind to.

"I'm worried Benton may be involved," Granville said. As a distraction, it worked better than he'd expected.

"Benton?" Scott said. "Why?"

"He didn't give me any names for our pursuers, but he did give me a veiled warning. And he tried to hire me."

"Hire you?" Scott thought about that for a moment. "That's either a compliment or a bad sign. And why now?"

"Probably both. And I confess it's the timing that worries me."

Granville could see Scott digesting this piece of information, examining its implications. "They send someone after you?"

"Trent and I had a tail the entire time. He made no effort to shoot at us, though."

"So they're after information."

"That's my thought. They aren't sure which of us has the map."

Scott nodded slowly. "Did you talk to Frances?"

"Yes. She hadn't heard anything."

"And Lizzie?" There was reluctance in Scott's tone, as if he was bracing himself for bad news about his youngest sister.

"Frances says she's eating. And has stopped smoking opium." Granville hoped that heartening news would distract Scott, keep him from asking about his niece.

"And little Sarah? Any news?" Scott asked.

He couldn't lie. Reluctantly, Granville pulled out the crumpled telegram, handed it over.

Scott's eyes scanned the few lines, met Granville's. "So that's what you're doing back here."

Granville grabbed back the paper, scanned it. He'd given Scott the wrong telegram. He hadn't meant to tell his partner about the threat on his own life.

Scott was watching him closely. "You might as well give me the other one," he said, holding out a hand.

Silently Granville handed over the telegram Emily had kept for him, watching his friend's face pale as he read it. When he'd finished, Scott's big hand fisted around the flimsy paper. "If you have this, why aren't you on the train to Denver?"

"We're no good to little Sarah if we're dead."

Scott gave him a hard stare. "I can take care of myself."

"That's not the issue. I don't think they'll give up easily, not with a gold mine at stake. If I thought it'd draw them out after me, I'd be on the next train to Denver."

"You think it wouldn't."

"Not as long as you're here," Granville said.

"I'm good to ride."

No, he wasn't. "We'll need money first, which means the gold. And I think we'll have to produce Cole's body before long, since there's a detective here. We can't get to Denver if we're in jail."

Scott ignored his attempt at humor. "So what's the plan?"

"I thought I'd hand the body over to the law, get out enough gold to look for little Sarah and re-hide the rest. Then we'll take ourselves and the map to Denver."

Not fooled by the explanation, Scott reached out and gripped his partner's shoulder hard. "Thanks."

"Don't thank me. I'm just tired of being shot at."

A commotion on the other side of the room captured Granville's attention. Scott followed his gaze.

"It looks like the dancing's about to start," Scott said.

"Now?"

"Yup. They've been feasting and preparing for two days. Look."

Granville watched in fascination as first one and then several gray haired Indian matrons stood up and began to sway, chanting as they did so. Nothing further from the waltz could be imagined, yet there was a stately grace to this form of dance.

"Are they Katzie?" he asked.

Scott squinted his eyes to see better down the length of the hall. "The middle one is. The others are relations from the Island. Sisters, cousins, who knows."

"The clans are closely related?"

"Tribes. And you're asking me?" He gave Granville a quick grin.

"Well, if you've been spending any time talking to Arbuthnot, I thought you might have picked up something."

"How do you think I know as much as I do? And that's another thing. What' d'you mean by inflicting him on me when I was too weak to get away?" Scott said with a scowl.

"Mr. Arbuthnot struck me as a very convivial gentleman," Granville said with a straight face.

"Huh. The man loves to talk. And he's fascinated with everything to do with the Indians in this region of the world, really a fount of knowledge on the subject. Problem is, the man's also a prosy bore."

He grinned. "I rather thought he might be. But for all that he's the epitome of the upright Victorian gentleman—I knew if you needed something he'd see to it."

"Hmmmph," Scott said. "Well, if you want to know about these dances, you can ask him yourself. The lecture you'll get will serve you right."

"This is fascinating," Granville said, his eyes on the slowly spinning figures.

"Yup, sure is. But I'm happy to watch it—I don't need to know the ins and outs of it all."

Granville watched as the women swayed and chanted. "I think I'll have that chat with Arbuthnot."

"You have that look in your eye again. I don't think it's dancing you're going to be asking about, is it?"

"I might start by asking about dancing."

"Hmmpf. Last time you got that look in your eye, you tricked a bunch of tenderfeet that had their eye on our claim into prospecting up the other end of Rabbit Creek. And look how well that turned out."

Granville glanced sideways at Scott. "You know full well it wasn't my fault they hit pay dirt on that supposedly worthless claim."

"All I know is our digging got us nothing but gravel and more gravel."

"We found enough color to buy our food. Most of the time."

"Well, I'm hoping you can do better this time," Scott said. "Maybe you can even avoid the black eye that you got as part of those negotiations."

"I hardly think Arbuthnot is going to punch me in the eye."

"Nope, but the ones you're hoping to trick will probably do worse to you."

"Not likely."

Scott chortled, but Granville noted in concern how pale he was under the weathered tan his face wore even in winter.

21

"Mr. Arbuthnot?"

The small man, dapper in spite of the fact he'd been living out of a trunk for the last week, turned away from the dancing to see who had addressed him. His face lit up when he saw Granville.

"Mr. Granville! You have seen how well your friend is doing?" He was nearly shouting to make himself heard over the drumming and the rhythmic stomping of moccasin-clad feet.

"Yes indeed, and I thank you for looking after him so well."

"Oh, I did nothing. It was the *olia's* doing. They say he's the last one amongst all the *Halkomellem* to truly know the old ways of medicine and of healing. In fact, he's the reason they're holding this dance."

The mention of the dancing momentarily distracted him. "Why is that?" he asked.

"They say Peter Pierre knows all of the old spirit chants."

Suddenly Granville lost all interest in the dance. "Pierre? Is he the same man who spent time with an old Indian named Slumach before he was hanged for murder?"

Arbuthnot nodded. "He is indeed. In fact, he's his nephew.

Slumach turned himself in to Pierre when he finally could hide no longer."

"Were you here then?"

"Not at all—I only brought my family out from England in '92. But the stories of what happened are everywhere."

"In '92? You have learned a great deal of the Indian culture for so short a time."

"Thank you. It is a passion of mine," he said.

"Have you heard of Slumach's lost mine, also?"

Arbuthnot smiled. "Everyone has heard those stories. But don't waste your time on them, there's no more truth in them than in most 'pot of gold' stories."

He gave Granville a penetrating look. "But did I not hear Mr. Scott say the two of you were in the Klondike?"

"That's right," Granville said, bracing himself for the endless questions that information usually evoked.

But Arbuthnot merely nodded. "You know whereof I speak, then."

"Yes. The gold was there, but for every man who came out with a fortune, thousands lost everything. For some poor souls that included their lives."

"I fear it is the same with the Lost Mine of Pitt Lake," Arbuthnot said. "Except that in this case, there *is* no gold, but still those who chase it lose everything."

Except that there was gold in the Lost Mine, and plenty of it. "Have you ever asked Pierre about it?"

Arbuthnot shook his head, lips firming a prim line under the little mustache he wore.

"I would not care to be so rude," he said. "The poor man has undoubtedly heard more than enough on the subject from others. He's been good enough to offer me the shelter of his home. I would not profane that with base enquiries. He has far more important information to impart."

Granville fought to hold back a smile at his tone—he rather liked the little man.

"Thank you. And where might I find Pierre? I want to thank him for his care of Scott," he hastened to add, for Arbuthnot was now giving him a disappointed look.

"He's over there," Arbuthnot said, waving towards a man of medium height with a broad, pleasant face and long black hair tied back in a braid and threaded through with eagle feathers.

It was the shaman who'd cut the bullet out of him and doctored Scott.

Granville made his way through the cheerful crowd to where the shaman stood. "Mr. Pierre?"

He turned to face Granville. "Ah. You are well? The arm is not painful?"

"Yes, I'm very well, and grateful to you for it. And for caring for my friend so well."

"He is most welcome here. A man of gentle spirit, I think."

Granville glanced over at where Scott towered above the others, thought of all the fights he'd won, yet Pierre had the right of it. "Yes. He is."

The Katzie man nodded. "And heals very fast."

"Which I am relieved to hear. I do have a question for you, though, and not related to Scott's healing."

"Ah?"

"You had an uncle, I hear?"

Dark eyes rested on his face for a long moment and Granville had an impression of great wisdom, surprising in a man who could not be much above forty. "You look for the mine."

"Actually, I look for the rightful owner of the mine."

Pierre's eyes again searched Granville's face, then he nodded slowly. "I see. You have found the mine."

Granville said nothing, knowing Pierre would understand the unspoken agreement.

"Then what question do you have for me?"

Instinctively Granville trusted the man, but still he kept his answers general. "The man who hired us to help him find the mine had a map."

"Oh?"

Granville looked sharply at Pierre. There was something knowing in his face. "My client's dying words charged me with finding the rightful owner of the map, or rather his heir."

"My uncle left such a map."

Had his instincts been wrong? "Indeed?"

"Yes. I have destroyed it. The mine is cursed, the cost of taking out gold too high. Anyone attempting to find that mine can expect injury or worse," Pierre said.

The skepticism Granville was feeling must have shown on his face. "The mine killed the old miner, I think?" Pierre said.

Granville wondered how the shaman had known. "It was not the mine that killed him, it was the men who ambushed us." Or rather, it was the men who had attacked them for the sake of the map.

"For me, it was a broken leg," Peter Pierre was saying. "Just as my party set out to search for my uncle's mine. The spirits spoke clearly. There are things more important than gold."

Granville nodded slowly in deference to the conviction in the man's words. "And have you heard of another map to this mine?"

"Rumors only. If you like, I will try to think of names I have heard."

"The only one I have is James."

"James." There was a thoughtful silence, or at least as much silence was possible in the din. "I will think on it."

"Thank you."

"You are serious about finding this heir, then?"

"I gave my word of honor," Granville said.

"I see. I will think on it, and after the dancing we will speak again."

"Does the dancing go on all day?"

"All day and all night, and sometimes the next day and night also."

It was hard to imagine dancing lasting so long. "I'll look forward to our conversation."

"Please, enjoy our hospitality and the dancing."

"Again, thank you. It is a great privilege to see it."

Pierre nodded and turned back to his companions. Feeling dismissed, Granville rejoined Scott, and was pleased to find Trent there.

"Horses stabled and fed?" he asked Trent.

Trent nodded. "And the mules."

Scott grinned, despite the lines of pain around his eyes. "Mules? Not those ornery critters we set loose just before the avalanche."

Trent nodded.

"So they survived. I'm glad to hear it."

"Too ornery not to," Granville said, and Scott let out a roar of laughter.

"You named them well, then," he said in an aside to Trent.

Granville just smiled.

"So what were you asking the shaman?" Scott asked.

"He might know something of our map. He'll let us know."

"Can't ask more than that, I guess. So what now?"

Granville shrugged. With Moore hot to see Cole's body, he needed to move the gold. Question was if he could do so without being shot at.

22

Emily frowned at the address she held. "Clara, I cannot see the number."

"Let me look." Clara pushed her bonnet back on her head a little, then made a minute adjustment of the brim, so that it more effectively framed her lovely face. Emily had to smile at the sight—it was so Clara. "Fifty-three? I don't see it either."

They looked from one house to the other. They were small houses, bungalows, really, lining a quiet side street in East Vancouver. Each had narrow windows and wood paneling, much less ostentatious than the houses in on the west side of town where they lived.

"But here is number 51 and number 55," Emily said. "It must be here somewhere."

"Is that a pathway?" Clara pointed to a narrow lane that ran between the two houses.

"Perhaps." It looked barely wide enough to accommodate the sweep of their skirts. "Let's try it."

"You didn't say come along," Clara complained as she followed.

Number Fifty-three was a very small cottage tucked in behind the two larger bungalows in front of it. Emily could see neat lace curtains hung at each of the small windows that looked directly into the back walls of the bungalows.

"It must be very dark inside," Clara said in a half whisper.

"Shhh," Emily said, raising her hand and giving a sharp rap on the white painted door.

They could hear the quick tap-tapping of heels on a wooden floor, then the door was opened by a small, tidy woman in late middle age. Graying hair puffed over her ears, and sharp gray eyes looked them over from head to foot. "Yes?"

"Pardon me," Emily said, with her best company smile. "Mrs. Anders?"

"Yes?

"We're looking for Mr. Morgan, and were told he might be here. I'm very sorry to disturb you, but it is a matter of some urgency."

"And how did you know to look here?"

"Your nephew's mother-in-law's second cousin told us," Clara said, "And she sold me this lovely bonnet." And she put a hand up to the confection of frills she was wearing.

The woman eyed the bonnet for a moment, then smiled, transforming her face from severity into an appealing openness. "It is attractive. You'd best come in, then" she said, holding the door for them. "I've just brewed tea. If you'd like to set for a moment, I'll bring it through."

And she waved them into a tiny formal parlor.

After a quick glance at looming furniture and neatly placed doilies, Emily turned to the woman. "This is a beautiful room," she said impulsively, "but we're already imposing and I hate to put you to more trouble. You'd have sat in your kitchen with your tea, would you not? May we not join you? Please?"

The woman looked slightly shocked, then pleased. "You know, it's my favorite room."

As she led them into a small room at the back of the house, Emily could see why the room was a favorite. Thin winter sunlight poured in through the kitchen windows, lighting the scarlet geraniums that bloomed in profusion. Every surface gleamed, and the well-scrubbed oilcloth bore a cheerful yellow and blue pattern. A heavy brown pottery teapot sat on the table beside a delicately fluted white china cup and matching saucer.

"It's lovely," Emily said. "But how did you get your geraniums to bloom at this time of year?"

"I get a lot of sun. And I feed them dried tea leaves. It seems to make them flower better. Please, have a seat."

And when they were all seated, cups of tea in front of them, plates of fresh scones declined, the little woman laced her fingers in front of her and leaned forward. "What can I do for you?"

The warmth and honesty of the kitchen had decided Emily in favor of trusting the woman. "I'm looking for the girl in this photograph," she said, pulling it out and passing it to her hostess. "I was hoping the photo was taken by your nephew."

The woman studied the photo, turned it over in her hands several times, as if checking for something.

"No, it wasn't taken by my nephew," she said. "It was taken by his father, also A.J.," she added, before Emily had a chance to feel disheartened. "A.J. was my brother.""

"Was? I'm sorry."

Mrs. Anders nodded. "Thank you. Three years ago, now. A.J. Junior tried to keep the shop going, but he didn't have the confidence his father had. He's been lucky to find work that still allows him to take pictures, keep his hand in. One day he'll reopen the studio, if all these newfangled Kodak cameras don't make taking pictures too easy for the amateurs. Do either of you own cameras?"

Emily and Clara exchanged glances, shook their heads."

"And a good thing too," Mrs. Anders said. "Making cameras so simple anyone thinks they can use them. A lot more goes into a professional photograph than looking through a lens and pushing a button, you know. A good photographer takes years to learn his trade, plus he has to have the eye, of course. It's a thing that troubled my brother deeply in his last illness, you understand."

Clara who nodded, saying, "Indeed we do understand," in sympathetic tones.

Emily was too busy considering the advantages that having a camera and knowing how to use it could give someone in the detective business. "How does a photographer learn his trade?" she asked. "Is there a school?"

"Oh my no. The usual route is to apprentice with another, more experienced photographer, which is what my nephew was doing. Unfortunately, he never got to finish his apprenticeship. Now, of course, the camera companies are offering tutorials, but they're meaningless for a true artist."

But not so meaningless for an investigator? Emily made a mental note to talk to Granville about it at the first opportunity. "Your brother would have taken that particular photo, then, and not your nephew?" she asked.

The little woman rubbed a finger along one edge of the photo. "Yes, this is my brother's work," she said. "He had a particular genius for capturing the light and shadow in a way to highlight the subject's attire. See how this lace trim shows up?"

Clara leaned forward and made an appreciative noise. Emily couldn't tell if she was being polite or if she really did see a difference. "Then the photo must have been taken at least three years ago?"

"Yes, that's right."

"I don't suppose there are records kept of the sitters?" she asked without much hope.

The little woman surprised her. "Why yes, of course. The inventory is the most valuable part of a photographer's business—how else can someone request more copies of a favorite photo? Some day young A.J. will open his father's shop again."

"Would your nephew be able to find the record of this sitter?"

"Yes, but he left just this morning."

Yet another wasted trip. "For New Westminster?"

Mrs. Anders shook her head. "No. He and his wife are on their way to the hot springs at Harrison. They've both struggled with the 'flu this year and she is inclined towards weak lungs. He's worried about her health."

Emily's heart sank. It was nearly eighty miles to Harrison and the only way to reach it was by train. She could think of no reason to go there that her father would accept. Now what could she do?

"But I might be able to identify the sitter for you."

"You could?"

"Oh yes. I have the records here. My brother's records, that is. I've room, you see—they're safe and dry in the basement."

"You have them here?" Emily couldn't believe her luck.

"Follow me," Mrs. Anders said. Rising, she made her way from the kitchen along a narrow hallway patterned in chintz to a white painted door.

Beyond the door was a steep narrow staircase, illumined only by a single bulb with a pull chain.

EMILY FOLLOWED Mrs. Andrews down the uneven stairs.

Clara, behind her, stopped at the top of the stairs. "I think I'll stay in the kitchen and finish my tea," she called down to Emily.

Emily nodded, her attention focused on the long rows of steel cabinets she could see filling most of the basement.

"Your friend didn't come down with you?" Mrs. Anders asked from below.

What was that note in her voice? Emily's gaze moved from the friendly woman they'd been chatting with to the very dark cellar beyond her.

Suddenly alert to a danger she'd never even considered, she said quickly, "No. She'll wait for us in the kitchen."

"Well then, let's get on with this, shall we? Let me see the photo for a moment, dear," Mrs. Anders said.

Emily handed it to her with reluctance, wondering how she intended to make out the features in this dim light.

To her relief, Mrs. Anders reached to switch on an angled lamp Emily hadn't seen.

Mrs. Anders turned the photo over and peered at the back of it.

"9564," she muttered to herself. "Taken in June of '95." And she scuttled over to one of the cabinets and began pulling drawers open. "Here we are."

So the photo was taken four and a half years ago. That meant Mary was likely twenty-two or three now, nearly four years older than Emily was herself, in fact the same age as her oldest sister Jane.

Trent would be disappointed that she was so much older than him, Emily thought absently, as she watched Mrs. Anders with a careful eye.

"Ah, yes," Mrs. Anders said, pulling out a large manila folder and shutting the drawer with a clang. "We can look at this in the kitchen if you'd rather. The light's better there."

"May I have my photo back, please?"

For a moment Mrs. Anders seemed to hesitate, then she smiled and handed it to her. "There you go, dearie. Now, up with you."

Emily climbed the staircase quickly, more than relieved to be out of the cellar and the darkness that descended behind them as Mrs. Anders clicked off the lights.

Only her desire to find out as much as she could for Granville kept her from collecting Clara and leaving immediately.

Still, she watched in fascination as Mrs. Anders opened the manila folder and spread out the contents.

They were surprisingly meager. Just a shiny black square and a form with less than half of the spaces filled in. Emily tried to read the neat writing, but Mrs. Anders had turned it so she couldn't quite see.

"Hmmm. This was taken three years ago, just before my dear brother passed. Her name is Mary Pearson, and she lives, or she did then, at Number 221 on Fourth Avenue in New Westminster."

Emily pulled out her notebook and jotted down the information, her mind racing.

The woman was lying to her.

Three years ago would make it 1897—the woman had clearly said the photo was taken in 1895 when she was searching for it.

Did she not realize she talked to herself? For some people it was a habit, Emily knew, so it was possible she didn't even hear herself anymore, didn't realize what she'd given away.

Was anything else she'd told them true?

Emily gave the woman her best company smile. "Thank you so much for your time and your trouble. I really do appreciate it, but we must be going now. Clara?"

"Can I not offer you another cup of tea?"

"Thank you, but no. My father will be most concerned if I am not home at my regular time."

"It was nothing. And if you've more questions, please come back."

"Indeed I will," Emily assured her, with another, even brighter smile. "Come along Clara."

WHEN THEY REACHED THE STREET, Emily set off at a brisk clip towards the streetcar stop on Georgia Street. Clara, keeping pace with her with some difficulty, slanted her a look. "What was all that about? As long as you're home by dinner, your father doesn't expect you."

"Clara, what made you decide not to accompany us to the cellar to look for the photos?" Emily asked, ignoring Clara's question.

"I dislike dark, enclosed spaces. Why?"

"Oh, I just wondered." Emily saw no reason to convey her uneasy feelings to Clara. She didn't want her friend to worry, nor did she want her to decide that accompanying Emily was too risky for her comfort.

"Hmmm." Clara gave her a skeptical look. "Now you have an address for the mysterious Mary, I suppose you'll want to go traipsing back to New Westminster?"

"I think this time I'll wait for Mr. Granville to accompany us."

Clara stopped dead, staring at Emily, and forcing her to stop also.

Emily avoided her gaze. "We'd best go, it's getting dark."

"Only if you tell me what's really going on."

"I don't know what you mean," Emily said.

"Then we'll be standing here until nightfall." Clara's jaw was set, and Emily didn't doubt she meant every word.

"Oh, very well. Though it's more of a suspicion than a fact. But let's walk on while I tell you."

"As long as you tell me," Clara said. "All of it."

23

"So, are we off?" Trent asked.

Sunset was still two or three hours off, but Scott had given in to the lines of pain Granville could see bracketing his mouth. It was just he and Trent standing watching the dancers weave in and out of the smoke that now completely filled the longhouse. Detective Moore had vanished somewhere, which was a relief.

Granville didn't plan on taking the boy with him. Too dangerous. "Not until Scott's ready to travel with us."

"I know that. I meant are we off to get Cole's body and the gold?" Trent said, lowering his voice.

Granville eyed Trent's enthusiastic face and raised a brow. He appreciated the boy's discretion in lowering his voice.

It was unlikely they could be overheard against the drumming and the chanting, but at least the boy had thought about it. "I suppose I've no chance of convincing you to stay and look out for Scott?"

"Then who would watch your back? Besides, with all the people here, and especially Mr. Moore, no one has a chance to get anywhere near Mr. Scott. Which is how I know you're about to go after the gold without him."

The boy didn't miss much, and he was a quick thinker. And a good shot. "Then I suppose you'd better come along."

"I'll harness the mules," Trent said, beaming. "Don't go anywhere."

Shaking his head, Granville went to collect their knapsacks and leave a message with Arbuthnot for Scott. He planned to be back in a day, two at the most, but he'd brought provisions for a week, just in case.

He hoped Moore wouldn't decide to come after them, though the storm that had been predicted should deter him. If he and Trent had any sense, it would deter them too, but Granville was hoping to throw off any pursuers.

He didn't need company, whether it was Moore or whoever had sent the ambushers.

"WHY'D you borrow these coats, anyway?" Trent asked as they began to climb.

Granville chuckled at the look of distaste on the boy's face as he plucked at the sleeve of the grimy stained mackinaw borrowed from Arbuthnot. He wore its twin, and he pulled it closer around him as the wind picked up, sighing through the cedars as they rode.

"This thing reeks," Trent said.

Granville drew in a breath. The air was clear and cold, but not cold enough to mask the smell of stale smoke, rotting mulch and old bones that clung to the jacket. "Yes, but it's preferable to being shot. And the hat is a particularly nice touch, don't you think?"

Trent grunted something under his breath that was probably extremely rude.

He grinned. The air was exhilarating, and it felt good to be away from the heat and noise of the longhouse. Fascinating though it was to glimpse a culture so different from his own, the lack of action had grated on him.

And with their gold cache to be re-hidden, having Moore

accompany them was too much of a risk, despite any protection from ambush he might have provided.

Trent led the mules up an increasingly narrow path, following a winding route he said would lead them back to where he and Scott had stashed the gold without signaling to anyone who might be watching where they were headed. Granville hoped he was right.

"What are we going to do with the old man's body?" Trent suddenly asked. 'When the police are through with him, I mean."

"I rather thought Cole would like to be buried near the mine, though we can't do that until spring.

"Yeah, I think he'd like that. Unless Mary wants to have him buried near her?"

Granville smiled at the concern in Trent's voice. He really was smitten by that photo. "I think our client killed someone important to Mary. She isn't going to care where he's buried."

"But won't she mind if it's at the mine?"

"I don't think she needs to know about it."

"Oh."

As the trail grew steeper, they climbed on in snow-cushioned silence. The only motion was the whiskey jacks, gliding from snowy branch to snowy branch in their wake.

It was hard going, but the pull and burn in his muscles and the harshly cold air made Granville feel alive.

As the trail wound higher, the snow fell faster, thick and heavy. The birds vanished. Their footsteps and even the occasional jingle of the mules' bridle were muffled.

Then the crack of a rifle broke the stillness.

Granville pushed a hand between Trent's shoulder blades, propelling both of them to the ground.

"I thought they wanted us alive," Trent said, spitting out a mouthful of snow.

"So did I. Maybe they're shooting only to wound."

"Shot is shot."

The boy had that right. And they were too exposed here, their clothing dark against the snow. "Deeper into the trees. Hurry."

Trent had grabbed the mule's bridles and was in motion almost before he'd finished speaking.

Granville followed him, diving behind a large cedar trunk just as another bullet whined over his head. "I think there's only one shooter."

"Yeah," Trent said. "I can't get a bead on him, though. Can you see him?"

"No, the angle's wrong."

Two bullets whined in quick succession, just to their left.

"He's trying to herd us," Trent said in his ear. "Like we're wild pigs or something."

Another bullet whined by, this one slightly above them. The boy was right. "So where does he want us to go?" Granville asked as they returned fire, then eased their way into deeper cover.

"Does it matter?"

"It might. Scott's told me he tries to think like whatever animal he's hunting. Do you do the same?" he said in an undertone.

"Yeah. You're thinking he wants us to run for the cave where we stashed the gold?" Trent whispered.

"I'd say it's a good guess," he said, ducking lower as another bullet whined overhead, then returning fire. "We need to do something he won't be expecting."

Trent's eyes darted from their flimsy cover to the shooter's well-concealed spot and he smiled broadly.

"I have an idea," he said. "Cover me," and he began wriggling his way through the underbrush, pulling the reluctant mules after him.

Granville's instinctive protest died unvoiced.

The boy was gone.

He aimed, shot, aimed again.

Trent knew these mountains better than he did. He just hoped the boy wasn't being foolhardy. And that he could keep the shooter focused on him.

He fired again, waited.

The shooter returned fire.

The shot missed him, but not by much.

Granville dug a little deeper into the brush, then fired back. Again his shot was returned.

Good. He needed the shooter focused on him, not on Trent.

A loud bray a short distance uphill from where he lay had him flinching. Cursed mule. Would it be enough to give Trent's location away?

Granville fired again, hoping to distract the shooter. His fire was returned, then—nothing.

He lay listening hard. Fired several more times. No response.

Where was Trent?

THE WIND SHUSHED through the trees. Granville's belly was freezing where he lay pressed against the snow. He couldn't hear Trent or the shooter, not even the mules.

No shots, no crashing of brush, no braying, not even a snapping twig.

Easing himself up to his knees, he absently brushed off the snow, still listening hard, reloaded the Winchester. And waited.

Forty-seven very tense minutes later, Trent crawled back to where Granville crouched behind an outcropping of granite. "It's done."

"I hope the man tracking us looks worse than you do," he said, eyeing Trent's scraped and grimy face. "You look as if you were breaking trail with your face."

"I slipped," Trent said, looking remarkably pleased with himself despite the scratches.

"And the mules?"

"I set the gray mule loose, hid the other. I think our shooter's following John the Mule."

"How do you hide a mule?"

"It ain't easy. Let's get out of here before he figures out he's been fooled."

"As long as you don't expect to get out of explaining how you lost him."

Trent's grin and look of pride nearly had Granville grinning back. With an effort he maintained the irritated expression he'd adopted. It didn't seem to worry Trent, who just smiled more broadly.

"Follow me," the boy said, as he slithered under the snow-covered branches of a cedar and was gone.

Granville didn't know how Trent had done it, but he seemed to have lost their pursuer, at least for the moment. Listening hard, all he could hear was the soft rustle of the wind in the upper branches of the pines and the occasional plop as a tree released its load of snow. He could hear nothing of the shooter, nor of the mules.

How had Trent managed to quiet the ornery creatures, anyway?

As they climbed steadily uphill, keeping Trent in sight didn't get any easier. The boy seemed to disdain anything resembling a path, slipping between close growing trees and through thick under-brush without a sound. Granville found himself hard pressed to keep up.

Scott would roar with laughter if he could see him now, he thought ruefully as he ducked the back swing of yet another pliant branch. It was all too reminiscent of their Klondike days, and the long slog of trekking the creeks, looking for any sign of color. In their early days, Scott had called him The London Swell, and mocked his ineptitude in the reality of the Alaskan wilderness, so different from anything he'd seen before.

That had changed when he'd saved Scott from drowning when their badly built boat had failed to navigate the rapids at Five Fingers. Still, he had been a London swell, like so many others completely unprepared for the realities of the Yukon wilderness.

His lips quirked at the likely reaction of some of his London friends, if they could see him now. They'd simply not believe their eyes. Even the hunting-mad ones would never stoop to crawling through actual bush. That was for the hounds in pursuit of the fox.

The huntsmen were well mounted and stayed that way, thank you very much.

"We'll get the mule now," Trent said, appearing at his elbow.

"After you tell me how you lost our pursuers."

Trent grinned at him. "Nope," he said, and vanished between two trees.

The brown mule was tied in the lee of a cliff, strips of cloth snugged around his jaw. His were flattened back and his eyes were wild. Granville eyed the mule. "You do know he'll make us pay the moment you release him?"

Trent dug into his pack. "It's why I brought these," he said, pulling out two scrawny carrots and a wrinkled apple.

Fresh produce. Granville's mouth watered. "Where'd you get those?"

"I've dealt with mules before. I brought them with me from the markets in town."

"They're wasted on the mule."

"Not if it keeps him from braying and giving us away."

The boy made sense. He watched with interest as Trent held the carrot where the mule could smell it, then dangled it just out of his reach. The mule's ears came forward and he focused intently on the proffered treat. Trent slowly released the cloth binding his mouth, and the mule flicked his tail, then without a sound reached for the apple.

"See?"

Granville kept a wary eye on the mule, which seemed to know his good behavior was being held hostage for the sake of a carrot. Only the movement of ears and tail expressed feelings that the day before had been accompanied by repeated, carrying braying.

He shook his head in amazement. "I can't believe it's working, but it is. Will it hold while we move the gold?"

"Should do," Trent said.

"Good enough. Though I'd still like to know how they had someone following us so quickly."

"They must've seen us leave Katzie."

"Or we may have been followed from town."

Trent let out a very low whistle. "He'd have to be good. I didn't spot anyone the whole way."

"Nor did I. Which could also mean that someone in town wired this fellow to watch for us. Which is the more worrying possibility."

"It is?"

Granville nodded. "Means they're very organized, which we'd already suspected, but also they're predicting where we'll go next. And that worries me. The mind that can anticipate what we're likely to do next is a very dangerous one."

"Oh. Like Mr. Benton?"

"It's a possibility. I still can't see Benton giving that much of his attention to a potential gold mine."

"Mr. Gipson?"

"Is underhanded and sneaky but doesn't work this efficiently."

"Then who?"

"Who, indeed?" Granville said.

24

SUNDAY, JANUARY 14, 1900

Despite a long hard climb through thigh deep snow, the actual retrieval of the sacks holding the gold and Cole's body was anticlimactic. They saw no one, and both gold and body were exactly where Trent and Scott had left them, hidden in a depression in the sidewall of a deep, narrow cave.

Together Trent and Granville filled the mules' empty saddlebags, then strapped the awkwardly frozen corpse of their late client on top, with Trent talking softly to the mule, whose ears flickered towards the sound.

Lifting the lantern higher, Granville hefted one of the eight sacks of gold that remained, then glanced around them. "We need to re-hide these, but not too far from here. Can you suggest somewhere?"

"Sure. But why? We could carry more now, and make two trips."

"It'll be safer not to bring it down all at once."

Trent nodded and took a grip on one of the bags. "Follow me."

Granville gripped two more and followed Trent toward the back of the cave, dragging the sacks behind him. In the flickering light, he couldn't see a hiding place large enough, but Trent didn't hesitate, moving directly towards the smooth rear wall.

Suddenly the boy vanished. Granville blinked, holding the lantern higher and staring at the unbroken line of rock. What had he missed?

"No-one'll find it there," Trent said cheerfully, popping back out, seemingly from nowhere.

"Why didn't you hide the gold here before?" Granville asked, moving closer to examine the all but invisible seam in the cave wall. His eyes still had trouble finding it, but his fingers could feel the opening behind the rough rock.

"Not big enough for the body and the gold," Trent said matter-of-factly. "And once they found the body, they'd have kept looking 'till they found the gold. The best thing about putting the gold here now is that even if they find the cave, they'll assume we took all the gold away. And there's no draft here to give this away."

"No draft?"

"If this seam opened out to fresh air somewhere further back, you'd feel an air flow. Makes it easier to find pockets like this. Only this doesn't have one."

"Good enough," Granville said, passing first one then the other sack of gold to the boy and going back for the next load. "Well done, Trent."

"We'll come back in the spring?" Trent asked in a low voice as he backed out of the cave, sweeping all trace of their passage away with a fir branch he'd cut for the purpose.

"For the rest of the gold or the mine?"

"What's the difference?"

"We'll come back for the rest of the gold once we get back from Denver. The mine we'll leave until after the ground's thawed enough to stake a claim."

"Up here, that mightn't be 'til June or even July. Why wait so long?" Trent gathered the leads for the burdened mule and turned back towards Katzie, avoiding the trail they'd made on the way up.

There was still no sign of the shooter, but neither of them was taking any chances.

"Because we need to start working the claim within twenty days of staking it," Granville said. "Which means the ground needs to have thawed."

"Oh. What happens if we don't work it right away?"

"Then someone else can stake it, based on the information we'll give when we register it."

"So the map becomes useless the minute we stake the claim."

"Exactly," Granville said.

"What if you stake a claim but don't have time to work it?"

"You hire someone to do it for you and pay them by the day or with a percentage of the claim. If a claim's rich enough, it works out fine."

Trent thought about that. "But you'd have to know if a claim is worth anything before you could find someone to work it for you, wouldn't you?"

Granville gestured towards the laden saddlebags. "I think we've proof enough."

"Yeah. Guess so." They walked for a few moments in silence.

"So we really need to find Mary fast," Trent said. "Before we register the claim, I mean."

"Exactly. As the majority owner, she needs to be the one to register it."

"Why? Can't you register it then transfer it to her?"

"It gets complicated," Granville said. "The simplest thing is to find her before the thaw."

"But once you bank this gold, won't word get out you've found something? Then everyone'll want to get hold of the map before you can register the claim."

The boy didn't miss much. "Yes. That's why I'm planning to go through Benton rather than a bank. He'll take his cut, but give us cash for gold."

"And since he already knows you have the map, it shouldn't make things worse for us."

"That's it. Plus there's Francis."

"Oh," Trent said. "Because you're searching for her niece. If you weren't, she might expect Mr. Benton to do so. Since she's his ladylove."

Or something. Granville hid a smile. Apparently Trent's soft spot for Frances continued—the boy had grown up rough, and didn't usually sugarcoat anything. "That's it."

Trent nodded, and they continued on in silence.

As the Katzie village came into sight below them, Granville noted Trent's expression changed to a look of worry. "All right, what is it now?" he asked.

"What about Mr. Moore? Is he going to arrest us?"

"Depends. Has he got a temper?"

Trent slanted a look at Granville. "He can't arrest us just because he's angry with us, can he?"

"Perhaps. Though I rather doubt he'd actually do it. He seems the methodical type."

"Yeah." Trent slanted a look at Granville. "I've been thinking about Mary. All we have is her photo and that letter fragment. So if finding her before the thaw is so important, how do we do it?"

Good question. "Through excellent investigation."

"But aren't we about to head for Denver?" Trent said.

"Sometimes you have to set priorities. We've months yet before the thaw." Granville said. But it didn't sit well with him.

Trent seemed content with his answer, though. "So how soon do we leave?"

"Scott will need a few more days."

"I wonder if he'll agree with you?"

"I'M READY TO RIDE NOW," Scott said, his voice nearly lost against the drumming and chanting that still filled the longhouse. In the center of the room, the Katzie matrons dipped and turned in stately circles.

"You'll open up your wound again," Granville said.

"Let me worry about that."

"That's easy for you to say. We're the ones who'll have to carry you."

"Nobody's carrying me anywhere."

Recognizing the stubborn look in Scott's eye, Granville gave up. "We can be ready in an hour."

"I'm ready now."

"I need to have another conversation with Pierre. Know where he is?"

Scott indicated a small knot of dark heads. "You might have to wait a bit. He looks a little busy. And Moore's been looking for you."

That figured. "Where is he?"

Scott pointed across the hall. "There. And I think he's spotted you."

"Right. I'll want to chat with Arbuthnot, too," Granville said, spotting the smaller man to one side of the group around Moore.

"I'll come with you," Trent volunteered.

"For this I don't need your assistance. There's no point giving Moore another target. You can help Scott pack."

Trent's face fell and Scott looked irritated. Granville grinned at both of them. "We need to travel light. And fast. And Scott needs to conserve his energy for the trip."

Scott gave him a deadpan look. "Good thing we're partners. I might have to shoot you otherwise."

Granville was laughing as he wove his way across the crowded floor to where Peter Pierre stood.

"I CANNOT HELP you with the name you seek, I'm afraid," Pierre said.

"I understand," Granville said.

"But perhaps I can describe the man. I have thought on it, and I think it must be one of two men. The old miner was often seen in company with one or the other in the last months."

"You knew Cole?"

The shaman nodded. "He spent much time in these mountains, searching for gold. For many years he found nothing."

"Until he got hold of that map from someone. Did either of these two men talk about the map?"

"No. And there are no new rumors of such a map."

"And the old rumors?" Granville asked, curious.

"They have spread since the death of my uncle. Each year they grow more elaborate."

"Right. Tell me about these two men, then."

"Both men had perhaps fifteen more years than you have, but they were very different. One was very tall and thin. Quiet. He did not care for the warmth of the fire, that one. The other was about so," and his hand measured to Granville's shoulder, "well fed, and he smiled. He sought the company of others, told stories and listened too. The tall one would be harder to kill."

"And their coloring?"

"Both were as you, with pale skin. Both had brown hair like the otter. The tall one had gray eyes, the shorter one brown."

"You saw Cole with both men?" Granville asked.

"Yes."

"Did he ever refer to one as his partner?"

Pierre shook his head.

"Was he more often with one than the other?"

"I am sorry, I did not see them often enough to be sure. But now I am afraid you must go."

For a moment Granville thought he had somehow transgressed on the Indian's hospitality and was being thrown out. Then he noted the light in Pierre's eyes as the man gestured towards Moore, who was approaching them with a determined set to his jaw.

"I thank you for your help," Granville said formally, then with a quick grin turned to face the inquisition.

25

MONDAY, JANUARY 15, 1900

Sally's Diner was as crowded and noisy as ever. No surprise, given the reasonable cost and huge portions. As Granville forked up a slice of steak, he looked across the table at his friends. Trent was slathering eggs onto a piece of toast, then dragging the resulting runny mess through the syrup left from the stack of flapjacks he'd just devoured. Granville shuddered.

Scott wasn't much better—he'd stacked flapjacks, eggs with ketchup and steak onto his fork and was conveying the resultant taste disaster to his mouth.

"My mother would be appalled," Granville said. His grin spread even further when they looked at him in total bewilderment. "More coffee?" He waved his empty cup at the tired-looking waitress, who bustled over at the sight of his smile.

"Get you anything else?" she asked as she poured the dark rich beverage into his cup.

"Scott? Trent?" When both of them shook their heads, mouths too full to talk, he turned back to the waitress and tucked a coin into her apron pocket. "Just keep the coffee flowing."

Her eyes widened. "You can have as much coffee as you want, sir."

Scott smiled. "You might want to rethink that. I've seen this here gent drink his own weight in coffee."

Granville laughed at Trent's expression. "A slight exaggeration, I assure you," he told the now giggling waitress. "But your coffee is very good, and I'm fond of the drink."

"I'll be back," she said, and hurried off, drawn by a bellow on the far side of the room.

"Now you've arranged for your coffee, what are you planning?" Scott asked, his voice suddenly serious and not a little tense.

For all his lack of sleep and recent wound, Scott looked capable of taking down a grizzly by himself, Granville thought, looking across at his friend. "Next train to Denver's tomorrow morning. And I need to talk to Emily as soon as possible. You?"

"I'll go see Frances and Lizzie, let them know we're going."

Granville nodded. It wouldn't be an easy conversation.

Scott reached for his coffee. "You know, you never did show me that letter you mentioned."

Glad to provide a distraction, Granville teased the letter out of its pouch and extracted the creased and grimy half-sheet.

Scott peered at the cramped writing on one side, frowned. Flipped it over. Peered again. Then his eyebrows rose. "Cripple Creek?"

"That means something to you?"

"Depends. How are you planning on finding this Mary?" A grin split his broad face. "Since you're so intent on giving away a fortune?"

"We've a few leads to track down. Once we get back from Denver."

"Not very good ones, from what I've heard. Maybe you should just give up."

"I gave my word, Scott."

Scott's grin vanished. "Yeah, I know. Just like you gave Lizzie your word that you'd find little Sarah. Which is why we're going to Denver rather than staying here and looking for Mary."

He shrugged. It was true, and Scott probably knew him well enough to know how uneasy that decision made him.

"So you might like to know that Cripple Creek is a gold mining town a hundred or so miles outside of Denver."

"What?"

"You mean we can look for Sarah and Mary at the same time?" Trent asked.

"Somethin' like that. James, if that's really his name, knew Colorado and so did whoever wrote this to him. See here," the big finger jabbed at a line of crabbed blue ink—"he says 'like the Portland? It's one of the big mines up on the Creek."

Scott flipped the page over again, contemplated it, then looked at Granville. "Guess it's a good thing we're going to Denver."

Granville set down his cup. "It is at that. Trent, Emily will likely be in class this morning. Can you get a message to her?"

"Sure can," Trent said, and leapt up, pausing only to stuff a last mouthful of syrup-sweet toast and eggs into his mouth. "You'll be here?" he asked indistinctly.

"No, I need a shower and a shave before I see her." He ignored the look Scott gave him. "Ask her to meet us at Stroh's Teashop at noon."

"Not the teashop again?" Scott said.

Trent didn't say a word, but his grin nearly matched Scott's.

Granville ignored both of them.

"I TRUST you are feeling better, Miss Turner?"

Emily jumped as Miss Richards's voice sounded from behind her.

She'd been ignoring the clattering typewriters echoing off the windows and high ceilings of the classroom, and hadn't even been aware of her teacher's approach over the rapid rattling sound of her own keyboard. It seemed she'd finally found the trick to typewriting quickly—don't think about what you're doing.

Most of her attention was focused on recalling her meeting with Mrs. Anders and wondering whether her sudden fears were the result of an overactive imagination, as Clara had seemed to think. After all, what connection could the woman have to the missing map and the men who were after Granville? It had been pure chance they'd found her.

Her mind went to the scrap of paper with Mary's address, carefully tucked in her handbag, awaiting her next trip to New Westminster. She couldn't go on Sunday—Sunday was church, followed by the traditional roast beef and Yorkshire pudding, then visiting. There would be no time to even think about her quest.

This morning she'd intended to telephone Clara and see if she was free to go to New Westminster. That plan was abandoned when Mama had unexpectedly decided to accompany her into town. Apparently there was some shopping she wanted to do.

Emily had no choice but to get off on Hastings and turn into the school, while her mother waved from the streetcar window. Well, at least she'd apparently learned how to typewrite at last.

"Yes, thank you, Miss Richards. I'm quite recovered."

"I'm glad to hear it. It will be difficult to catch up if you fall too far behind. You must work hard to see that doesn't happen."

Emily nodded. This was as bad as being at home and lectured by her mother. Where was the independence she'd expected to be earning? "I'll try to do so."

"Very well then," said Miss Richards as she moved on.

Emily knew she'd missed several days of classes and she felt guilty about it, but she rather resented Miss Richards's disapproving looks. How was she to find Mary and keep up with her lessons? And why hadn't she heard from Granville? Surely he should have been back by now?

"There's a message for you, Miss Turner," Miss Richards said some twenty minutes later, breaking Emily's concentration so her fingers tangled in the keys once again. "I gather it's a matter of some urgency."

Her tone implied that only a death in the family would be sufficient reason for interrupting her class.

Emily took the folded piece of paper from Miss Richards. Over her teacher's starched cotton shoulder she could see Trent's broad smile and quick wink.

They were back!

Scanning the message, she saw Granville was proposing they meet at Stroh's at noon. She needed to let Clara know. And Tim.

"Oh dear," she said, composing her face into lines of sadness. "I must send a reply."

"Very well," Miss Richards said. "I shall ask the messenger to stay.

He'd stay anyway, but there was no need to upset Miss Richards further.

Dashing off two notes, Emily walked over and handed them to Trent with a quick smile. "Tell Mr. Granville I'll be there. And these notes are for Clara and O'Hearn," she said in a low voice.

His answering smile told her he'd probably anticipated the request.

Good. She gave him a little nod and he winked at her and left.

NOON FOUND Emily and Clara seated at a table for six near the back of the teashop, feeling decidedly conspicuous. Emily was sure several of the ladies had turned to follow their progress to their table, but when she'd looked no one seemed to be looking at them.

"Why is it we're always the first to arrive?" Clara asked.

"I suspect the gentlemen find themselves out of their element here. At least with us present they've a reason for being here."

Clara looked around them at the tables filled with stylishly dressed women sipping tea, discussing fashion and catching up on the latest gossip. "I suppose. It doesn't seem to bother Mr. O'Hearn, though."

Emily held back the comment that sprang to her lips. "As a reporter, he must be used to going anywhere there's a story."

"He had another byline on page three. Did you see it?"

"The one on the police investigation of the man shot a few days ago? Yes, I thought it was good reporting. But Clara, never tell me you are reading the paper now?"

Clara blushed, and smoothed out her gloves. "Not exactly. I do glance through it when my Papa is finished."

"Looking for a certain byline, perhaps?" Emily said with a quick smile. "And your father permits it? Mine still pretends he doesn't know I read the newspaper. And if I weren't engaged to Mr. Granville, he would still be trying to break me of the habit, as he terms it."

"My father doesn't know. He leaves the paper in his study, and I've taken on overseeing the cleaning of that room. Mother thinks I am finally learning to like housekeeping duties, and is most pleased with me. Which is convenient at times," Clara said with a conspiratorial smile.

"May we join you ladies?"

Emily looked up to smile at Granville.

Running her eyes over him, she could see he was undamaged. He looked tired, but his eyes gleamed. "I'm so glad you're back safely. And Mr. Scott. Trent. Please be seated, all of you."

"Thank you for meeting us on such short notice," he said as he pulled out the chair opposite hers.

"It was arranged last time we met, remember? Only delayed."

He smiled at that, and she was annoyed to find herself flushed and a little nervous. "You didn't have any more trouble?" she asked in a rush.

"No, none."

She noted the glance Trent shot at him.

So there had been trouble. Granville was trying to protect her, and she wished he wouldn't. "Is there further news of little Sarah?"

"We may have another lead," Granville said, and related what Benton had told him.

"Oh, how awful," she said when he was done. "You can find her though, can't you? And bring her back to her mother?"

"We certainly hope to. It is the strongest lead we've had to date."

"If those villains have her, we'll find her," Scott said.

The big man's voice was determined, but she could see the lines of tension and strain about his mouth.

His face was too pale, and there were tiny beads of moisture along his brow. She could see how ill he'd been, and hoped he was well enough to undertake such a long journey and all the danger they were going into.

Granville would look after him, though. "I'm sure you will."

"And how have you been getting on?" Granville asked her.

Her search for Mary hardly seemed important compared to their determination to rescue little Sarah. "Clara and I found out that the photography studio was in New Westminster, but has been closed for several years now. The photo was taken in '95, so Mary must be twenty or twenty-one by now." Emily carefully didn't look at Trent as she said it.

"Were you able to get a last name for Mary?" Granville asked, smoothing over the awkward moment.

Emily leaned forward. "I was told her name is Mary Pearson. We've an address too, also in New Westminster. We haven't had a chance to visit there yet, so I don't know if it is still good."

"I'm amazed by much you have learned in such a short time. That is very well done, ladies," Granville said.

Emily felt her cheeks heating again, and Clara beamed.

"How'd you learn all that?" Trent blurted out.

Emily smiled at him. "Clara and I were able to find the photographer's sister, a Mrs. Anders. She still had all his photo files and records stored in her basement."

"Mary Pearson," Granville said thoughtfully. "So Cole lied about James being a surname, after all. Presumably the man's name was James Pearson."

Scott nodded. "Our late, unlamented client wasn't straight about anything else, so why would he be about this?"

"True. And if Mary is twenty-one, she could be either Pearson's widow or his daughter."

"Didn't your client say she was his daughter?" Clara asked.

"He did. But I'm not inclined to believe anything he said without further proof."

"And in either case, she could be married by now, with a different last name," Scott said.

It was true, Emily realized. Why had she not thought of that? "So we may be no further ahead."

"Not at all," Granville said, smiling at her. "Each step leads to the next, and you've moved us a long way forward in finding our missing heiress. Thank you both."

"Well, I'm glad to have helped," Emily said. She still felt like an idiot for not thinking Mary might have changed her name, no matter what he said.

"How old is the address?" he asked.

"Five years. So she is not likely to be still living there."

"Perhaps not, but someone there may be able to tell you more about her."

It was the same thought she'd had. "I'm not sure I trust my informant on either Mary's last name or her address. I got a most uneasy feeling from the woman and I wasn't sure that she was telling me the truth about either."

Granville frowned. "What do you mean by uneasy?"

"She seemed—angry." That didn't quite capture it, but surely she'd imagined that feeling of danger?

"Angry? And you'd just asked about the subject of a photograph her brother took?"

Emily nodded.

"I felt it too," Clara said.

Emily gave her friend a quick smile, grateful for the support. She felt a bit foolish, and she didn't much like the feeling.

Granville's face was tense and his eyes held hers across the table. "Emily, I don't think you should be asking any more questions about Mary Pearson without my being there."

"What do you mean?"

"I'm not sure who is looking for the map and the mine, but they killed Cole and tried to kill us. I want you safe. If this woman is somehow involved with our pursuers, then you can't trust her or anything she might have said. I don't want you anywhere near her, or her associates, whoever they are."

Emily was suddenly glad she hadn't said more. "There was nothing more she could tell us in any case," she said, making her tone light.

"Someone out there is willing to kill because of this gold mine." His gaze was intense. "Until we know how Mary is connected, I must have your promise that you'll do no more investigating. It's too dangerous."

"Very well," Emily said with a shiver. She certainly had no intention of talking with Mrs. Anders again, nor Mr. Gipson. Looking for an address wasn't really investigating, after all.

And how dangerous could a few questions be?

Granville nodded, apparently satisfied.

Clara looked uneasy, but then Clara had known her far longer than her pretend fiancé.

Before Clara could say anything, an out of breath O'Hearn slid into the seat opposite her. "Sorry I'm late," he said. "I couldn't get away. That story about the man who was shot? They think they might have found the shooter."

Emily watched Granville and Mr. Scott exchange glances, and she suddenly put the pieces together. "That was your client, was it not? The man who was ambushed and murdered, the one the police are investigating?"

O'Hearn leaned forward eagerly as Granville nodded. "Indeed."

"Your client?" O'Hearn's ubiquitous notebook appeared. "You were with him when he was shot? What happened? Why was he shot?"

Granville held up a hand. "Why don't you start by telling us the news? It may be a matter of some urgency to us. We'll fill you in later."

"I've your word on it?" O'Hearn clearly wasn't going to lose sight of the possibility of another front-page story.

"You have my word."

"All right then. The police are now expressing interest in talking with a man named Morgan."

Emily jumped at the name, and exchanged glances with Granville, who suddenly looked fierce.

"You aren't to go anywhere near New Westminster, do you hear me?" he said to her.

Emily nodded. She heard him. She hadn't promised anything, though.

"What did I miss?" O'Hearn asked.

26

TUESDAY, JANUARY 16, 1900

As they descended from the streetcar in New Westminster, Emily drew her jacket more closely around her. A fierce wind gusted off the river, and seemed to search out every patch of bare skin. Ignoring it, she gestured to the east along Columbia Street. "Clara, since we're here, we should at least walk over to Fourth Avenue. It shouldn't be difficult to find that address Mrs. Morgan gave us."

"In this cold? And I thought you promised Mr. Granville that you wouldn't do this," Clara protested.

"A brisk walk will do us good. And I only agreed that I heard his concerns."

"I knew it."

"Just walking past won't do any harm. And we should be out of the wind on Fourth. Besides, I suspect Mrs. Morgan lied. There's no danger if it isn't even the right address for Mary."

Clara muttered something, which Emily knew better than to ask her to repeat.

And Emily was right—the address was neither difficult to find nor Mary Pearson's. The current owner had rebuilt after the fire, and had been in residence for a total of nine years.

He had never heard of Mary Pearson."

"You see, it was safe enough," Emily said as they left. "Now shall we have another look at that bonnet?"

Clara shot Emily a look that said she saw right through her. Then she linked their arms and began to walk briskly in the direction of the milliners.

Ten minutes later, they were surrounded by bright, frothy confections, with feathers and wisps of netting everywhere. At the tinkling of the door chimes, the shop clerk hurried over to them.

"Good morning. You came back," she said to Clara with obvious delight. "Did you decide on the bonnet after all?"

"I need to look at it again, as I brought my material," Clara said, bringing out a small swatch of silk.

"Perfect. Please let me know if I can be of assistance."

"Actually, while Clara considers the color, perhaps you could answer a question or two?" Emily said with a smile. "I did manage to find Mr. Morgan's aunt the other day."

"Oh, I'm glad," the saleslady said. "Was she of any help?"

"She was most helpful. But unfortunately the address she gave me was an old one, so I still need to speak with Mr. Morgan. Have you any further suggestions as to where we might look for him?"

"I'm afraid not," was the reply. Then, "Oh, isn't that bonnet marvelous on you!"

"Thank you," said Clara, doing a little twirl to show it off.

Emily tilted her head to one side as she considered her friend. "I like it even better than I did the other day," she decided. "I think you must buy it, Clara."

"Then I shall," Clara said. "And perhaps I'll have my photo taken in it. I do wish you could remember something that would help us find him," she finished, handing the bonnet to the saleslady.

"You know, I think I may have seen an advertisement about having photos taken," the saleslady said, pausing in writing up Clara's receipt.

"Really? And was it Mr. Morgan who advertised?" Emily asked.

"It might have been. It was several months ago, but I remember thinking it was odd."

"Odd?"

"Well, Mr. Morgan had just started with Butler and Resnick. I don't know when he'd have time to take photographs."

"And do you recall where you saw the ad?" Emily asked.

"I think it was a flyer, in one of the shop windows. I don't know why I didn't think of it when you were in the other day."

It didn't sound particularly useful, Emily thought. A flyer would be long gone. Along with Mr. Morgan, it seemed.

She didn't put much faith in Mrs. Morgan's claim he'd gone to Harrison, though. "Have you any idea which shop it might have been?"

She frowned, tapped her pencil against her forefinger. "No, I'm sorry. But I passed by on my way to the store."

"On Sixth Avenue?"

"Possibly, or along Seventh..."

As Clara paid for her bonnet, Emily thanked the woman most sincerely.

They found the flyer in the window of the bakery on Sixth. Faded lettering and curling edges said it had been there for quite some time. Morgan's name was listed, and a telephone number.

Emily made careful note of the information.

"What now?" Clara asked. "I'm freezing, Emily. We need to get out of this wind."

"After we call him," Emily said.

She had seen one of the new, bright red telephone booths at the end of the block. Clara stood in a doorway out of the wind while Emily phoned, since with their wide skirts, the booth was not big enough for both of them.

The number rang hollowly. Emily was just about to hang up when it was answered.

"Hello?"

A man's voice, quick and a little shallow, as though he'd hurried.

"Is this Mr. Morgan?" she said.

"Who's asking?"

He sounded anxious. It had to be him. "I am Emily—Richards. I would like to have a formal photograph taken for my fiancé, and your work has been highly recommended. Is this Mr. Morgan?"

"Yes, I'm Morgan," he said, some of the tension gone from his tone.

"And you could take such a picture for me?"

There was a pause, then Morgan said, "A formal photograph? Yes, I can take one for you, but it will have to be this afternoon. And I'll require payment in advance."

He must need money. "That would be perfect. Where and when?"

"Number seven Begbie Street, at three o'clock. The studio is on the second floor."

"Very well. I will see you at three."

There was no answer, only the click of the phone disconnecting. Emily considered it thoughtfully.

"That seemed almost too easy," she said to Clara as she rejoined her. "I wonder if he will actually keep the appointment this afternoon?"

Clara had compressed her lips, and she was giving Emily the look that said she was about to be lectured to.

"Emily, have you gone mad?" Clara said. "This man is a suspect in a murder. Mr. Granville has told us these people are dangerous. You yourself said that this man's aunt made you nervous. And now you're proposing to see him on your own?"

"Not at all. You will be with me, will you not?" Emily said, just to see her friend's expression.

Clara's face was flushed and she seemed to be having trouble forming words.

Emily smiled and patted Clara's arm. "Do you think Mr. O'Hearn could be here by three o'clock? If we told him were had an opportunity to meet with a man that the police want for questioning? We could meet him at that little café that serves such wonderful cocoa."

Now Clara looked intrigued. "Do you have the number for the *World?*"

JUST BEFORE THREE, Emily followed Tim O'Hearn up the narrow stairwell to the second floor of number seven, which was indeed a photography studio. The morning's thick clouds had cleared and the pallid sunlight reaching in through the studio's south-facing windows provided just enough light to see by.

The room was large and open, with shelves along two walls and equipment stacked randomly. A fading sign identified the establishment as Gladstone and Son, Photographers. Except for the harsh stink of chemicals, it seemed deserted, even abandoned. There was no sign of A.J. Morgan, Jr.

Four steps into the room, Mr. O'Hearn came to an abrupt halt.

Emily stopped too, and Clara bumped into her from behind.

"What is it?" Clara whispered.

"I don't know," she whispered back.

Mr. O'Hearn's gaze was fixed on the far wall.

Her eyes followed.

At first, she couldn't see what he was staring at, but then her mind registered something wrong with the stacks of equipment along the far wall.

As she stared into the dimmest part of the room, she realized that backdrops and lights had been over-turned, and tins and jars swept off the pine shelving. Either there had been a struggle, or someone had been very angry.

"Stay here," Mr. O'Hearn said in an undertone as he began to make his way through the mess.

Ignoring the command, Emily followed, careful not to trip.

His gaze was focused downwards.

"What are you looking for?" she asked softly.

He jumped. "I thought I said—oh, never mind. I'm trying to see what happened here."

Emily's gaze had moved past him and fixed on the shadowy wall. "Is that…?" she began, and found she could not finish, mutely pointing.

Mr. O'Hearn spun around and as he did so, the electric lights overhead came on, bathing the blood-spattered wall in clear light.

Emily had to force back a scream. She pretended not to hear the curse that Mr. O'Hearn uttered.

"I found the light switch," came Clara's voice. "Does that help?"

There was no body, only drying blood, overturned equipment and dark puddles of noxious-smelling liquids.

MR. O'HEARN WAS DETERMINED to report the whole matter to the police, though Emily had wanted to telegraph Granville first. She then insisted on accompanying him to the station house, despite his protests.

The police station, in a temporary building near just off Columbia, was easy to find. Once the patrolman at the front desk understood why they were there, he ushered them into a small office with an even smaller window looking out on yet more construction. They were offered chairs and cups of very bad coffee.

The detective in charge, a Mr. Moore, listened to the story of the appointment for a portrait, and their discovery at the studio with a startled and somewhat wary expression. When they finished, he looked at them consideringly for a moment.

"Morgan is dead," he finally said. "Beg pardon for the shock, ladies. I'll need to know when you last spoke with him."

Emily felt suddenly cold, and she could hear Clara drawing in a sharp breath. A cold hand slipped into hers and she held it tight.

She'd been dreading this news from the moment she'd seen the blood spatters, but hoped she was wrong. She hadn't known how much until this moment.

Even though she hadn't known Mr. Morgan, even though he'd probably been less than honest, the news that someone she'd spoken to just hours ago was now dead was overwhelming. She clutched her friend's hand harder.

Mr. O'Hearn pulled out a pencil and notepad. "When did this happen?"

"An hour ago. Maybe less," the sheriff was saying.

That was what it meant to be a reporter. You had authority to ask questions about everything that happened, and people gave you answers. But there was still the reality of dealing with bloodstained rooms and death.

"When was it you talked to him?" the sheriff continued.

"I spoke with him," Emily said, concentrating hard so the words would come out without wavering. "It was just after ten this morning."

"And he was alone then?"

"He gave no indication otherwise, just agreed to the appointment."

"How did he die?" Mr. O'Hearn asked.

"Shot."

"And the weapon?"

The detective regarded his busy pencil with suspicion. "Why do you ask?"

"I'm a reporter, with the *World*. I'm covering this story."

"With these ladies along?"

"They asked me to meet them to give a man's opinion on a portrait. We certainly never expected to find blood and mayhem in the studio. The link to my ongoing story is purely coincidental."

"Coincidental, is it?" Detective Moore gave him a skeptical look.

"I assure you it is. But since I'm here, and happened across the scene of the crime, would it be possible to view the body?"

Moore looked shocked.

"The ladies would remain here, of course," Mr. O'Hearn hastened to assure him.

"I'm afraid not."

"But…" Mr. O'Hearn began, then seemed to change his mind. "Did you find anything on the body? Anything unusual, I mean?"

"No. Not unless you consider a laundry ticket unusual."

"Which laundry did he frequent?"

That earned him another considering look. "Why?"

Mr. O'Hearn shrugged. "It adds local color."

"You're not thinking of investigating this death yourself, now are you?"

"No. I'm just looking to capture the details that bring the story to life for our readers. Human interest, you know."

"I see. In that case, it was Chang's on Eighth."

Mr. O'Hearn extended his hand. "Thank you for that. We'll be on our way now."

"You told the sheriff you wouldn't investigate Morgan's death," Clara protested as they stopped on the muddy path outside the laundry shop. It was one of several poorly built buildings along a narrow street still lit by gas lanterns in New Westminster's Chinatown.

"The public has a right to know," O'Hearn said with a grin and a wink.

"I hope they speak at least a little English," Emily said as she followed him into the steamy interior, which was filled with a babble of rising and falling tones.

They did, or at least one of them did. But no one remembered Morgan.

"Early twenties, medium height, brown hair and eyes," Emily said, remembering the shop girl's description.

It wasn't much to go on, and it brought forth another round of shaking heads. Another dead end.

Too bad they didn't have a photo of Morgan. It was so much more effective than describing someone you'd never met. That thought led to another, and on an impulse, she pulled out Mary's photo. "Do you know this woman?"

The photo was examined carefully, and what seemed to be a

conference held. Emily felt a moment of hope, dashed when the man with the longer pigtail shook his head. Then the shorter man nodded just as vigorously.

"Do you know her?" Emily asked him.

He said something to the other man in quick tones.

"He say she look different, but eyes still same," they were told.

"She may be older now. This..." Emily said, tapping the photo. "Is five years old."

"Ah." He turned, spoke with the first man, nodding as he listened to the response. "Yes, she come here, sometime. Not soon."

"Do you know her name?"

Another conference. This time, the answer was no.

"Does she come here regularly?" O'Hearn asked.

Blank faces met his look. He rephrased his question. "Is this lady," he indicated the photo Emily held, "here on a Monday? A Wednesday?"

"Ah. No. Different day." He conferred with his fellow countryman. "She collect laundry for other lady."

"She collects another lady's laundry?" Emily asked. Perhaps Mary was working as a maid. "Do you have a name for the other lady?"

Another conference, and the first man brought out a black bound ledger book and flipped through the pages. Emily caught a glimpse of neat columns of incomprehensible symbols. She was impressed by the orderly pages, particularly when contrasted to the chaos of heat, steam and stacks of clothing around them.

He seemed to have found the page he sought, and was running a finger down it. The finger stopped. "Missee Laynor," he said.

"Do you have an address for her?" O'Hearn asked, notepad at the ready. But that, it seemed, was too much to hope for.

"When was she last here? What day?"

"Tuesday. Week ago, then four-five more."

"Four or five weeks ago last Tuesday?"

Both men nodded. Emily thanked them and turned to go.

As soon as they were outside, Clara asked "What now?"

It was O'Hearn who answered. "I'd suggest we visit City Hall, see if they have records for a Laynor."

"Why not just check the telephone listings?" Emily asked.

"We could, but since few households actually have a telephone, the city records are a better bet."

"Oh."

When they reached the city hall, housed in yet another temporary building, the clerk was inclined to be suspicious of their request to see the property rolls, until Mr. O'Hearn explained he was a reporter with the *World* and mentioned a murder investigation. Then he was more than helpful.

Escorting them to a long table in a dusty side room, he disappeared, then returned with a large stack of the ledgers they'd asked for.

Some time and no little degree of eyestrain later, Emily looked up from a list where she was not finding Laynor to see Clara watching her, one finger marking her place in a slim paperbound volume. The look in her friends' eye told her she was up to something. She waited to be told what.

"Emily, I've been thinking about something. Our houseboy has trouble with his 'R's'. So does your Bertie. They come out more like 'L's'. So I thought Laynor might be Raynor. And I found a listing," Clara said.

She put the phone book she was holding in front of Emily, opened to the R's, and pointed. There was one Raynor listed.

Mr. O'Hearn moved to stand beside Emily and together they flipped through the ledger she had been reading to the appropriate page.

One Raynor.

"That's brilliant, Cl—Miss Miles," Mr. O'Hearn said. "I'll need to interview her."

"I think you mean 'we', do you not, Mr. O'Hearn?" said Emily firmly.

27

WEDNESDAY, JANUARY 17, 1900

"Emily, you are going to fail your typing class," Clara said as they walked briskly towards the interurban station. The streets were crowded with carriages and delivery wagons at this hour, and the sidewalks thronged with workers and shoppers as Vancouverites began their day.

"Miss Richards will assume I have my monthly. She may lecture me on the importance of reliability in a typewriter, but she won't ask embarrassing questions."

"Emily!" Clara said, casting a shocked look around them.

"Don't worry, no-one is listening. And it isn't as if you don't have them too, so stop pretending to be shocked."

"I'm not pretending!"

And judging by the pink in her cheeks, perhaps she wasn't. How odd. Emily had thought that such prudery was limited to her mother's generation, though come to think of it her sisters weren't much better. "I wonder where Mr. O'Hearn is?"

"I'm sure he'll be here momentarily," Clara said, straightening her newest bonnet and patting at the curls that surrounded her face. "The tram isn't due for another ten minutes."

"Stop fussing, Clara. You look very nice, but this is a murder investigation, not a fashion show."

Clara drew in a quick breath, letting it out in a puff of indignation that hung in a frosty cloud for a moment. "We're supposed to be looking for Mary Pearson. I don't want anything to do with murder, Emily Turner. Seeing that poor man's blood was bad enough. I may have nightmares for weeks!"

Emily was relieved to see Mr. O'Hearn rounding the corner. In this mood, Clara was likely to refuse to go another step, but she'd never do so in front of O'Hearn.

"Good morning, ladies," he said as he drew closer. "Are you ready to brave the wilds of New Westminster to pay a call on Mrs. Raynor?"

NEARLY TWO HOURS later the trio stood on the plank walk outside a large biscuit-colored house with elaborate gingerbread in shades of garnet and cream. "I'm sorry to have dragged you on a wild-goose chase, Mr. O'Hearn," Emily said.

"Think nothing of it. It's part of being a reporter, tracking down sources. You'd be surprised how many of them are dead ends."

"Well, I find it odd that this Mary would have left so suddenly, and without leaving a forwarding address," Clara said.

Emily suppressed a smile. For all her protestations, Clara was enjoying this nearly as much as she was herself. "I've heard Mama complain about the utter unreliability of female domestics. It's one of the reasons she is so pleased with Bertie."

"I suppose so. But after working nearly five years for Mrs. Raynor, she suddenly gives notice six weeks ago? You must admit that is suspicious."

"Not at all," Tim O'Hearn broke in. "She may have taken another position, or gone to nurse relatives, or..."

"Or she may not have wanted someone to find her. Someone like Mr. Morgan, perhaps?" Emily said.

Clara looked disgusted, but Tim's expression grew intent, and he drew out his notepad. "Tell me more about the link between Mary Pearson and the photographer," he said.

28

THURSDAY, JANUARY 18, 1900

Emily sat behind the heavy black typewriting machine, hands in her lap, listening to yet another lecture. All around her, the other students were typing industriously, almost drowning out the sound of commerce on the street one floor below the Pitman School.

Apparently she had been wrong when she told Clara that Miss Richards wouldn't question her.

"There is already reluctance to hire women typewriters," Miss Richards said in a forceful undertone. "You are one of the pioneers. If you don't set a good example, you are hurting not only your own career but those of the women who would follow after you. Pioneers can't afford the luxury of feeling unwell each month."

Emily cast down her eyes so Miss Richards could not see the expression in them.

She'd begun to question her plan of becoming an assistant in someone's office. The idea of spending her days following a rigid routine, recording and transcribing someone else's thoughts, was stifling. And it might not be her only way to be part of the business world after all.

Perhaps she could become a reporter like Mr. O'Hearn. It was true there were very few women reporters, but Mrs. McLagan was a reporter as well as being the manager of the *Daily World*. There was no reason she couldn't be a reporter too.

Her father would argue the point, of course. He was already worried by her desire to engage in trade. In his eyes, the business world was no place for a lady. But given Papa's restricted definition of a lady, Emily had long been sure that was the last thing she wanted to be.

In fact, it was probably a good thing her engagement to Granville wasn't real. His wife, when he eventually chose her, needed to be every inch a lady, someone who'd never even consider taking typewriting lessons. So why did that thought make her hands clench?

"You need to be committed," Miss Richards finished.

"I'm sorry. I'll try to do better."

"I know you will," Miss Richards said, patting her shoulder. "It isn't easy, but I know you have the persistence to do well."

Her kindness made Emily feel guilty, and she gave the woman a weak smile. Her teacher walked on, leaving Emily to wrestle with the typing exercises she'd missed in the last few days.

As her fingers flew, her mind was equally busy. Granville hadn't settled for a career that stifled him. Why should she? She was enjoying the challenge of searching for Mary. Could that become an option for her?

She'd love to work with Granville and Mr. Scott as a detective, or perhaps as a detective's assistant, since she didn't think she'd ever heard of a woman detective. Still, there was no real reason a detective had to be a man. All she had to do was convince Granville of that fact.

It was a new century and it was time for things to change. Surely he would see that? After all, he was an English aristocrat working as a detective in the colonies—it wasn't like he was a stickler for the old ways.

Thinking about Granville brought back her worries as to how

he was faring in Denver, and whether they'd found little Sarah. Would it be dangerous for him?

"Oh, drat it," she muttered as a clump of keys stuck together again.

"Miss Turner?"

Emily jumped. She'd been concentrating so hard she hadn't heard Miss Richards come up behind her again. Now what had she done? "Yes?"

"A message for you."

Emily opened it, scanned the few lines. O'Hearn had some information he thought she'd want to hear immediately. Had something happened to Granville?

Emily stood up and shook out her skirts. "My mother is ill. I must go," she said, the words out of her mouth before she'd even thought what to say.

"Of course. I hope it isn't serious," Miss Richards was saying, standing aside to let her pass.

Emily hoped so too.

"You got me out of class to tell me you've tracked down Mr. Morgan's mother?" Emily asked Tim O'Hearn in a fierce undertone. She was glad to see he looked even more uncomfortable than usual, sitting at the small table set for high tea.

Much as she enjoyed the occasional visit to Stroh's Tearoom, it was becoming far too frequent a haunt. She was getting tired of the attention it drew from some of her mother's friends, who were fond of the place, and the little buzz of gossip that seemed to follow in her wake.

Not to mention the questions she had to dodge from her mother, who was alert for any sign that Emily wasn't serious about what Mama called "Emily's typewriting nonsense."

"I thought you'd want to know," O'Hearn said.

"You thought it would be good for your story, you mean." She sipped her tea and gave him a social smile, just to keep the gossips quiet.

He looked chagrined. "She'll more readily talk to you. And it's to help Granville, after all.

"I don't see how."

Clara, who had been watching them, felt the need to intervene. "Now Emily, you know you were looking for information on Mr. Morgan."

"Only as a route to Mary Pearson. We've learned all we can there."

"I don't agree," O'Hearn broke in. "I think it most significant that he was murdered after you began looking for her."

Emily went pale. "Do you think my questions are responsible for Mr. Morgan's death?"

Tim O'Hearn took a hasty sip of tea. "No, no. I'm not saying that at all. I'm simply emphasizing that these things may be related. In fact, I suspect that Morgan's murderers are the same crew who've been after Granville."

Clara threw a quick glance at Emily's drawn face, then leaned towards O'Hearn. "What makes you think so? And how would they be related?"

"I did a little research into our Mr. Morgan. His father was quite a prominent photographer before his untimely death, worked with all the society ladies, doing portraits and such."

"Then why would he have taken the photo of Mary Pearson, who for the last five years was a maid for Mrs. Raynor? And how could she have afforded him?" asked Emily, intrigued despite her determination not to be drawn into his need for a story.

"Exactly what I asked myself. Especially when I discovered that quite a number of photos of the Raynor clan are credited to Morgan, Sr."

"You think Mrs. Raynor paid for the portrait? But..." Emily began, her voice tailing off as her mind darted from one conclusion to the next. "If she valued her that much, why would Mary have left so abruptly? And surely Mrs. Raynor must know where she went. So why didn't she tell us?"

"Mrs. Raynor might have been protecting Mary," Clara said. "Think about it. If Mrs. Raynor paid for the portrait, wouldn't that have been her address that Mr. Morgan had on file? Why would Mrs. Anders go to such lengths to give us the wrong information?"

"If the two of you worked at the *World*, you'd beat me out of too many headlines," O'Hearn.

Emily gave him a speculative look. "Do you think your editor would consider…?"

"Your father would never allow it," Clara said.

O'Hearn just shook his head.

Emily wasn't giving up that easily, not when Mr. O'Hearn had brought the subject up himself. But now was not the time.

"Will you come with me to speak with Morgan's mother?" O'Hearn was asking. "I think she may speak more readily to the two of you than she will to me."

"Of course we'll come," Clara said. "Won't we, Emily?"

EMILY STOOD beside Clara on the scrubbed stoop of the careworn little house on Seventh Avenue, hoping there would be an answer to O'Hearn's confident knock. Finally, the door screeched open.

The woman facing them had thin cheeks and red-rimmed eyes. She hid behind the half opened door, staring at them in horror when O'Hearn identified himself as a reporter for the *World*.

Emily gave O'Hearn a look, then stepped forward so the woman could see her clearly. "Mrs. Morgan? I'm so sorry for your loss. I hate to bother you at such a time, but we haven't much time. We're looking for a woman your husband once photographed. Her life may be at risk, and your information could save it."

The door wavered open another inch.

Emily stepped forward and held up the photo. "Do you recognize her?"

"Perhaps." Lines deepened around the woman's eyes as she peered at the photo, then a shaky hand reached out.

"May we come in?" Emily asked.

"Better not." The voice was soft but the tone was firm. "The photo?"

With a mental shrug, Emily passed it to her. She hoped it would not be the last she'd see of it, but they needed information.

"Mary Pearson."

"You recognize her?"

"She worked for the Raynors in New Westminster for some years. Mrs. Raynor herself requested this photo be taken. My husband couldn't believe it."

"Why not?"

"The girl was a thief."

"A thief?" It was O'Hearn's voice, and out of the side of her eye Emily could see him scribbling frantically in his notebook.

She was pleased to see Clara poke him in the side, and hoped he'd take the hint. What was needed here was back stoop gossip, not a reporter's interrogation.

"Oh?"

"The Raynors wouldn't ever believe it of her, of course, felt sorry for her, with her ma dead and her pa off chasing Klondike gold. But there was no getting around that things kept vanishing from that house."

Emily wasn't quite sure which tidbit of information to ask about first, but she knew she had to play this just right, or the door would close in their face. "Things went missing?"

"Bits of silver, trinkets, a gold thimble."

"Who *did* they suspect?"

"Everyone for a time. Eventually, they settled on my husband. Ruined his business. He died from the shame of it. And now it's killed my son." Her voice was bitter and her eyes burned in her sallow face.

Beside her, Emily sensed O'Hearn stir, but he subsided without saying anything. "I am truly sorry for your loss, and for disturbing you at such a time" Emily said. "But can you tell me anything of what happened to the girl?"

"Mary?" Mrs. Morgan gave a bitter laugh. "She stayed on, never a whisper against her. I had to leave town and that little liar stayed on."

"She's not there any longer," O'Hearn said.

Mrs. Morgan's lips thinned. "Good."

"Do you know where she went?" Emily asked quickly. "I know you don't live there any longer, but I hoped you might have heard."

"Course I heard. She left with her uncle, didn't she? Him as came back with stories of gold and making her rich."

"And her uncle? Is his name Pearson too?" O'Hearn asked. It earned him a glare.

"How would I know?" Mrs. Morgan said, and slammed the door.

29

FRIDAY, JANUARY 19, 1900

Granville stepped stiffly off the train in Denver, tired and gritty. Scott and Trent didn't look much better, thought Scott's color had improved. All three of them had spent the journey alert for any sign of attack, sleeping half-dressed, revolvers at the ready.

He'd startled awake the first night when the train stopped dead. As he lay listening, one hand on his gun, there was a great banging and clattering. The carriage shuddered several times, then they moved forward. And stopped again.

Shoving his feet into his boots, he'd leapt from his berth—and crashed into Trent. When they'd sorted themselves out, they'd peered out the windows, to see the train, section by section, being loaded onto a ferry.

"What the…" he'd muttered.

A smothered chuckle had him glaring at Scott, who'd drawn back the curtains on his berth far enough to watch them. "You should see your faces," his partner had said.

"What is this?"

"Track through to Portland's on the other side of the Columbia.

There's no railroad bridge, so the train gets loaded onto the car ferry."

There was no obvious danger, and still no sign of a shooter, so he'd gone back to bed, shaking his head. No challenge the landscape threw at them seemed to daunt these North Americans. It was amazing.

The rest of the trip had been incident free, but not more restful. By the third day, he'd have welcomed a chance to take on their pursuers, just to decrease the tension.

Finally arriving at their destination was a relief, but they stepped off the train into organized chaos. Union Station was huge, with high ceilings, fluted pillars and marble floors. Crowded and noisy, it was the clearly the hub of the city, with people and trains flowing in all directions.

Much as Granville craved a shower and a change of clothes, both he and Scott were impatient to find out what Harris knew about little Sarah. After taking a moment to get their bearings, and downing a beer to clear the grit from their throats, they turned their feet towards the police station.

Inside the two-story brick building, they found the bustle common to police stations everywhere. Granville eyed a few rough types being hustled along a narrow hallway, and wondered what they'd been arrested for. It took a few minutes before the burly policeman behind the main desk so much as nodded at them, but eventually their presence was acknowledged.

When they were shown into his cluttered office, Detective Mitchell Harris was on the phone. He glanced at them, held up a finger. "Uh huh. Got it," he said, scribbling something on the page in front of him. "Thanks."

Hanging up, he braced his hands against the edge of his desk and leaned back in his chair, regarding them. "Glad to see you finally made it."

Granville came forward, hand outstretched. "It's good to see you, Harris. I gather you have news for us?"

Harris stood up, gripped Granville's hand with his own.

Nearly as tall as Scott, but lean and wiry, the detective had sandy hair and a direct gaze. "Good to see you both."

Harris's eyes moved to Trent. "And who is this?"

"Our assistant, Trent Davis. Trent, Detective Mitchell Harris." Granville noted something odd in the boy's expression as he made the introduction, and filed the information away for later.

"What I have isn't solid news, I'm afraid, so much as a possible lead," Harris said. "I haven't liked what I've been hearing about an increase in the number of baby farms."

"Baby farms? And what exactly is a baby farm?" Granville could barely restrain his revulsion at the term.

"Not something you're familiar with in England? Or Canada?"

"No."

"They look after young children, for pay, when their parents can't. Often it's children of doxies or the like, who can't care for the young'uns. And conditions can be pretty bad."

"I heard about them in Chicago," Scott said. "The way some of them treated the little ones..." His face was hard and set. "So how do these baby farms connect to little Sarah?"

"We've investigated some of these places on rumors that they're selling babies and young children, mostly for servants, but we haven't been able to prove anything."

"Why didn't you mention these baby farms last time we were here?" Scott demanded.

The detective shrugged. "Didn't think it would be worth your time."

The look on Scott's face had Granville stepping forward. "Go on."

"There've also been rumors for a while now of a smuggling gang with some kind of mysterious trade, operating from here to California."

"And...?"

"When we began hearing rumblings about illegal adoptions, I started putting some things together. If the baby farms are connected to some kind of adoption racket it explains the growth and why we can't pin anything on them. And if the children are being taken out of state, it'd explain why they're leaving so little trace."

The words he hadn't spoken hung between them.

"Surely something can be done to stop it?" Scott's voice was tight with anger.

"Most of the victims either aren't missed or the parent is afraid to come to us about it."

"Unlike my niece."

Harris' face was unreadable. "I said most."

Scott's expression darkened and Granville was afraid he'd lash out, but the big man clamped his lips tight.

"So you think Scott's niece might've been sent out of the state?" Granville said, cutting into the tension.

"It could explain why we've found no trace of her here," the detective said.

"How likely is it she's still alive?" he asked bluntly. He hated saying the words in front of Scott, but it had to be asked.

"If they saw a way to make money from her, they'll have treated her well," Harris said. "If she's part of this thing, the odds of her being alive are better than if she isn't."

People undoubtedly disappeared in cities like Denver all the time. Granville could think of a number of ways a baby could vanish, none of them pleasant. "Why the urgent telegram?"

"The more time passes, the harder she'll be to trace," Harris said. "And I don't have the resources to follow the few leads I do have."

"And you hadn't heard any of this when we were here in December?" Scott asked.

"We knew about the baby farms, but to be blunt, three years is too long for them to hold onto a child if no-one's paying the bills."

Scott's face went white. "This is my niece we're talking about.

And maybe my sister, too. If we don't find little Sarah, I don't think Lizzie is going to make it."

Granville hadn't known that Scott realized how precarious Lizzie's attachment to living was. Without her child, she could too easily give in to her wasted body and the siren call of opium. "And what leads do you have now?" he asked Harris.

The detective pulled a file off a stack on one corner of his desk, flipped it open. Pulling out a sheet half covered with spiky writing, he handed it to Scott.

"These are the orphanages we talked to. They're all legit, and none of them had any record of a child who could be your niece. These ones," and he handed him another list, slightly longer, "are other facilities we know about—they're legal too, but they skirt the edge of the law. Again, no child resembling your niece."

Scott's gaze was fixed on the pages. "Thanks."

"Also, a couple of names keep coming up in relation to the smuggling—Dale Androchuck and Peter Mather. Mather is a low-rent crook. Androchuck is of the same ilk, but brighter. And I hear your Jackson had dealings with Androchuck when he was in this part of the world."

"So where do I find these two?" Scott growled.

"You're keeping in mind that murder is still murder in this town, no matter the reason," Harris said.

"I'll make sure he remembers," Granville said.

"See that you do." Harris pinned them both with a hard look, then relented. "You can probably find Mather at a dive called the Red Mule. You know it?"

Granville nodded, remembering a dimly lit speakeasy, the roughness of the whiskey only exceeded by the roughness of the clientele. Perfect hunting grounds. He glanced over at Scott, who grimaced. "We know it."

"Watch your back," the detective said.

"That's what I'm here for," Trent said suddenly, from his position behind Granville.

Granville started. There was a warning note in the boy's voice and his gaze was hard and flat. Aimed at Harris?

Granville's gaze fixed on the detective, who had a half frown between his brows and looked as if he was trying to remember something. What was going on here?

"Is there anything else you might not have mentioned?" Scott asked into the ensuing silence. His tone made the words an insult.

What was this? Scott was desperate to find his missing niece, but where was this animosity towards Harris coming from? Granville knew his partner and the detective had known each other before—Scott had said as much when he introduced them last year—but "we worked together, once" didn't explain the undercurrents in Scott's voice now.

Looking from one to the other, he wondered just what his partner had neglected to tell him. This time.

Scott's innate privacy and determination to protect those he considered his to protect had nearly got him hung for murder a few weeks ago. What were they likely to get them into now?

Granville needed have a long chat with his partner, and soon.

His gaze slid to Trent, who was watching Harris intently. And the boy, too.

30

"I thought you cared about becoming a typewriter?"

Emily started and her index finger jammed between the 'F' and the 'G'. "Darn," she muttered, and looked up to meet Laura's accusing stare. "No, it isn't that," she said, tripping a little over the words. "I was ill."

Ignoring the looks the other students were giving her, Laura gave Emily a frigid look. "I know the truth, remember? You've been gone for three and a half days, and you just come back and start typing without a word? Are you forgetting I helped you?"

Emily glanced around and was relieved to see that their teacher was busy on the far side of the room, helping Andy Riggs. She let out a little breath. "You're right, you deserve the truth, but not now. Wait until Miss Richards calls a break."

"I feel faint," Laura said, putting the back of her hand against her forehead. "Help me to the ladies room?"

"Yes, of course," Emily said, standing up and casting a glance around. "Only please try to be a little less dramatic or she'll guess we're up lo something."

As soon as the door closed behind them, Laura turned to Emily. "So?"

Emily's gaze had gone to the mirror behind Laura, where one of the doors was not entirely closed. Holding a finger to her lips, she tiptoed over and eased it open.

No one was there. She tipped her head towards the other door. Laura nodded, and banged on the door. "Excuse me. I'm feeling ill and need to get in."

Nothing. Laura banged again, without result. With a half smile at Emily, she twisted the knob. It was locked. There was someone inside.

Emily touched Laura's arm and gestured towards the long hallway that ran to the front of the building and the interior stairwell. Laura nodded, and the two girls tiptoed out.

Stopping halfway down the stairs, out of sight from both directions, Emily began to tell Laura everything that had happened, speaking in a hushed tone that had the other girl leaning towards her. When she finished, Laura's eyes were huge.

"No wonder you missed class," she said. "I'm surprised you're here today."

"We reached a dead end," Emily said. "No new leads on Mary, and not even a name for her uncle."

"You said you had a photo of this Mary. May I see it?"

"Yes, of course." Emily reached into her silk bag and removed the photo, handing it to Laura.

Laura glanced at the photo, then looked harder, carefully examining each feature. "But I know her!" she said. "Or at least I think I do. The woman I'm thinking of is somewhat older."

"You recognize her? This photo was taken some five years ago."

"That sounds right. It's Mary Pearson, right?"

So her last name was Pearson. "Yes! But why do you know her? And when did you meet?"

"She was one of the other maids at the Howe's ball on New Year's Day.

"Really?" Emily searched her memory, but couldn't remember seeing anyone that resembled the photo she held. "Do you know how to find her?"

Laura shook her head. "We were hired just for the evening. I haven't seen her since. She seemed nice enough, though she kept herself to herself."

But if Mary's uncle had enough money for Mary to leave Mrs. Raynor's employ, why had Mary taken that job? "Who hired you?"

"Mrs. Howe herself. She advertised in the *World*."

"So Mrs. Howe might have a current address for Mary." She gave Laura a rueful smile. "Here I've been looking everywhere for information on her, and you knew all the time. I should have shown you the photo days ago."

Laura looked pleased and a trifle smug. "But Emily, what about the men who killed the photographer, and tried to kill your fiancé?"

"We've no leads at all."

"Except whatever information our classmates might have."

Emily stared at Laura. "You're right. I was forgetting about our Mr. Riggs. You'll help me?"

"Yes, of course. Where do we start?"

Her eyes narrowed. "Which one the three do you think is the weakest?"

Laura considered her for a moment. "You really care about Mr. Granville, don't you?"

Emily could only nod.

"AND, FINGERS UP," said Miss Richards. "Please take out your notebooks."

Emily sat back with a sigh, flexing sore fingers. It was a good thing she was better at learning shorthand than she was at typewriting, or she'd probably quit, and she hated giving up on things.

At least the odd squiggles invented by Mr. Richard's friend Isaac Pitman were interesting. When she knew enough of them, she'd be able to take down whole conversations without missing a word.

She could envision herself interviewing someone for a story or capturing every word as she interviewed a suspect.

Emily's pencil, which had been flying to capture the symbols that Miss Richards was putting up on the chalkboard, suddenly faltered. Could that be why she was learning this Pitman method so easily, because she saw a purpose for it?

She had a sudden image of O'Hearn when she had first met him, hammering away on the keys of a large Underwood in the newsroom of the *World*. Reporters had to typewrite their own stories.

If she decided she wanted to be a reporter, she had to learn to be as good a typewriter as she was a stenographer. And if she were working with Granville, she'd need to transcribe her shorthand, wouldn't she?

Emily bent to her typewriter with renewed concentration.

After that, typing practice went surprisingly well, as if the break from classes had somehow helped her brain integrate what her fingers already knew. Waiting for the luncheon break was hard, though.

When it was finally called, Emily and Laura raced to get their jackets and followed Wally Sutton down the stairs, joining the lunchtime crowd walking briskly along Hastings. Once Wally was out of sight of the building, they came up on either side of him.

"Wally? I mean, Mr. Sutton," Laura said. "Could we speak with you a moment?"

He looked from Emily to Laura and flushed. "Miss Turner. Miss Kent," he said with a stammer. "Why are you—I mean what do you —I mean..."

"We wanted to talk to you, Mr. Sutton," Emily said. "We felt we could trust you."

His flush deepened. "Me?"

"Yes," Laura said with a smile. "I've been watching you, and of all our classmates, I told Emily you were the one we could trust."

"But..."

"Is Laura right? Can we trust you?" Emily asked before he could summon his arguments.

"Well…"

"We need a man's help," Laura said, putting her hand on his arm. "I fear it is too dangerous for just the two of us."

"Dangerous?" He looked like he wanted to run, but someone had trained him too well to allow him to leave two women on their own.

"It's just information we need, but ladies can't ask the questions that need to be asked."

"Oh. Questions."

He seemed incapable of forming a complete sentence, but at least he hadn't said no. This was the tricky bit. Emily glanced at Laura, who gave her a little nod. "I know you're friends with Mr. Riggs. His father is involved in a plot against my fiancé."

Sutton's eyes widened, and she thought for a moment he might bolt despite his training. "But…"

Laura put her hand on his arm again. "It's why you are the perfect person to help us. You'll be helping Mr. Riggs too."

"How will it help him?"

At least it was a complete sentence. This might just work.

"Once my fiancé is—gone," Emily swallowed hard. It was hard to say, even as part of her story. "The man who hired Mr. Riggs' father will have to deal with everyone involved."

Sutton went pale. "Deal with?"

Really, this was too easy. "Kill them. Get rid of anyone who knows of the conspiracy. My fiancé is very well connected, and his family will not let his death go unavenged, once they learn the truth."

"It frightens me, all this violence. Where will it end?" Laura had her hand on his arm again. "I'm so glad we have you to turn to."

He gulped, then his shoulders straightened. "How can I help?"

Emily thought it sounded more like a plea than a declaration, but he hadn't said no. "We need the name of the man who is really behind all this. That way, we can make sure he will be arrested quickly, saving both my fiancé and your friend's father."

"That's all you want? Just his name?"

She didn't think it was going to be quite that simple, but Emily nodded. "Just the name. And where he can be found."

Wally Sutton stood a little taller. "I can do that."

31

In the run-down hotel room they'd found just off Market Street in downtown Denver, Granville, Scott and Trent had showered and changed. Granville could have used a couple of hours sleep, but he was anxious to get started, now they finally were here. Finding the child was more important than sleep.

He looked from Scott to Trent. "Which one of you wants to tell me what's going on with Harris?"

Trent picked at a strip of wallpaper that was dangling forlornly near his head. "What d'you mean?" he asked.

Scott just shrugged.

Granville knew from experience that getting either of them to talk was going to be a struggle.

And he didn't have the time.

"Never mind." He glanced at Scott. "D'you know anything about either of these men? Androchuck or Mather?"

"I've heard of Mather," Scott said, looking up from the lists he was still studying. "I knew his cousin, back in Chicago. Craddock used to run with him."

"Which could explain how Craddock found out what Jackson had done with the child."

"Assuming he wasn't bluffing," Granville said.

"Assuming that, of course."

"He didn't tell you anything? Craddock, I mean," Trent asked.

"Not a word. Just looked at me and sniggered," Scott said.

"Even though he faced the noose?" Trent said. "I thought he was trying to work a deal?"

Scott grimaced. "Yeah, around Gipson's crimes."

"But Gipson's out of jail already." Trent said.

"Exactly. And Craddock's still alive," Scott said. "With us still not knowing what he knows about little Sarah, if he indeed knows anything."

"But that's wrong," Trent said.

"Yeah. So?"

"So do we start with the lawyer Benton told us about or the Red Mule?" Granville asked.

Scott looked at him. "I need a drink. You?"

He nodded. "Think you'll recognize Mather?"

"If he's anything like his cousin," Scott said. "He'll have ears like jug handles."

"We need a plan," Granville said.

"You go in low, I'll go in high," Scott said.

"Not that kind of plan. We won't get answers from dead men. And I think Harris was serious about arresting us if there's any shooting."

Scott muttered something under his breath.

"What was that?"

"Nothin'."

His partner wouldn't meet his eyes.

Granville glanced at Trent, but the boy was seemingly intent on re-loading his rifle. Great. Neither of them was in any hurry to admit what was going on.

"Then let's go," he said.

THE RED MULE was every bit as sleazy as Granville had remembered. Only half-full, it was still noisy and so smoky it was like seeing the room through a thick London fog. Patrons stood two deep along the bar, casting suspicious glances at the three of them. This was not a place to ask too many questions.

On his left, Scott's eyes were scanning the room, while on his right he sensed Trent's tension. "Scott?"

"Nothing. No-one I recognize."

"What are you drinking?"

"Beer."

"Why don't you and Trent find somewhere to stand." Granville said, and made his way to the bar.

After ignoring him just long enough to make it clear he was an outsider, the bartender finally turned to him. "Yeah?"

"Three beers."

"Denver Ale?"

"Fine. And can you point me towards Mather?"

The man's small eyes ran over him. "Not sure he's here. You got business with him?"

"A message from his cousin."

The bartender nodded towards a tall table in the corner, where three men stood. They'd been there a while, judging by bottles covering the tabletop. "Yellow-haired one's Mather."

Obviously jug-ears did not run in his side of the family. "Thanks." Dropping two coins on the grimy bar, Granville made his way back to where Scott and Trent stood.

They'd chosen a spot that let them keep their backs to the wall and their eyes on the door. In a place like this, it was only prudent.

"Mather's over there in the corner," he said, low-voiced, handing them each a bottle. "You want to talk to him? I told the bartender we had a message from his cousin."

"Since I'm the one who knows the cousin, I'd better do it," Scott said.

"Keep in mind that we need information more than you need vengeance."

Scott frowned at him. "You coming or not?"

With a shrug, Granville followed Scott across the room.

"Mather?" Scott asked as he stood looking down on the narrow features and bleached looking hair of the man who might be able to lead him to his niece. Might have sold his niece.

"Yeah?" the man with yellow hair said.

Granville noted the fellow's hand moving to rest near his gun, the wary alertness of his two companions, and he moved to stand at Scott's elbow.

"I knew your cousin Dean back in Chicago," Scott was saying.

Mather grunted.

"He said if I was ever in town and looking to make some money, you had a sweet deal going," Scott said.

Granville could only hope that the cousins still shared information on their various deals.

"You run with Dean?" Mather asked.

"Not exactly. We clashed a few times, had the same target."

Oddly, Scott's honesty seemed to satisfy Mather.

"Yeah?" Mather said. "Sounds like Dean. What'd he tell you?"

"No details. Just said talk to you if I was out this way. See if you needed a few more guns."

"Huh." Mather eyes slid to the revolver at Scott's hip, then to Granville standing silently behind him. "And who's this?"

"My partner, Granville."

"You'd better join us." Mather waved them towards the table. His eyes slid to his own friends, then back to Scott. "We lost a couple guys a week or so ago. Maybe we can use you. Or maybe you should just be movin' on."

Granville hoped Scott knew what he was doing.

When he'd suggested Scott do the talking, he hadn't anticipated the offer to join Mather's gang. The potential for disaster loomed, but if they could pull it off, it was possibly the fastest way to get the information they needed.

And they both knew that the more time that passed, the less

chance they'd have of finding little Sarah. And the more chance that Lizzie would just fade away.

With a grim smile, Granville stepped to a spot beside Scott.

His attention was fixed on the wiry runt he figured was Androchuck, who seemed to be weighing every expression that crossed Scott's face. Granville was willing to bet he was the more dangerous of the two.

"So why're you here?" the short man asked suddenly.

"It seemed a good time to get out of town," Granville said.

"You're a Brit?"

"Yes. And you are?"

"Androchuck. The quiet one's Berger. How'd you end up with him?" Androchuck nodded toward Scott.

"Partnered up in the Klondike."

Mather laughed, a short, hard sound. "I'm guessing you didn't find gold."

Having made a quick assessment of both men's character and weighed the risks, he chose his words with care. "Not there."

"You found gold someplace else?"

"Let's just say we found a map that'll make us rich," Granville said.

"Then why d'you want to join with us?" Mather asked. "If you've got gold, you don't need more."

"A man can always use more," Granville said. "But as it happens, we don't have gold."

"Just the map?" asked Androchuck, clearly suspicious.

"Just the map."

"So what're you doing here? Is the mine near Denver?" Mather asked.

"Nope. Oregon," Scott said.

Granville was relieved his partner had picked up on his plan.

Androchuck was looking from one to the other. "So who ran you out of town?"

"We aren't sure—we were ambushed," Granville answered. "Leaving town for a time seemed the smart choice."

"Why here?" Androchuck asked sharply.

Were they buying it? Granville shrugged. "Easy train ride. And Scott here remembered what your cousin said. Plus no-one would think to look for us here."

Well, that much was true. Unless Benton told them, of course.

"And meanwhile you've got this map," Androchuck said slowly. "We could maybe work out a deal, if you throw in with us."

"The mine's not part of the deal," Scott said.

Androchuck eyes narrowed. "So you'd make money on us, but not return the favor?"

"We thought to sign on as hired guns, now 'til spring."

"I think I'd trust you more if we were partners. That way we've all got somethin' to lose."

They'd taken the bait. Now could they pull it off? Granville glanced at Scott. "We'll have to discuss this. We'll meet you tomorrow with our answer. Here?"

Androchuck nodded slowly. "Same time. And make sure you show up. This is our town, and we can find you."

"We'll be here," Granville said. Signaling to Trent, they left the bar.

As they stepped out onto the snow-covered sidewalk, Scott turned to Granville. "What've you got us into?"

"As I recall, I'm not the one who offered them our services."

"Yeah, but you're the one talked about the map. Now they won't rest 'til they get it."

"Exactly. And we're guaranteed entry into their scam," Granville said.

"At what price?"

He shrugged. He'd promised Lizzie to bring her daughter back. "An acceptable one."

"Assuming they don't just decide to kill us and take the map," Scott said flatly.

Granville winked at him. "Life was getting dull."

Scott shook his head, but he clapped Granville on the shoulder hard enough to make him wince.

32

SATURDAY, JANUARY 20, 1900

After donning the tailor-made suit of heavy worsted and adding a wool overcoat, cashmere scarf and fur-lined gloves, Granville eyed his elegant reflection with some cynicism. It was in stark contrast to the foxed mirror and the dilapidated hotel room he stood in.

Only the tightness around his eyes showed signs of too many whiskeys downed in too many bars the previous night, while they chased rumors of smugglers and illegal adoptions. His clothes and the bearing drilled into him by a series of governesses conveyed confident prosperity. He hoped it would convince Baxter.

Tipping his hat to the reflected image, Granville thought of his father at his most imperial, and was disconcerted to see his own features settle into something resembling the authority of the fifth Baron.

Scott's face swam into the wavery glass behind him. "You look like you ate something didn't agree with you."

"Baxter needs to be convinced I'm a serious businessman," Granville said.

Scott nodded thoughtfully. "He sees you lookin' like that, he might be laughing too hard to answer any questions."

Granville's answering grin erased all traces of the fifth baron. "Let's go."

As the three of them exited the hotel, Trent glanced up and down the street. "Which way?"

"I'm heading for the business district. I don't know about you two."

"Depends. I could spend time in a higher rent district." Scott waved a hand at the seedy buildings on both sides of the street as they headed east. "But I don't want to queer your pitch, as you Brits say. What's the plan?"

The stealthy movement of a curtain in a run down hotel across the street caught Granville's eye. "Duck," he shouted.

Granville suited action to words as a bullet slammed into the wood siding of the tavern behind them. He crouched behind the wooden railings of the porch, his revolver drawn. Scott did the same, while Trent had rolled to sight his gun under the lowest rung of the railings.

Glancing back over his shoulder, wincing as the movement pulled on his barely healed wound, Granville could see the bullet had hit precisely where he'd been standing, centered on his heart.

Whoever the shooter was, he was good.

Very good.

He risked a glance over the railing, ducking just in time to avoid the bullet that whined by his ear. "There's only one shooter. He's in the hotel opposite us, second floor."

"And he's good. I can't get a shot in," Scott said.

"Me neither," Trent said.

For a long minute, none of them moved.

It was intensely cold, and the wind that came straight off the mountains that circled the city seemed to find every gap in their clothing.

"Get inside," Granville said to the other two in a low voice. "I'll cover you."

Ten minutes later, the three of them were seated in a dark corner of the Drunken Pheasant, mugs of ale in front of them. They still had their revolvers drawn, but there was no further sign of the shooter.

Granville took a deep pull on his ale, his eyes moving quickly around the dim, fetid interior. Neither the exchange of shots nor their hurried entrance seemed to have interested the bar's few patrons. The bartender was still watching them with one hand out of sight, undoubtedly on the rifle he'd have below the bar, but he hadn't hesitated to pull the ale or accept their coin.

It was good ale, too. Much better than he'd had expected from the look of the place.

"So who's after us now?" Scott had drained his tanker and was conducting the same visual search Granville was.

"Could be our friends from home or our new partners looking for a shortcut to the map," Granville said.

"But if it's one of the guys from Vancouver, how'd they find us?" Trent asked. "We weren't followed."

"That we know of. Maybe Benton told someone where we were going. Maybe someone heard us purchasing our tickets. This fellow seems to have a network of informants. And I find it interesting that there's only one shooter again."

"Yeah, but he's a deadeye," Scott said. "Know anyone other than Benton with a network like that?"

"I'm still new in town, remember? What do you think?"

"No-one I can think of. You think Benton sent him?"

"We both know he's capable of it. I can't see any gain for him in doing so, though."

"Doesn't seem his style, either."

"I agree, but we've too many unknowns. Starting with our late client and his partner, or whatever Pearson was to him. *If* that's even his name."

"Yeah. Guess we'll just have to keep a low profile 'till we can figure it out."

"Unless we can get a shot at him."

"Doubt it—he seems pretty wary. All I've seen so far is the glint of a rifle behind a curtain."

Trent was looking from one to the other. "You don't suspect Harris is in on this?"

The two men turned to look at him.

"I gather you do?" Granville asked.

Trent hurriedly lifted his ale, drank down a mouthful. "Well, he knows we're in town. And where we're staying," he said, wiping his mouth on his sleeve.

"What's between you and the detective, Trent?"

"Nothin'. I never met him before."

"Yet he almost seemed to recognize you," Granville said, regarding their assistant's suddenly pale features closely. "Or d'you just look like someone he does know?"

Trent flushed. "Well—he might know my Pa."

"Your father? The man who left town after that fiasco when he tried to break into the silk train?"

Trent bristled. "You know it is."

"And where is he now, Trent?"

"Here."

"Denver?"

"Yeah."

"He's had a run-in with Harris?" Scott asked.

"He's trying to go straight, but there's no work. An' he says most of the police are crooked."

"Scott?"

"Far's I know, Harris is a straight arrow. But he doesn't hold out much hope of finding little Sarah, does he?" Scott's voice was harsh.

"So we may not be able to count on him for much help." Privately Granville wondered about the expression he'd seen cross the detective's face when he mentioned the kidnapping ring. It was something to think about. Later. "You're planning to check out the rest of the places on his lists?"

Scott nodded.

Granville turned to Trent. "Would your father know anything about baby farms?"

Trent shrugged. "I doubt it, but I'll ask. If I can find him."

"And if we don't get shot getting out of here," Scott put in.

He grinned at them. "We won't if this establishment has a back door."

THEY EMERGED CAUTIOUSLY from the alley the rear entrance opened into, but there was no sign of the shooter.

Guns drawn and ready, they made their way towards the center of town. As they turned onto Sixteenth, Trent gazed up at the six and seven story buildings that lined it, a nervous crease between his brows.

A loud report had him ducking, but Granville's hand on his arm kept him upright.

"That wasn't a gun," Granville said.

"Then what…?" Trent started to ask, then stopped mid-sentence, eyes wide, to watch the black Daimler chugging down the street.

"A motor car," Granville said. "You have an address for your father?"

Trent shook his head. "Care of General Delivery. I'd no idea Denver was so big."

It seemed small to Granville, but then his idea of a city was London. Viewing Denver from Trent's perspective, Granville could imagine his sense of dislocation. The place was at least twice the size of Vancouver, maybe more.

"Time to split up. We'll be less conspicuous if we separate. Scott will help you look for your father. I'll visit Baxter, then stop in at a stationers. I'll meet you back at the hotel," Granville said.

That drew Trent's attention away from the street. "A stationers? Whatever for?"

"So he can write to his fiancée," Scott said with a chuckle.

"Just watch your backs," Granville said.

All senses alert, Granville covered the remaining few blocks quickly, finding Baxter's office without incident. It was located on the fourth floor of a six-story tower just south of Curtis.

Nothing about the location, the starchy receptionist or the expensively furnished office gave a hint of the nature of Baxter's business. As he considered the large oil of a hunting scene in the reception area, Granville found himself wondering what else the man was involved in, and whether any part of his business was legitimate.

A gesture from the attractive woman behind the reception desk caught his attention. "Mr. Gordon? If you'll come this way?"

"Thank you." He met her sideways look with a smile.

The hallway she led him down was paneled in mahogany, the Turkey carpeting thick enough to muffle their footsteps. If this was a cover, it was an effective one. And Baxter's appearance only solidified the impression.

The lawyer advanced around his desk, one hand outstretched. His dark business suit, hearty manner and richly rounded tones were designed to inspire confidence. Baxter's office was as polished as he was, but the rich woods and dark brown leather were much warmer than his gaze.

His brother William would like this man, Granville thought. It made him even warier.

"Mr. Baxter? A pleasure, sir. I'm in town on business, from the coast, and I was advised that you were the man in Denver whom I had to see."

"I'm honored, Mr. Gordon. May I ask who spoke so highly of me?"

"Several of my acquaintances have done so. All men with hopeful new families, you know."

"In general, I prefer to deal with family men. I find them more reliable."

"As do I. Indeed, my wife and I plan a large family, but our hopes are as yet unrewarded."

"That is unfortunate indeed." The lawyer paused, seemingly waiting for something.

"Are you a family man yourself, Mr. Baxter?"

"I'm afraid not. Someday, I hope to be that fortunate."

"I'm sure you will." Granville said. He wasn't sure how much more of this small talk he could stand, but without knowing what cue Baxter was looking for, he was feeling his way. Was it too soon to mention adoption?

"Thank you. Family is so important, is it not?"

"Yes, yes it is," Granville said, thinking quickly. He leaned forward slightly, dropped his voice. "In fact, so important that my wife and I are considering adopting a child. If we could be sure of his bloodlines, of course."

"You're thinking of a boy?"

Granville nodded, letting an expansive smile cross his face. "Must have that heir, you know. Followed, perhaps, by a little girl to please the wife."

"Hmmm." Baxter played with his pen as if making a weighty decision, then leaned forward. "Mr. Gordon, I may be able to suggest a solution to your dilemma."

"Yes?"

"A cousin of mine, from a very good family, has run into—difficulties. The child is due any day now, and all indications are that it will be a boy child."

"I see." Granville sat back, steepled his fingers. "And the father?"

"Too young for responsibility, but with a very good bloodline."

As if they were discussing horses, Granville thought in disgust, as he let a little calculated eagerness show on his face. "It sounds perfect."

"There is the matter of the lying-in expenses..."

Granville waved a dismissive hand. "Not a consideration."

"And the legal fees for registering the birth—to your lady wife, of course."

Granville leaned forward again. "Is such a thing possible?"

"Indeed it is. It is more expensive, of course."

Naturally, given that it was illegal, and likely required large bribes in the right places. "In this matter, money is available for whatever is required. It's a matter of great importance to m—my wife, you know."

Greed gleamed in Baxter's eyes then was gone. "I understand," he said.

"Since this is my heir, I'd like to accompany you at every step of the legal process. Would that be possible?"

"I'm afraid not. I must protect the reputation of my young relative."

"I realize there may be additional costs, and I'm more than happy to bear them."

"I'm sorry, the answer is still no."

"I see."

"I must honor her confidence as I will honor yours," Baxter said smoothly.

Honor had nothing to do with it. Did Baxter already know of a male infant, or would it be up to his cohorts to find one for him? "And the next step?"

"The baby, your son, will be born soon. You'll need to make another appointment for the day after tomorrow. At ten."

"Ten o'clock, day after tomorrow." Granville extended his hand and left the office, feeling as if he'd stepped too close to a snake pit.

Had he convinced Baxter? He'd done what he could, and would be here as requested.

Then they'd see.

AFTER LEAVING BAXTER, Granville walked briskly back across town towards their hotel.

When he turned onto Sixteenth, he had the uneasy feeling of being watched, but he saw no-one paying particular attention to him. Every sense alert, he took advantage of every awning and hanging sign that might interfere with a shooter's aim.

He was acutely aware of every spot he passed that provided potential cover for an ambush. There were far too many of them.

It was a relief to turn into Cobley's Stationary, which catered to the amateur naturalists and artists who stopped in Denver on their way to exploring the Colorado wilderness. The young clerk was both helpful and knowledgeable, and Granville had no difficulty obtaining the paper and inks he needed.

As he left, he scanned the street. Still no sign of the shooter. And the sensation of being watched was gone.

Had the fellow gone looking for Scott and Trent?

Back in their cramped hotel room, Granville removed his tailored coat and starched shirt, hanging them in the small clothes press and shrugging into a dark wool shirt. He replaced the gun holster, then spent several hours making a copy of the map of the lost mine, with a few strategic alterations. When Trent and then Scott returned, empty-handed, he was painstakingly aging the result with dirt and cold tea.

Scott headed straight for the whiskey bottle, poured a shot, and tossed it back.

"No luck with Harris's lists?" Granville asked.

"Nope. Just confirmed what he told us. Little Sarah isn't at any of these places."

"Any sign of the shooter?"

"Nope. You?"

"It felt like I was being watched for a time, but I saw nothing and there were no shots taken."

"Huh. Wonder where he got to?"

That was indeed the question, and it was one he didn't have an answer for.

Trent was standing by Granville's elbow, watching silently as he continued his work on the map. "That's what you wanted the stationary store for?" the boy finally asked. "It's amazing! If I didn't see the real one, I'd believe this one."

Scott looked from the original map to his copy and raised a brow. "Misspent youth?" he quipped as he poured himself another drink.

"Something like that," Granville said, youthful pirate hunts and treasure maps flickering through his mind. "We need something to bargain with, but we hold the map in trust for Mary Pearson."

"Interesting sense of fair play you've got," Scott said. He regarded the false map critically. "This is good, except that you seem to be missing a few pieces. Place names, for one."

"Exactly."

"So they can't decide they don't need us?"

"Right. I've left out everything that identifies where the map is actually located. To find the mine, they're going to need us. Alive."

"Good thinking."

"Thanks. I thought so."

"But they won't, will they? Find the mine, I mean?" Trent asked.

"No. Take a look at where this map ends."

Trent looked closer, compared it to the original and let out a low whistle. "They'd never get out again."

Scott took the map from him, glanced at it, then winked at Granville. "Serve 'em right if they steal it from us."

"Plus they think it's in Oregon." Granville rubbed the last smudge of dirt into his map.

"So how'd it go with Baxter?"

"I think he believed me. I'm to meet him again day after tomorrow. Then we'll see."

"What d'you think of him?"

"He was exactly as Benton said—slick as a snake."

Scott's hands tightened into fists.

"Snakes aren't exactly slick, you know," Trent's voice came from the narrow bed along the wall where he'd perched. "Their skin is smooth and dry, not slimy at all."

He hid a grin. "Think about how they move."

"What? Oh—they're fast, and they writhe." The boy thought for a moment. "This guy, Baxter. He's like that?"

"Exactly like that. Deceptively innocent, until you see him move."

"Huh. So what's next?" the boy asked.

"Next I let this dry in the sun for an hour or so."

"And then?"

"Then I think it's time for our return visit to the Red Mule."

THE SPEAKEASY WAS LESS crowded than the previous day, but looked even dirtier in the shafts of sunlight stabbing through the grimy windows. Mather and Androchuk were in their usual spot, and from the looks of it, they'd been there a while. They didn't look too pleased by Granville's news.

"So why don't we just go get the gold?" Mather demanded.

"The ground's frozen—too hard to dig," Granville said.

"Not to mention the blizzards," Scott added.

"Oh," said Mather. "But what about ..."

"Let it go," Androchuck said. "They've already told us." He turned to Granville. "You got that map?"

After a show of reluctance, Granville handed over the copy he'd made. Androchuck held it up to the flickering gas lantern. "Can't see much here. I'll need to see this under a better light. And show it to our backer."

"And who might that be?" Granville asked, holding out his hand for the map.

"He's by way of being a partner of ours," Androchuck said. "And you'll get the map back after I talk to him."

Granville opened his mouth as if to protest, let his gaze move to where Mather's hand rested lightly on his gun, and sat back.

"I'll be counting on that," he said, pointedly glancing at Scott's hand, also resting on his revolver. "Especially as you'll need us to find the area where the map's set."

Mather looked startled. Androchuck considered the map for a moment more, then tucked it in an inner pocket. “Can’t say I’m surprised.”

“Why exactly are you meeting with this partner of yours?” Scott asked.

“He has the say on who we take on and who we don’t,” Androchuck said.

It had to be Baxter. “What happens then?” Granville asked, hoping a meeting with Baxter wasn’t in the plan.

“Then we talk. Tomorrow morning. Ten.”

Granville gave a curt nod. “We’ll be here.”

33

SUNDAY, JANUARY 21, 1900

Ten o'clock found Granville and Scott back at the Red Mule. At this hour, it still reeked of last night's revelries—stale smoke, stale beer and unwashed males. Sitting at their usual table, Mather and Androchuk each had a half-empty tankard in front of them. They looked like they hadn't ever left.

"OK, you're in," Mather said, looking pleased with himself.

"His cousin vouched for you," Androchuck told Scott. "Said you're almost as ruthless as he is, and a crack shot. But you've new partners in your gold mine."

"Yeah. Us," Mather said.

"Uh huh. Done much digging?" Scott asked.

"We've done our share," Mather said. "Both of us were at Cripple Creek, and I spent some time at Leadville."

Mather might know James Pearson, then—if his name was indeed Pearson. They'd have to think of a way to ask about him that wouldn't raise Mather's suspicions.

"Different kind of mining," Scot was saying. "Might come in handy, but you'll have a lot to learn."

"I think we need to know what business we're getting into. If we're to be partners," Granville said.

"It's no fail," Mather said with a smirk. "We're relocating kids." He emphasized the second word and glanced sideways at them as if inviting them to share the joke.

The man was despicable. Granville vowed to himself that he'd see Mather and his partners behind bars before they were done, but allowed no trace of his feelings to show on his face. "And there's money in that?"

"Good money, on both ends. And more when they need papers so it looks like their own child. Ba..." he began then hurriedly changed his words when Androchuck cleared his throat loudly. "Our partner set it up brilliantly," he finished.

So it was Baxter. And as he'd guessed, Mather was the weak link in this partnership. That could prove useful. "When do we get to meet this partner of yours?"

"You don't," Androchuck said. "The fewer people know who he is, the safer for him."

That was a relief—they couldn't afford to have his own double role exposed. "Fine with me, as long as the money's good," Granville said.

"When do we start?" Scott asked.

"Tomorrow night. Meet us here around eight. And come armed. We'll fill you in then."

"Good enough. Scott?"

Scott shrugged. "Long as they pay us, I'll follow orders."

Granville knew that for a blatant lie, but if it fooled these two, that was all he cared about.

Back in their nondescript room, Granville headed straight for the whiskey. Early as it was, he needed to get the taste of their new partners out of his mouth. He held the bottle out to Scott.

Ignoring the invitation, Scott jabbed a finger into his chest. "Why'd you give up so easy? They'll start suspecting us if we're not careful."

"I had to get out of there, before I told them what I really thought," Granville said. "I can't believe Harris had word of this and didn't do anything."

"Not like you to be an idealist. There's not much the law can do."

"These are children," Granville said, then regretted it when he saw the misery in Scott's eyes. "We will find her, Scott," he said, wishing he were certain of it.

"Yeah," the big man said, reaching for the bottle and pouring a good four fingers.

Granville watched, concerned. Scott had been drinking steadily since they got here. And there was little more they could do until the following night. If he kept drinking like this, he'd be useless by then. "Mather said he used to dig at Cripple Creek."

"Yeah. I heard that. Too bad we can't just ask him about Pearson."

"So we ask someone else. We can't get any further in finding little Sarah until I meet with Baxter tomorrow. Might as well spend time looking for someone who knew Pearson."

Scott frowned. "I used to know some men who'd spent time in Cripple Creek. Wonder if they're still in town?"

"You never worked there, did you?"

"No. But when they found gold in the early 90's, the Creek drew would-be miners from all over. Then mining went soft and a bunch of 'em headed for the Klondike in '97 and '98. Remember Soapy Smith?"

Granville nodded, scowling at the memory of the notorious "King of Skagway," who had plucked many an unwary pigeon before his final, and fatal, duel with the law.

"He was from Denver."

"Since he's dead, I hardly see how he can be of help to us."

Scott ignored him. "Carter was from here too. And so was Rogers. Might as well see if any of 'em are still around."

"I don't think Rogers made it back. Remember?"

"Was he the one froze to death?"

"That's him."

"Shame. What about Kendrick? And Bailey. They made it out, didn't they?"

"Bailey shipped out of Skagway same time we did. And I last saw Kendrick in the bar in Sheep Camp, but he looked pretty hearty then. They both from Denver?"

"Yup."

"So how do you propose to go about finding them?"

"We'll need to split up. And we'll need Trent."

"Where is the boy?" Granville asked with a sudden spurt of worry. Just because they hadn't seen the shooter today didn't mean he wasn't still after them.

"Damned if I know," Scott said. "He can't have gone far."

No sooner had he said this than the door flung open and Trent hurried into the room, red-faced and panting.

Granville's hand was poised on his revolver, and he noted Scott's alert readiness. "What's wrong?"

"They—they—"

"Is someone after you?" Scott asked, rising to his feet.

"No," he gasped.

"Then wait until you get your breath back," Granville advised.

Trent nodded, bending over and putting his hands on his knees. Gradually his breathing slowed. "I think I've got a lead on what happened to little Sarah," he said at last, standing upright.

"What?"

"How?"

"I was down along Market Street, lookin' for my Pa. I saw a couple police officers, acting odd. So I followed them."

The boy had expected to find his father in the red light district, dangerous even in daylight? "Odd? In what way?"

"Never mind that. What about Sarah?" Scott demanded.

Trent darted an apologetic glance at Granville, but answered Scott. "They went into a large yellow house off Twentieth. It was nearly half an hour before they came out again."

"Officers visiting brothels is hardly news."

"From what I saw, I think it's a baby farm. One not on your list."

"So I was right. Harris is involved." Scott's big hands clenched until the knuckles gleamed white.

"I don't think he is," Trent said.

"I thought you didn't trust the fellow either."

"I don't. But these cops were too sneaky. If the detective knew, they wouldn't have to hide."

"The lad's right," Scott said. "But how many other places weren't on that list of Harris's? We'll have to find every one of them."

"No, you won't," Trent burst out.

Granville gave him a sharp look. "What did you do?"

"I went in, told them I was looking for my little sister. I said my Mam died a couple years ago while I was working back east, and I'd heard they'd taken in little Nan."

"Did they believe you?"

Trent shrugged. "I said all I wanted was a chance to see her, say hello, and that I had money for any boarding costs that might be owing, so they didn't throw me out. Just asked how old she was, what she looked like."

"What did you say?" Scott asked.

"I didn't see any harm in telling the truth, but when I said she was nearly three, with dark hair, blue eyes, and a birthmark on her arm shaped like a seahorse, their eyes went kinda funny and they couldn't rush me out of there quick enough."

"They knew her." Scott's face seemed lit from inside.

"Sounds like it." Granville's mind raced. "And now they know someone is looking for her." He looked at Trent. "They'll know her background, and that she has no siblings, much less a brother your age."

Trent's face fell. "Oh."

"We'll have to move fast," Scott said, easily following Granville's thinking. "Else they'll move her, maybe send her out of state."

"If she's still there. She may have been adopted out before now."

"So I've made things worse?" Trent's fists clenched and his jaw thrust out. "Then I'll just have to get an answer out of them."

Granville fought back a grin at the boy's dramatics. "Don't blame yourself. This is the first solid lead we've had since we arrived."

"And we can force the rest out of them," Scott growled, grabbing his hat off the bed.

"Not so fast."

Scott and Trent both stared at Granville, but it was Scott who spoke. "What d'you mean?"

"Do you want your niece back or not?" he asked Scott.

"Of course."

"Then you can't just rush in."

"Why not?"

"Cause they might do somethin' stupid. Right?" Trent said.

Granville smiled at Trent, nodded. "Right. This is where we need to be smart. If we are, we'll not only take little Sarah home with us, Baxter and company will be in jail and the smuggling ring scattered."

Scott glowered at him. "Yeah, that's easy to say. But how? And what about the baby? Huh?"

"We can't alert them until we have our plans in place," Granville told him.

"What plans? We ask questions till we find little Sarah, then grab her and take the nearest train out of here."

"With our shooter still out there? And while Baxter and his boys might try anything to stop us? It's too risky. And I couldn't sleep nights if we just leave Baxter and his henchmen with their filthy business."

Convincing his friend not to head straight for the baby farm was hard. It took a good fifteen minutes of arguing, but Scott finally agreed to take it one step at a time, once Trent had satisfied him that the little ones had appeared well fed, warm and clean.

"You sure 'bout that? Cause most baby farms I heard about, they weren't looked after right," Scott had growled.

Only Trent's repeated assurances had convinced him.

"So now what?" Scott asked.

"We keep working with Baxter and Mather, and we follow up on this lead Trent's given us. Scott, you need to ask the sheriff about this latest baby farm, see what he knows. Trent and I will keep looking for word on Pearson."

34

"I can't believe we're here under the guise of making afternoon calls," Clara whispered. She and Emily stood in a tiny but painfully neat parlor in a house that couldn't have more than four rooms and an attic. The air smelled of lavender and carbolic, as if it had been thoroughly scrubbed just that morning.

"Shhhh. They'll hear us," Emily said.

"I also don't believe the way you dragged the information out of Mrs. Howe. And to do so at church!"

"It was just social conversation," Emily said. "Perfectly acceptable."

"I don't think your Mama found it so. I saw her face when you announced that one of those maids was a fellow-student at your typewriting class."

Clara was right, and Emily knew it. "But Mrs. Howe remembered Mary. *And* her address."

"You were just lucky she's got an amazing memory," Clara said. "Still, I wonder if this Mary even gave her the correct address."

"Well, the landlady didn't say Mary Pearson wasn't here," Emily said. "Surely that must mean she is, and therefore this *is* the right address."

"Or she thinks we're addled and didn't like to say anything. I wish you'd let us bring Mr. O'Hearn."

"If he were calling on you, we would have a reason to include him on our Sunday afternoon jaunts," Emily said with a sideways glance.

Clara frowned at her. "Don't make me regret I told you."

"Oh, very well. I'll say no more. Though it was difficult enough to convince Mama to let me go with you after church."

"Especially after your little revelations. I suppose I should be grateful you gave up the idea of trying to attend Mr. Pearson's church service," Clara began, but the return of the elderly woman who'd answered the door kept her from continuing.

"Miss Pearson is away just now," that lady said. "My sister says she has no idea when she'll be returning."

"And it is Miss Mary Pearson?"

The faded eyes took in the two well-dressed girls, whose attire put them out of place in this shabby parlor with its tired fabrics and mismatched furniture.

Seeing the dawning suspicion, Emily answered the unspoken question. "We're helping my aunt hire a new parlor maid and Mary's name was given to us by a previous employer." Which had the added benefit of being true. "Do you know if she's currently employed?"

"I wouldn't like to say. She may well be."

Emily smiled. "Perhaps her uncle would know? She really came very well recommended."

"He left town yesterday, but I believe we are expecting him back later in the week."

"We'll come back then and speak to him," Emily said. "Perhaps Wednesday?"

Her story had obviously been believed, for the landlady nodded. "Yes, we had a telegram that he'll be back that morning."

Emily thanked her, and linking arms with Clara, turned towards the door.

"I can't believe it. You found her," Clara said as they proceeded down the walk.

"If it is she."

"Well, who else could it be?"

"We won't know for sure until we talk to her. Perhaps I should have left a note, or mentioned having news to her advantage."

"Surely saying too much is worse than saying too little? Especially in a situation where a potential fortune is at stake?"

"You're right, Clara. Mary will have to prove who she is to claim the mine."

"I'm often right," Clara said loftily, then spoiled the effect with a giggle. "And I'm sure your Mr. Granville will be as pleased that you didn't endanger yourself as that you found his heiress. And there's the streetcar."

"Good. I think we deserve a leisurely afternoon tea, don't you?" said Emily.

GRANVILLE MET Scott back at the Drunken Pheasant. It wasn't the most inviting of establishments, but it was convenient to their hotel and the beer was cheap and good. Scott was already there, a half-empty whiskey in front of him.

Granville couldn't read Scott's expression, and that worried him. "No sign of Bailey?"

"Oh, I found him, alright. He just couldn't help us. What about you?"

"Same." He glanced at the glass Scott was gripping and signaled to the bartender to bring him the same. "I found Kendrick in the fourth place I tried. You?"

"First one for me. Bailey was clerking in the same dry goods shop he'd worked in before he left for the Yukon. Any sign of the shooter?"

"None. You?"

"Nothing," Scott said, draining his whiskey and signaling for another. "What d'ye reckon?"

"Either we weren't his target, or for some reason he's given up on us."

"Huh. Doesn't make sense."

"It might, if we knew why we were targets in the first place." Granville downed half the shot the bartender put in front of him. "You've been here a while?"

"Nope, just got here. Bailey suggested a couple other names he knew from the Creek. He even knew where to find them."

"Useful. I gather none of them panned out, either?"

"You gather right," Scott said, and drained his glass.

"And what did Harris say?"

His partner shrugged, looked away. "Not much. He seemed kinda embarrassed we'd found an establishment he didn't know about."

What was this? "You weren't there long?"

Scott shook his head, but he wouldn't meet Granville's eyes.

Granville eyed the evasive look on his friend's face with something close to alarm. "Where did you go after you left the police station?"

"Nowhere in particular."

That's what he'd been afraid of. "You didn't go asking questions about your niece, did you?"

"I had to know," Scott said.

Granville couldn't blame him, even if his actions might have made rescuing the little girl even more difficult. "And?"

"Trent was right. Little Sarah was there. She was adopted a couple years ago."

Granville debated asking how Scott had wrung the information from them, then decided he probably didn't want to know. "Adopted. They have a name?"

"Yeah. Seems it was a Mr. and Mrs. Baxter."

"Baxter?"

"That's what I was told."

"Not Darren Baxter?"

"Yup."

"Why that slimy, double-dealing son of a... he told me he wasn't married." For a moment Granville wondered about that marriage, and just how the greedy lawyer had been persuaded to do something as dangerous as personally adopting one of the infants he smuggled for profit. What kind of woman could convince a man like that to take such a risk?

"I don't guess the truth is a strong point for our Mr. Baxter."

"You have that right." Granville took a deep breath, glanced at his partner. Now he had to ask. "You can't tell me you simply walked into that baby farm and they answered your every question."

Scott looked irritated. "I didn't just waltz in there asking questions. You don't think I'd jeopardize everything we're trying to do here, do you?"

"So what did you do?"

"I had a little help."

Granville let the silence stretch.

"Once I knew little Sarah had been there...I've old friends here."

"Go on."

"Julia White was just another soiled dove when I know her back in Chicago—she's a madam now. Runs one of the better houses in town. She has real presence, and connections that it's better not to ask about. I asked her if she'd see what she could find out."

"And they simply told her about the adoption?"

Scott shrugged. "I didn't ask how she found out."

Granville nodded. Some things they were better off not knowing, especially in mob-controlled Denver. "But you trust this Julia? And her information?"

"Yeah. She saved my life once. And I saved hers a couple of times. She used to have a pimp, beat her up pretty bad."

Granville glanced at Scott, saw the shadows and the certainty in his face. "All right, then. After I talk to Baxter again, we'll come up with a strategy for getting little Sarah back."

"I still say we should be grabbing her and getting out of here."

"One more day, then we can make plans. Believe me, I don't want to spend a minute here I don't have to. Not when it leaves Emily alone in Vancouver with all that's going on, and when she'd just met with that strange woman."

"One more day then."

Granville signaled the barkeep another round, then checked his pocket watch. "Where's Trent?"

"Dunno. He should've been back by now—I sent him to follow up on a couple of the names Bailey gave me."

"Let's hope his lucky streak continues."

"Yeah."

Scott was on his third whiskey and Granville was working on his second when Trent finally arrived.

"Well?" Granville said.

Trent beamed at them. "I found a connection."

"Where?"

"And who?" Scott asked.

"Third name you gave me, Homer Norton."

"The tailor?"

Trent nodded. "Yeah. He used to work for one of the big mining firms in Cripple Creek, and he got to know some of the miners real well. He recognized Pearson's name and description, even remembered a daughter named Mary."

"He know anything about where Mary is now?"

"Nope, just that she left when he did."

"Where did they go?"

"He didn't know about her, but he said Pearson headed for the Klondike."

"For the Klondike?" Granville repeated in surprise. It was the last thing he'd expected to hear.

"James Pearson," Scott said thoughtfully. "Trent, you said you had a description?"

"Scott, there were thousands of us headed north," Granville said. "We didn't know the fellow."

Scott ignored him. "Trent?"

"Medium height, skinny, sandy hair, gray eyes."

"Like hundreds of others," Granville said.

Scott was shaking his head. "Nope, doesn't ring a bell…"

"His brother Albin went too."

"What?" Scott said at the same moment Granville said "Albin?"

"Does that help?" Trent asked. He looked pleased with himself.

And so he should, thought Granville. Albin Pearson, alive, might be easier to find than either a dead man or his daughter, who might have married and not even be going by Pearson any longer.

"Granville…"

Something in Scott's tone made the hairs on the back of his neck rise. "You've remembered someone?"

"Do you remember the Pike Twins? We met them in Skagway when we first got there."

Granville did remember them. He'd thought the nickname ironic, because the two had looked nothing like brothers, let alone twins. "Slim Jim and Mad Al?"

Scott was nodding. "That's them."

Everyone had liked Jim, who always had a joke and a smile. Al was another story—he was a man on the edge and he was deadly. Pistol, rifle, it didn't matter—he never missed. And the brothers were never apart.

"I don't think I ever heard their real names. Are you saying…?"

"I came up with them on the steamer. I can't swear, but I think I'd heard Mad Al's real name was Albin. Can't be too many of them around. And Cripple Creek's near Pike's Peak."

The back of Granville's neck prickled at the thought. If Slim Jim was their James Pearson, where had Mad Al been when Jim was killed? And did he know about his brother's death?

Granville thought about Jim, all that good humor lost under six feet of frozen ground. It was wrong. If it was the same man, the Klondike hadn't killed him, but gold had, by way of their former client.

Suddenly he was truly sorry Cole was dead, and that he couldn't be the one to bring him to justice. If he could find Mary and help her register the mine, perhaps that was a different form of justice. Unless Mad Al had already delivered his own form of frontier justice? "Any way we can confirm that?"

Trent sat tall. "I got another name, somebody the brothers used to be friendly with here."

"Go on," Granville said.

"His name's Carl Berger and he hangs at the Red Mule."

Scott glanced at Granville and grimaced.

Trent looked from one to the other. "What?"

"Berger was the man with Mather and Androchuck the day we met them," Granville said.

"So how you going to ask him about the Pearsons without giving away that the map's theirs by right?"

"If you don't have a good hand, you bluff. Cheers." And Granville raised his glass, tipped it at Trent and drained it.

"I SEE BERGER, but I don't see Mather or Androchuck," Scott said in an undertone as the two of them strolled into the Red Mule.

Granville's gaze swept the dim, crowded room. It reeked of spilled beer and unwashed bodies. A certain humming tension told him there would be a brawl later on. "Good. Let's join him. Maybe we can find out what we need to know before the others show up."

They sauntered across the room, boots squeaking on the sawdust underfoot, until they reached the table where Berger stood with another man Granville didn't recognize. "Mind if we join you?"

Berger looked up. "Can if you like."

"Thanks. Expecting Mather tonight?"

"Why d'you care?"

"I thought to stand him a beer, that's all."

Berger shrugged. "Nah, he and Androchuck are busy tonight. You'll have to wait till tomorrow."

Interesting. Busy doing what? "In that case, can I buy you both another beer?"

"Won't say no."

Granville got up and headed for the bar. Placing the order, he half turned so he could see the table he'd left. He watched Scott lean forward, say something to Berger. The fellow grinned and nodded in return. Scott said something else and Berger seemed taken aback, then clapped him on the shoulder.

Grabbing two foaming steins of draft in each hand, Granville wound his way back to the table. He slid two beers across the table, passed the third to Scott and raised the last to his lips.

"Did y'know Jim too? James Pearson?" Berger asked.

So Slim Jim was their James Pearson. "I did, yes," Granville said, and took a long swallow of the cold, bitter brew.

"Sorry to hear he's gone."

"You hadn't heard?"

"Nah." Berger drained his stein and started on the fresh one. "Damn shame. He was a good man. Don't know how that brother of his is going to survive, though."

"Albin?" Scott asked. "They called him Mad Al, up north."

"Huh. And with reason, I'd bet. I swear it was Jim kept him sane, even when I knew him."

"He'd a pretty quick temper, all right."

At Scott's words, Granville had a sudden and vivid mental picture of walking into Doyle's in Dawson City and seeing Mad Al with his fingers wrapped around another fellow's throat. Such outbursts weren't uncommon, and the Mounties usually restored order pretty quickly.

Usually the arguments were over one of the dancehall girls or a claim dispute. This had been different, he thought, though the details escaped him. He'd have to ask Scott later.

The memory increased the uneasy feeling he'd had since Scott reminded him about the twins. Could Mad Al be their shooter, fixed on vengeance for his brother's death? If so, why had he suddenly stopped? They hadn't been shot at since Saturday. Which should be a relief, but the illogic of it had been nagging at him ever since.

"I'll drink to that," Berger said, raising his mug and draining half of it.

"Any idea what happened to him? Albin, I mean?" Scott asked, signaling the barkeep for another round.

"Thanks. Wal, I heard the two of them'd settled on the coast. They had people there, but..."

"Whereabouts? San Francisco?"

"Near Seattle, I think."

It was what they'd been looking for all day, a lead that might take them to Mary Pearson.

"But Albin was here, day or so ago," Berger finished.

"What?" Scott said.

Mad Al was their shooter.

Granville finished off his tankard in one swallow. They were lucky to be alive. Denver wasn't that big—he could have found them easily, and at least one of them would be dead by now. In fact, if it was Mad Al on their trail, they were lucky not to have been killed long before they reached Denver. What was going on?

"Yup, he wandered into the Mule one afternoon," Berger said. "Too bad I didn't know you were lookin' for him."

"He say where he was going?" Scott asked.

Berger shrugged. "Seemed like he'd been lookin' for work, but after he had a couple drinks with us he said he'd be heading north the next day."

"Back to Seattle?" Granville asked.

Berger looked surprised. "I think he said he was goin' to Vancouver. But that's Canada, ain't it?"

"There's two," Scott said. "One in Washington State, one in British Columbia."

"Ah." Berger nodded, apparently satisfied.

Which Vancouver would Mad Al be headed for? If he was their shooter, he'd come from Canada and would likely return there.

And Emily was there, looking for Mary Pearson. Granville felt a sudden unease.

Now he thought about it, Emily hadn't actually agreed not to investigate the case further. Was there any possibility she would actually find Mad Al? He couldn't risk that happening.

"You sure he said Vancouver?" he asked.

Berger was nodding. "Yup, cause I asked him about it. He said it was a pretty place but it rained too much."

That could still be either city. They needed to rescue little Sarah, deal with these villains, then get back to Vancouver.

Except he wasn't even seeing Baxter until the following day.

Perhaps he'd stop at the telegraph office and send Emily a wire, urging her to be careful. And hope she wouldn't simply ignore it.

35

Clara and Emily sat in the Turner's cozy front parlor, with a pot of tea and a plate of currant scones between them. It was a cold, blustery day and the often over-heated room felt comforting. Mama and her sisters had gone shopping, despite the weather, so they could talk freely. As Emily lifted the cup of fragrant Souchong tea to her lips, Bertie appeared at her elbow. Startled, she nearly spilled her tea. "Bertie, what is it?"

"Telegram, Miss Emily. From Denver." He handed it to her.

Emily's heart leapt into her mouth. "Thank you, Bertie," she managed to say before ripping it open.

"It's not bad news, Emily?" Clara asked.

"No indeed. Good news, I think."

Clara leaned forward. "You're not sure?"

Suddenly remembering Bertie's presence, Emily smiled at him. "There'll be no answer."

He bowed and turned to go.

"Emily! What does it say?" Clara asked.

She lowered her voice. "It says: Progress here. Stop. Home Friday with parcel. Stop. Keep safe. Stop. Granville."

"Oh. I see why you weren't sure."

"He's worded it carefully in case Papa reads it, but I think it means they've found little Sarah."

"You think the parcel is little Sarah?"

"What else could it be? And I know how determined Gr—Mr. Granville is."

"Oh, for heaven's sakes. You needn't be so formal with me. But if the parcel is little Sarah, what is the "progress"?"

Emily smiled. "I knew you'd catch that. I think he must have learned something about Mary."

"In Denver?"

"Why not? And at least I know he's well."

Clara was staring straight ahead, one gloved finger tapping the opposite wrist.

"Clara?"

"Keep safe—that's a peculiar ending. Do you think he is warning you against further involvement in looking for Mary?"

"I'm sure it means no more than it says."

Clara gave her a shrewd look. "Neither of us believes that, Emily. Perhaps you should simply leave it alone until he returns."

Emily heaved a sigh. "It's no use, Clara. I can't pretend to be fascinated with things that bore me. It was bad enough when Mama was wanting me to embroider every piece of linen for my trousseau..."

"With your embroidery skills?"

"Exactly. Now Miriam has taken up burning designs into leather, and Mama has hoping I'll do the same."

"A year ago you might have enjoyed it."

"It's a complicated process—you heat the burning point over an alcohol lamp, then keep it hot with a bellows while you burn the design into the leather. Which smells awful, by the way. And all to create objects for your loved ones that they'll hate but have to display every time you come to visit."

Clara giggled.

"Well they will. It seems so pointless."

"As compared to investigating, perhaps?" Clara bit into a dainty watercress sandwich.

Emily blushed. "Not at all. But doesn't it make you feel good to know that you're part of returning a legacy?"

"You don't have to justify yourself to me, Emily. I know how you feel about your Granville."

How could she know, when Emily wasn't entirely sure herself? "This isn't just about him."

"No, it isn't, is it? Your life might be easier if it were."

Emily didn't have to ask what she meant. She had a feeling Clara might be right, though she'd never admit that. But she couldn't be someone other than who she was.

"Have you heard anything from Mr. O'Hearn about Mary's uncle?" she asked. "It would be such a good thing if we could find him before they get back from Denver."

"How would I have heard from him? It isn't as if Mr. O'Hearn is calling on me," Clara said.

"Clara, you're blushing. What haven't you told me?"

"He may have asked if he could call," her friend said.

"When?"

"After we came back from New Westminster. It was while you were watching for the streetcar. But I said no."

"Oh Clara, why?" Emily considered her friend's expression. "You're afraid your father would object."

Clara nodded. "I'm expected to marry well, and Mr. O'Hearn doesn't meet my father's criteria."

"There must be a way," Emily said.

"I don't think so. Besides, I don't really care for him, nor he for me. It's only the excitement of Mr. Granville's investigations that connects us, really."

Emily gave her a sideways glance, but said nothing. She'd find some way to help her friend.

Clara caught the look. "Really, Emily, it is better this way. Now, what are you planning next? I'm sure you have a plan."

"No, not really."

Clara's eyes narrowed at the odd tone in her friend's voice. "Emily?"

"Really, it's nothing."

"We've been friends too long for me to believe that. What are you up to?"

Emily sipped her tea and tried to decide how much to tell Clara. There was no point in worrying her.

"Emily! What are you planning? And exactly how dangerous is it?"

"What makes you think it dangerous?"

"I know you. And since you met your Granville, I've come to know that look in your eye. So tell me."

"Oh, very well, if you must know." And Emily related her conversations with Laura and Wally Sutton.

Clara heard her out in silence, only a sharply indrawn breath indicating her emotions. When Emily finished, she eyes searched her friend's face. Such restraint was unlike her.

"It truly isn't dangerous," Emily said.

"Of course not," Clara said. "You're merely searching for a deadly killer by having a naïve fool ask questions on your behalf."

"Clara, there's no need to take that sarcastic tone. And it isn't like that."

"It's exactly like that. I can't believe you were rabbiting on about embroidery and leather burning when you've just set yourself up as a target for a killer."

Emily gave a strained little laugh. "I haven't done that at all. Whoever is trying to kill Granville can have no interest in me. And it's exactly because Wally is so naïve that no-one will suspect his questions to be dangerous."

Even to her own ears the explanation sounded weak. She really hadn't been thinking beyond to the need to do something, anything, to help Granville. A few questions asked of Andy Rigg's relative had seemed harmless enough—how dangerous could it be to confirm that Mr. Gipson was the culprit?

"Besides, you and I went to talk with Mr. Riggs," Emily said firmly. "*And* Mr. Gipson. How is this different?"

Clara shook her head. "Don't remind me. We should never have gone there. But this is different because someone might actually tell this Wally Sutton something of import."

"Are you saying there was no possibility I would learn something?"

"You didn't, did you?"

Since this was unarguably true, Emily thought it wise to change the subject. If Clara thought about this too long, she might refuse to help in future, and that would be most unfortunate.

36

MONDAY, JANUARY 22, 1900

Clad in his best suit, Granville sat on the other side of Baxter's ostentatious desk and waited impatiently for the lawyer. He wanted these animals who dealt in little children behind bars, and quickly.

Sending the telegram to Emily had not calmed his fear for her. Had Mad Al gone back to Vancouver? But surely he'd have no reason to hurt her. The thought distracted him at odd moments.

Drawing in a deep breath, Granville willed his features impassive. He knew it might be asking too much to see Baxter, Androchuck and Mather arrested, knew he might have to settle for getting little Sarah back. Perhaps he even should do so.

But something in him rebelled at just grabbing the child and running. Somehow he'd managed to convince Scott. Now he had to be equally convincing with Baxter.

And he'd need luck on his side.

A side door opened and Baxter came in, hand outstretched and an annoying smile stretching his lips. "Mr. Gordon. How nice to see you again."

"And you, Mr. Baxter. Is there word of the child?"

"Yes, I'm glad to say. A healthy boy, born last night."

His luck had come through! Granville swallowed hard. "My son. Can I see him? Now?"

"Perhaps this evening."

"And when can I take him home?"

"It will be a week, perhaps two, before he'll be able to travel."

Granville suspected this was a lie. "My wife is in such suspense, it's worth any amount to get my son home earlier than that."

Baxter tapped his lips. "Perhaps something can be arranged. You can afford a wet nurse?"

"Of course."

"Very well." Baxter scribbled several lines and handed the page to Granville. "Be at this address tonight at eight. Come alone. And bring a bank draft in that amount."

Granville pursed his lips in a silent whistle, then nodded. "Alright, yes. This is, after all, my heir. You'll be there?"

"No, you'll be dealing with several of my associates from this point on."

Granville narrowed his eyes, set his jaw. "For this much money, I'd expect to deal directly with you, not some associate."

"I assure you, they're very competent."

"Nonetheless." He waited. Would it be enough?

Baxter moved his gold pen into precise alignment with the blotter. "That isn't how I do things."

"I'd not be comfortable dealing with anyone else on so sensitive a matter. But I do realize the value of your time." He crossed out Baxter's original figure, wrote in one substantially higher. "Would this be sufficient?"

Baxter's eyes gleamed. "Very well. I'll see you at eight."

"Thank you, sir. It's been a pleasure," Granville said as he rose.

EMILY ARRIVED at class very early on Monday morning, to be greeted by Miss Richard's look of surprise and an empty classroom. But Emily hadn't been able to wait a moment longer. Would Wally Sutton have learned anything?

She tried to look busy with her shorthand notes as the other students arrived by ones and twos. She nodded and smiled at each, but avoided meeting their eyes. With so much at stake, she felt too restless to make conversation.

By three minutes to eight, there was still no sign of Wally, nor of Laura.

Andy Riggs and Ada Parker had arrived, but not Wally. Was this usual? Since Emily herself normally arrived right on the hour, she had no idea whether they usually arrived together.

Finally, at one minute to eight, Laura hurried in, smiling when she saw Emily and heading straight for her table.

"Is he here?" she whispered as she got closer.

"No. Is he usually this late?" Emily whispered back.

"No, usually he's early. He gets here with Riggs and Ada."

Emily nodded towards them. "They've been here fifteen minutes or more."

"Do you think something has gone wrong?"

"Surely not. He was just asking questions," Emily said, feeling a sinking in her stomach. Could he have got into trouble? But Andy Riggs was here.

"What could have happened?"

"I don't know…"

"Seat yourselves quietly, please ladies. And—fingers up!"

The command from Miss Richards had Laura scurrying for her seat.

Emily automatically moved her fingers into place above the keys of the typewriting machine, while her mind raced. What would she do if Wally didn't come to class today? Should they go looking for him? She couldn't just assume he was fine, not when she'd put him up to doing something that might have proven dangerous. If…

The banging of a door broke into her thoughts. Emily looked up to see Wally dashing into the room. His hair was tousled and he had a bruise high on his cheek, but otherwise looked much as normal.

She breathed a sigh of relief. At least he was alive, and relatively undamaged. But had he learned anything?

As he seated himself with stammering apologies to Miss Richards, he glanced towards Emily and gave a tiny nod. Emily nearly knocked the typewriting manual onto the floor. He'd learned something!

Now she'd have to wait until the break to find out what it was.

At the end of the hour, Miss Richards announced that since the class had been delayed, they would continue for another half-hour. Several groans were heard. Emily could barely contain her frustration. She glared at the neatly typed page on the platen, then looked again.

Every word, every punctuation mark was perfect. Even the spacing was correct. Somehow, while she had been speculating on what Wally might tell them, her fingers had been typing perfectly. There might be hope for her typewriting career after all, she decided as she rose, shaking out her creased skirts.

As long as she didn't have to spend it in an office taking dictation. Or typing out long and boring lists.

"So what did you learn?" Emily asked as soon as she, Laura and Wally reached the relative privacy of the stairwell.

"And how did you come by that bruise?" Laura asked.

Wally Sutton fingered the dark red center of the mark with a combination of embarrassment and pride. "It was nothing," he said, his gaze falling to his neatly polished shoes.

"But...?" Emily prompted.

"Well...."

"Go on," Laura said, and he smiled at her.

"Well. I did ask, but Riggs thought I was insulting his father, saying he took orders from someone else. That's how I got this," he said, touching the bruise.

"And?" Emily asked.

"We sorted it out and everything's fine now."

"No, I meant did he give you a name?"

He looked surprised. "You must see I couldn't ask him again. It would be like confirming the insult."

"How can it be an insult if it's true?"

Wally just shook his head. "Riggs said you wouldn't understand."

Laura went pale. "You told him?"

"Well, naturally. I had to explain, didn't I?"

Emily silently muttered a phrase she'd heard Papa use when he didn't know she was listening. Clara was right. She should have known better than to involve this nitwit.

So what would this mean? "I'll have to talk to Mr. Riggs myself," she said.

"Oh, Emily. Are you sure there isn't another way?"

"I'm sure, Laura." She turned to Wally. "Thank you for your help." It was a struggle to get the words out. "Did you tell Andy Riggs about Laura's involvement, too?"

He gave Laura a devoted look. "She wasn't involved, so how could I tell him? You were asking the questions."

Emily nodded. "True enough."

"I'll be involved now," Laura said.

"No, I'd rather any problems not fall on you," Emily said. "Thank you, though."

"What problems could there be?" Wally asked.

Behind his back, Laura rolled her eyes. Emily smiled, despite the twisting feeling in her stomach.

AT QUARTER to eight that evening, Granville stood outside the run-down warehouse in the worst section of town. His breath steamed on the crisp air and he jammed his hands further into his wool overcoat. The lighting was poor here, and shadows clung thickly between the buildings, each one more decrepit than the last.

He was all too aware of the risks he ran, walking alone into such a setup. Scott and Trent were somewhere in the darkness behind him, weapons held ready, but in a fight, their help could come too late.

The warehouse stood quiet, seemingly empty. Nothing moved in the darkness around him. A cloud drifted across the half moon, and the shadows thickened.

There was a sudden rustle of movement to his left—a rat?—then silence again. Granville stamped his feet on the snow, more in defiance of the stillness than in a futile effort to warm them.

Somewhere a door creaked, and he heard a baby's thin wail. He snapped to attention. The cry came again, then was stifled.

He hoped they were treating the poor mite carefully and had bundled him well against this cold.

"Mr. Granville?"

It was Baxter's voice. Granville tensed. He'd been worried the lawyer would sense something amiss and not show up.

He hoped Scott and Trent were well hidden. "Yes, I'm here."

"You've the money?"

"Yes."

A shaft of light appeared as the door creaked wider, Baxter silhouetted against the lamp lit interior. He was holding a gun. "Come in then, and hurry. This isn't the safest of areas."

It was an understatement, from what he'd seen. But what lay in wait for him had the potential to be even more dangerous. Especially if Androchuck and Mather were waiting inside. "Is that my son I heard?" he asked as he walked forward.

"It is."

"I can't wait to see him," he said as he entered a room that was brighter but still cold. Which was true, though not for the reasons Baxter might have assumed.

"Hmmm. All it needs is the money, and he's yours," Baxter said.

"And there's no possibility the mother will come after him? Or me?"

"None. Everything will show him your own son, born of your wife."

Granville wasn't sure if it was arrogance that allowed Baxter to be so open, or just confidence that the only ears within hearing belonged to his men. A quick glance confirmed that Baxter had brought along four others, including Mather, Androchuck and Berger.

All were armed, and he recognized the alertness that meant he was seconds away from death.

He had to forcibly stop himself from reaching for his own revolver.

Mather was holding an infant with the off-hand ease of familiarity. It made Granville shudder.

They hadn't recognized him yet. In the poor light he looked too different, and they didn't expect to know him. But it wouldn't be long.

He needed to get this right, and quickly.

"Here's your check," he said, handing it to Baxter. As he'd expected, the action focused all their attention on that bit of paper for a few critical moments.

"However, I've had difficulty securing a wet nurse here, and my office has called me home early," Granville said. "I'll easily be able to arrange a wet nurse once I arrive there. Is it possible for you to deliver the babe to my home next week, rather than my taking him tonight?"

"Yes, of course. For an additional consideration," Baxter said as he folded the check and slid it into an inner pocket.

"Naturally. But there'll be no difficulty in delivering the babe? You are remembering I live in San Francisco?"

Baxter waved in the direction of the others. "Not at all. They've made similar deliveries to your city in the past."

It was what he'd been hoping to hear. "Delivering babies across state lines, for cash? Surely that's illegal?"

His tone had Baxter's expression changing from complacency to the beginnings of alarm. The click of a hammer being drawn back echoed loudly in the stillness.

Granville braced himself.

Before either man could react, the door burst open and Detective Harris stepped in, followed by a half dozen of his men, carefully chosen and heavily armed. "Don't move. You're all under arrest."

Androchuck took aim and fired.

Granville leaped to one side just as the bullet whined by him.

He hit the floor and rolled as a second bullet missed by inches, drawing his revolver and squeezing off a shot as he did so.

Androchuck winced as the bullet winged his arm, then fired again. A deputy stepped forward and traded shots with the runty man.

A sound from the side had Granville turning to fire. In the jumpy light of the lanterns, his shot went wide.

Squinting into the shadows, Granville could just make out Mather raising a rifle and aiming directly at him.

Before he could get off another shot, a voice from directly behind Mather froze the blackguard where he stood. "He means you, too, Mather," Scott said.

Granville grinned at the sight as his eyes scanned the room. All around him stood crooks with their hands in the air and their guns at their feet. One of the policemen was awkwardly holding the baby, and patting its back.

The child's frightened wailing was dying to the occasional hiccup.

37

TUESDAY, JANUARY 23, 1900

Harris had insisted that Granville and Scott be in court that morning to testify at the arraignment of Baxter and his men, so it was already mid-afternoon when Granville walked towards the imposing white house with its gleaming black shutters and door. Baxter had been doing very nicely for himself. It was an affluent neighborhood—lawns were manicured, shrubberies pruned in fanciful shapes.

With Baxter facing a jail sentence and the loss of his profession, to say nothing of his illegal income, what would become of the house and its inhabitants now?

Beside him, the normally calm Scott was practically jittering with impatience. "Little Sarah will be here, won't she? She's too young to be at school, isn't she?"

"Yes, I think she'll likely be at home. But it won't be easy to tell Mrs. Baxter we've come to take away her daughter. And to convince her to let the child go."

Scott's face set and his jaw thrust forward. "Not her daughter. Lizzie's."

"Mrs. Baxter is the one who's been raising her, the one who

convinced her husband to give the child a home. And she's just learned of her husband's arrest and criminal activities."

"For all we know she's been in on them."

"And if she hasn't?"

"Doesn't matter. She'll survive the loss. Lizzie won't. And Lizzie is the child's mother."

Granville nodded. There was nothing more to say.

A very crisp and proper maid opened the door to them, then ushered them into a luxurious front parlor and announced them. One glance at the chestnut-haired woman seated amongst the greenery told him Mrs. Baxter had already heard the news about her husband.

Granville had never seen a woman more devastated. White to the lips, she seemed to be waiting to hear the next word of trouble. He hated to be the one to deliver it.

"Mrs. Baxter?"

She rose gracefully, coming forward with a hand outstretched in greeting, a strained smile on her full lips. "Yes. Please, won't you sit down?"

Once they were seated, she on the brocaded sofa, he and Scott in plush wing chairs facing her, and had declined tea, she inclined her head. "How may I help you?"

He glanced at Scott, but the big man was mute in the face of the woman's evident grief. "It's about your daughter."

One hand flew to her lips. "Ellen? Has something happened to her?"

"It's Sarah," Scott burst out.

With a glance at his partner, who had subsided back into silence, Granville said soothingly, "Nothing has happened to her. She's fine."

"Oh, thank goodness. Then…?"

"I don't know how much you knew about your husband's business, ma'am? The—other side of his business?"

Mutely she shook her head, but her eyes were wary, and her fingers slowly clenched tight.

"You know he's been charged with selling children, adopting them away from their parents?"

"Yes." The word sounded as if it had been dragged from her.

"Your daughter is adopted, is she not?" he said, his tone gentle.

The woman's face took on a gray tone and she swallowed hard, slumping back against the sofa. For a moment he thought she'd fainted and was about to call the maid when her green eyes opened and met his.

Swimming with tears, they didn't waver. "Ellen has living parents?"

He nodded.

"How do you know it is indeed she?"

"The little girl we seek has a small brown birthmark on her right arm in the shape of a seahorse."

"Yes, it is she." The words were all but inaudible.

"My younger sister is her mother, ma'am." In the face of Mrs. Baxter's grief, Scott had found his tongue, and his deep voice was gentle. "Her health is poor, and finding her lost baby Sarah is all she can think of."

"Sarah." She shook her head. "It sounds so wrong. She has always been Ellen to me." The words caught on a sob, quickly muffled in a dainty handkerchief.

"I know how hard it must be, ma'am," Scott said. "But my sister grieves her child."

"So you'll take her from me. And leave me to mourn?"

Watching the two of them, Granville had a sudden sense something wasn't right. He couldn't quite say what it was, but he observed the lovely, fragile-seeming woman closely.

"My sister suffers from a—serious illness. The thought of regaining her daughter is what keeps her clinging to life."

"And if your sister dies? What happens to the child then?"

"She won't die," Scott said, but there was more conviction in his tone than in his expression.

"And what of my Ellen?" Mrs. Baxter said. "Have you thought

what it will do to her to be wrested from the only mother she has known?"

Scott's face reflected his confusion. "But—Lizzie is her mother."

"Yet I am the one who rescued her from that terrible place, who made sure she had good food to gain the weight she needed, who held her while she cried."

"A child belongs with its mother," Scott said.

"Does giving birth give a woman permanent rights over a child she abandons?"

"Lizzie didn't abandon little Sarah! The child was torn from her by the father, and left behind when he forced my sister to move to another city, another country. She had neither the means nor the opportunity to search for the child. Until now."

"No? She was left in a baby farm! The conditions were intolerable!"

Granville watched as Scott's shoulders sagged. His friend seemed unable to find a response. Mrs. Baxter still looked grief-stricken, but he hadn't missed the tiny satisfied quirk of her lips while Scott struggled to find answers.

There was more to the woman than she showed on the surface. Granville had begun to wonder if she and her husband were not well matched after all.

"A baby farm run by your husband and his associates," he said.

If he hadn't been looking, he would have missed the flash of annoyance, before Mrs. Baxter composed her features. "I cannot speak for what my husband might or might not have done. All I care about now is Ellen's welfare." Her voice was clear and compelling.

"Her name's Sarah," Scott said in a low voice.

Mrs. Baxter ignored him, her attention focused on Granville.

"And it is to ensure her welfare that we are her," He said. "But you must know you have no legal right to her."

An angry frown, quickly hidden behind the dainty handkerchief. "So what do you propose, since you say you are concerned for Ellen's welfare?"

"I propose you bring the child her so we may meet her," Granville said.

"Now?" Mrs. Baxter asked.

"I see no reason for delay."

Her eyes flickered, then she gave a slight nod. "Very well," she said, and reached for the bell-pull.

THE LITTLE GIRL who walked in clutching her nanny's hand was beautiful. With big dark eyes and soft golden curls, she was dressed in a gown of crisp white cotton with lace everywhere. Even her booties matched.

Granville glanced from the child to Mrs. Baxter and back, just in time to see Sarah drop a slightly wavery curtsey to her. Mrs. Baxter gave a little nod, and the child's face lit up.

"Come to Mama," Mrs. Baxter said, and opened her arms.

Sarah half danced across the room, and gave her a kiss on the cheek.

Mrs. Baxter tightened her arms around her, and Sarah stiffened, a startled look on her face. Quickly Mrs. Baxter turned the child so that she faced him and Scott.

"These are friends," she said. "Mr. Granville and Mr. Scott. Say hello."

"Hello," said the little girl with another curtsey. She glanced at Granville, but seemed fascinated by Scott, who had given her a broad smile and a bow in return.

Scott crouched down, so he would be at her level. "Do you like living here?" he asked.

She nodded.

"And is your mama good to you?"

Another nod.

"Do you see her often?" Granville asked.

She looked uncertain.

"Do you and your mama do things together?" he continued.

After a quick glance at Mrs. Baxter and another at the nanny, Sarah said softly. "Sometimes."

Mrs. Baxter began to say something, but Granville gave her a hard look and the words died unsaid.

Scott had picked up on Granville's line of questioning. "Do you like going to the park?" he was asking the little girl.

"Oh, yes," she said with a huge smile.

"Do you go with your mama?"

A look of surprise and a shake of the head.

"Does your mama tuck you in at night?"

"No."

"Or kiss you goodnight?"

She cast another glance at Mrs. Baxter, bit her lip, and slowly shook her head.

"Thank you," Scott said. "It is a real pleasure to meet you, and I hope to see you again soon."

He stood up, glanced at Granville. "I think I've heard all I need to know."

Mrs. Baxter, very pale now, gave a nod to the nanny, who escorted the little girl from the room. Granville watched them go, then turned to their hostess. "The child comes with us. We'll take the nanny, too. Do you want to tell them, or shall I?"

She started to speak, noted Scott's unflinching expression, and stopped. Finally, she found her voice. "I will."

LITTLE SARAH DIDN'T LIKE the train. She sobbed unceasingly for nearly an hour, then drifted into an uneasy sleep.

Granville woke some hours later to find a pair of thickly lashed eyes staring at him. Thumb stuck firmly in her mouth, she was awake, her curious gaze darting from him to Trent and back.

Scott was awake too, still holding the child carefully in his arms. Beside them, the nanny snoozed, worn out by the trauma of getting herself and the child packed and aboard. Something in the big man's strength and gentleness seemed to have calmed her fear.

She'd be home soon, Granville thought. Hoping little Sarah would give Lizzie reason to live.

And that Lizzie had enough love left in her to give little Sarah the love she'd never known.

38

WEDNESDAY, JANUARY 24, 1900

After an unexplained absence, Andy Riggs was back in class, looking no different than he had any other day. As the morning wore on, Emily was frequently aware of him glancing at her. What was he thinking?

Her stomach churned, and she longed for the lunch break and a chance to talk to him.

When Miss Richards finally called the break, Emily hurried to get her coat, then waited for Mr. Riggs to leave and followed him to the stair.

He stopped dead and turned to face her, taking her by surprise. "So you're asking questions about my father again," he said harshly.

Emily took a step back, noting he had one fist clenched at the same time she realized they were out of sight of the others. Surely he'd not strike her?

"It isn't your father I'm interested in, but the man who hired him. The one who means harm to my fiancé," she said. "Surely you can understand that? In any case," she added quickly when his expression darkened further, "anything you tell me can only deflect interest from your father."

"Seems to me you're the only one who has an 'interest' in my father's doings," he said, advancing a step towards her.

For the first time Emily felt real fear. There were others near, but if he lost the temper she could see simmering in his face, he could hurt her badly before anyone could reach her.

Gathering her skirts with one hand in case she had to run, she drew a calming breath and forced the fear back. "My only interest is in my fiancé and his continued health," she said. "Two men are dead. The police in New Westminster have an ongoing investigation into the matter. Surely you wouldn't want your father's name to be part of that investigation?"

Andy's brow clouded further. "Are you threatening to…" He stopped, looked at her. "*Two* men?"

She nodded. The fact that the murders might not be related was something she'd keep to herself. "An old miner and a photographer from New Westminster."

"But he never…" He stopped himself, looked at her. "I must talk to my father. I might have something for you. Tomorrow, here, before class."

"Very well."

"If I give you a name, you'll see him clear of this?"

"My fiancé would do so. As long as he stays alive."

Andy Riggs gave a short nod and continued down the stairs.

Emily released the breath she hadn't realized she'd been holding and half fell against the wall as her knees gave way. She knew Riggs was a bully, but she hadn't expected him to be dangerous.

Straightening, she brushed back the locks that had fallen into her eyes, just as Laura dashed through the door. "Miss Turner? Emily? Are you all right?"

"I'm fine," said Emily. "Can you be here early tomorrow morning?"

Clara and Emily stood in the tidy but shabby parlor on Oppenheimer Street, waiting for the landlady to fetch Mr. Pearson.

"I'm just glad he's back," Emily whispered. "I don't think I could convince Miss Richards I had the headache again tomorrow afternoon."

"You're going to fail that class, you know."

"I'm getting better…" Emily began, then broke off as the landlady returned. A tall man with gaunt features and dark hair stood behind her.

"This is Mr. Pearson," the elderly woman said. "He may be able to help you."

"Thank you," Emily said, and the woman nodded and left the room. Turning to the tall man, she said, "Mr. Pearson, I am looking for a Mary Pearson. Is she a relative?"

"My niece." His eyes considered them. If he thought they looked out of place here in their modish gowns, he didn't say so.

Emily hurried to explain. "My cousin and I are assisting my aunt in hiring a new parlor maid and your niece came very highly recommended. Can you tell us if she is currently looking for employment?"

Mr. Pearson appeared to accept her story. His expression grew somewhat less fierce and the suspicious glint died out of his eyes. "No, she's no longer seeking work."

"I also have the respects of Mrs. Raynor to pass on to her, and would very much like to do so in person. Is she here?"

"She is still out of town, I'm afraid."

He didn't ask them to sit, Emily noted.

She really wanted to ask about Mary's father, but she didn't quite dare. There was something in the tense alertness of his stance that made her uneasy, though she quite liked his eyes, which were a dark gray.

Surely this was the right Mary?

Unable to think of a question that would clarify it without raising Mr. Pearson's suspicions, she thanked him for his time.

"Not at all."

"And could you please pass on Mrs. Raynor's respects for me?"

"Yes."

"She is such a lovely lady, and she thinks so highly of your niece." Emily knew she was babbling, but she'd had the sudden thought that perhaps Mr. Pearson had met Mrs. Raynor, and she could confirm the connection that way. But no.

"I'll do so," he said, and politely stood back so they could precede him to the door. There was no possible reason for them to linger.

"Good day," Emily said, accepting the inevitable.

"It does seem to be our Mary," Clara said as soon as they were out of earshot. "I wonder why she no longer has to work?"

"I don't know," Emily said, still pondering the odd feeling she'd experienced in talking with Mr. Pearson. "Perhaps she *isn't* the right one at all."

"What makes you say that?"

"I just wish I'd asked him more questions."

"There wasn't much you could ask."

"I suppose not."

"Well, I for one am glad you didn't ask any more questions—I think Mr. Pearson could be more than a little frightening if angered."

"I quite liked him."

Clara gave her a look, but said only "We'd best be going or we'll be late for dinner."

"In my father's eyes, that is a fate worse than death," Emily said, straight-faced.

39

THURSDAY, JANUARY 25, 1900

Early the following morning, Emily paced the hallway outside their classroom. She was anxious to hear what Andy Riggs had to say. She glanced again at the large clock over the stairs. Where was Laura? She'd promised to be here.

She rubbed her hands together, trying to warm them. The stove had not yet taken the chill out of the air, but mostly she was nervous. The door to the street banged open, and she jumped.

Then relaxed as Laura's light tread raced up the stairs. "Emily?"

"I'm here. Thank you so much for coming early."

"I wouldn't leave you to meet that bully alone. I'm just sorry I'm late. He's not here yet?" she asked as she rounded the corner, nearly out of breath.

"No. You're the first."

"Good." Laura half-rested against the wall, panting slightly. "I really hate my new corset. I've told Mother I can't breathe properly, but she just says I'll get used to it."

Emily nodded, but before she could commiserate the door slammed. They stared towards the stairs. The heavy tread of booted feet climbed towards them.

Emily braced herself, then relaxed when she saw Wally Sutton, who looked startled to see them.

"You two are here early," he said, then flushed and looked away. "I mean—I'll just go on through."

"No, stay," Laura said, clutching at his arm. "We're just waiting for Mr. Riggs. He's promised Emily news."

"If you're sure?"

"Very sure," said Laura, releasing his arm but holding him with her smile just as tightly.

Emily was glad she'd done so. Wally was too smitten with Laura to take part in Riggs' bullying of them, and his presence might help keep Riggs in line.

Her nerves were still tense, but she breathed a little easier.

The door slammed again, and a new set of boots ascended.

This time it was Riggs, who looked a little taken aback to see the three of them. His gaze narrowed on Wally.

"I need to talk to these ladies alone," he told him.

Wally began to turn away, but Laura put her hand on his arm.

He stopped, glanced at her. "I'll stay, if you don't mind," he said.

It was clear Riggs did mind, but it was a neat trap, Emily thought, with some sympathy for the treatment Wally would undoubtedly receive later. If it separated him from Riggs, though, it might serve him well in the end.

"You had something to tell me?" she said to Riggs to distract his attention away from Wally.

"We don't need witnesses," he growled.

He was nice-looking, showing fair promise to be an extremely attractive man, once he'd grown into his shoulders, but his surly expression undermined that. "They're my friends. They stay," she said.

Laura looked pleased, and Wally looked abashed.

Riggs's mouth curled down. "You call these friends?" he said with a nasty laugh.

Emily ignored him. "I believe you have a name for me?"

"If I give it to you, your fiancé will protect my father's good name?"

What he had of one. "Yes."

"Very well. It's Pearson."

Mr. Pearson was a murderer? The same man she'd talked to the day before? For a moment a gray cloud swung before Emily's eyes, and she thought she might faint. "This Mr. Pearson hired your father..."

"Hired my father's men."

"...To kill my fiancé and his party?"

"Yes."

Beyond Riggs Emily could see Laura's face, too pale, and Wally seemed to be supporting her. Seeing the other girl so stricken by the news made Emily feel a little better, for some reason.

"Are you certain?" The words came out strong and clear, and she felt proud of herself.

He nodded, but wouldn't meet her gaze. "I'm sure," he said.

The noisy arrival of several other students ended the conversation. No matter, thought Emily. She had what she needed.

But how to warn Granville? He'd be on the train somewhere between here and Denver by now. And Mr. Pearson was here.

Did that mean Granville was safe? Or had Mr. Pearson hired someone else to follow them to Denver?

Surely Granville was fine—his telegram held no hint of danger. Not that he'd tell her if he *were* in danger.

But had she put Clara in danger along with herself when they'd gone to visit Pearson? The thought made her feel ill.

But no, she reassured herself. Mr. Pearson had no reason to know about her connection to Granville. Or to think she and Clara were anything other than what they'd said they were.

Another thought struck her. What if Mr. Pearson left town? What could she do?

She could send Granville a telegram, warning him. Beyond that, there was probably nothing more she could do. She'd have to wait for his return.

Emily hated waiting.

40

FRIDAY, JANUARY 26, 1900

"There's a message for you." Miss Richard's disapproving tones cut into Emily's confused thoughts. Emily could feel every eye on her as she dropped her hands, glanced at the perfect page she'd just typed, then looked up.

"Thank you." It was hard to focus when she was so worried about the threat Mr. Pearson might pose for Granville. Looking beyond Miss Richards, she could see Trent's excited face. They were back!

"Oh..." she said, trying to contain the mixture of excitement and fear that rose in her. Judging by Miss Richard's raised eyebrows, she hadn't succeeded. "Please excuse me. My mother must be unwell."

Only an effort of will kept her gait sedate as she crossed the room to where Trent waited. "How is he?" she whispered.

"Fine, we're all fine. But..."

"I must see him."

"They're waiting for you at Stroh's," Trent said. "Can you get away?"

"Yes. Wait a moment." Turning to her teacher, who hovered

nearby, Emily swallowed hard and said in a breaking voice "It is as I feared. Mama is—taken ill again. I am sorry, I must go."

Miss Richard's expression softened. "Of course, my dear. I wish her well in her recovery."

Emily gave her a faint, brave smile. "Thank you."

Two minutes later, cloaked and hatted, she was following Trent down the stairs.

GRANVILLE RELEASED a breath when he saw Emily come through the door with Trent, and cursed the fact that the amber liquid in his teacup was not whiskey. Strong whiskey. She looked unharmed, if a little pale, but the green eyes were as vibrant as ever.

As she handed her gray wool jacket and gray velvet bonnet to an attentive waiter, Granville's eyes searched that slim figure for any change. He found none. She was fine.

It was ridiculous to have been so concerned—despite Emily's spirit, how could a well-brought up young lady have learned of Mad Al Pearson, much less found him?

Emily sat down as gracefully as she did everything, poured a cup of tea for herself and Trent and smiled at them. "I'm so relieved to see all of you well."

She gave him a look and a smile that he swore had a dimple attached. But Emily didn't have dimples, did she?

He smiled back, meeting her eyes. "And I you."

"I have news."

"So have we."

Her eyes widened, her gaze moving from face to face, lingering on Scott's wide grin. "Little Sarah? You found her?"

"She was returned to her mother early this morning."

"I'm so glad. And—how does her mother?"

"You should've seen Lizzie's face, when she saw her daughter," Scott said. "I've never seen such joy. And the child almost seemed to know her." His voice choked. "I think Lizzie'll be fine now. I think she'll get well."

Granville thought so too. The change in Lizzie was astounding—it was as if some smoldering ember had been rekindled. Her face and body were still gaunt but her eyes had come alive and her voice held purpose. And she held her little girl with such tenderness he'd had to look away.

"So now we can turn our energies to our search for Mary Pearson," he said.

Emily drew in a deep breath and folded her hands in her lap. The demure posture was so unlike her it immediately focused his attention. He had a sudden uneasy feeling.

She didn't disappoint him. "I think you'll find Mary in a rooming house on the East Side," she said. "On Oppenheimer, near Gore. She's living with her uncle, a Mr. Pearson."

She'd found both of them. This was worse than he'd imagined, but at least she had no idea whom she was dealing with.

"I believe Mr. Pearson to be the man behind the attempts on your life, and the death of your client," she continued, shattering his last comfort. "And I can see he might be dangerous, though I thought him rather kind."

"You met the man?" Granville asked, then moderated his voice when every head turned in their direction. "Suspecting what he was, you met with him? And how did you find out all this since we've been gone?"

Emily hid a smile behind her teacup. "You obviously learned the same, or you would be asking different questions. And I didn't know when Clara and I met with him. I've only this morning learned he's the one who hired the men to follow and ambush you."

So that explained why they'd survived the first attack. It hadn't been Mad Al himself shooting at them.

But why only shoot at them once in Denver?

Trent's eyes had grown wider and wider, and Scott was an alarming shade of purple.

Granville took a deep breath. "You've done amazing work. But I thought you agreed not to pursue this any further."

"Well, what I actually promised was not to investigate. I just asked a few questions," Emily said. She did have a dimple.

What was he going to do about her?

Granville picked up her hand and pressed a kiss into the palm of it, watching with interest as she blushed and snatched it back.

"We will discuss that at a later date," he said. "As you've done half my work for me and located the fellow, I only need to work with the local officials to have him arrested. Promise me you'll stay away from anyone involved until then?"

"Yes, if you'll promise to be careful," Emily said. "And perhaps it might be possible not to shoot Mr. Pearson? I rather liked him."

41

SATURDAY, JANUARY 27, 1900

Standing on the tidy porch of 153 Oppenheimer, Granville tightened all the muscles in his neck and shoulders, then released them. He checked the fit of his gun in the holster strapped to his thigh.

Out of the corner of his eye he could see Scott, Detective Moore and several heavily armed New Westminster police—Vancouver's Chief of Police had declined to be involved in this little exercise. Moore had argued strongly for he and his men to be standing right beside Granville and Scott, but in the end they'd conceded.

Granville just hoped his reading of the situation had been right.

Mad Al Pearson himself answered the door to Granville's knock. He didn't seem surprised—gave them a nod of recognition. Though the fellow didn't appear to be armed, Granville let his hand rest on his own revolver.

It earned him a hard stare but Pearson stepped back to allow him entry.

"My name is John Granville and I've come..."

"I know why you're here."

"Then you'll know I didn't come alone."

"Yes."

"So why are you still here?"

"My brother is dead. I've avenged him," Pearson said.

"You could have fled."

"My niece needed me."

"Your niece is about to become a very wealthy woman."

"So I understand."

Granville gave him a hard stare. "How did you know we meant to give the map to her? That is why you didn't pursue us in Denver, isn't it?"

Mad Al nodded.

"How did you find out?"

"You had the map, but you didn't register the mine. At first, I thought you'd sell it to the highest bidder, but then I learned you were asking questions about my brother and looking for me."

"So?"

"If you'd killed my brother for the map, or partnered with that old villain, it wouldn't have served you to look for Jim." The depth of pain in the man's eyes as he uttered his dead brother's name made Granville's gut clench. "And then there was the child."

"Child?"

Mad Al smiled, and Granville suddenly saw exactly what Emily had meant when she said she rather liked the man. "Scott's niece. Men who sought so hard to find a lost child, against such odds, would not knowingly do my niece wrong. Even an ambush didn't deter you."

"I'd give much to know how you came by your information."

The deep-set eyes regarded him. "I'm well known there," was the only answer Mad Al gave.

Granville nodded. "You did kill my client, did you not? Cole?"

"He killed my brother. He deserved to die," Pearson said.

"He would have hung. Now you will."

Mad Al shrugged. There was a look in his eyes that made Granville uneasy.

"Did you kill Cole?" Granville asked.

"Yes."

"And the photographer?"

"Fool thought he'd try a spot of blackmail."

It wasn't the answer Granville had found himself hoping for. "What about Jim's daughter? What about Mary? She'll need someone to look after her."

Mad Al tilted his head slightly and contemplated Granville. "And here I thought you'd promised your late client to make sure she got the mine. Way I figure it, means you'll have to protect her, too."

"Where d'you hear that?"

"Your young assistant talks too much. Like I said, I know people."

Trent. The boy was lucky to be alive, and probably didn't even know it. "So why didn't you just light out? Head north?" Granville asked.

Mad Al shrugged. "I figured this was justice."

"AND MR. PEARSON just let himself be handcuffed?" Emily asked. They sat in her mother's overheated parlor, armchairs pulled close together, heavy drapes drawn against the weather.

Emily expected to be interrupted at any moment, so she spoke quickly. "But why? Does he expect to be acquitted?"

"I think he really doesn't want to live without his brother," Granville said.

"Oh. You liked him, didn't you?"

"Yes. He wasn't mean spirited, and he has a clear sense of justice, even if it's a little old testament for my taste. He wasn't what I'd expected."

She thought about it for a moment. "Then why did he kill Mr. Morgan?"

"Morgan and his aunt were blackmailing former clients. And Morgan tried to blackmail Mary with the thefts at the Raynors."

Emily's eyes searched his face. "Blackmail her how?"

She didn't miss a thing. He'd hoped to avoid telling her this part, but it didn't surprise him if she'd guessed. "He was pressuring her for her favors."

She nodded. "It had to be something like that to make her uncle commit another murder."

"I think Pearson had already decided to die for avenging his brother—to him this was the surest way of taking care of his brother's daughter too."

"And Mary?"

"Still in Seattle. Scott's gone to get her back."

"It's so sad." She was looking down, tracing little patterns on her skirts. "All those deaths, for gold."

"Yes."

She looked up, met his eyes. Her own were steady and serious. "Would you kill? I mean, is there anything that would make you kill someone?"

"Not for gold."

"For what?"

"For the people I care about. If I had to save you, for instance." He tried to turn it into a joke, but couldn't quite pull it off.

Her cheeks flamed, but her eyes were steady. "Even when our engagement is over?"

"Even then. If it is over. I like you, Emily."

Her lips quirked. "That's good," she said, "because we may be engaged for a time yet. I'm proving to be a dreadful typewriter."

Her eyes were telling him something quite different.

42

MONDAY, JANUARY 29, 1900

Emily sat at the typing table and stared at her clenched hands. The soft voices and stifled laughter around her as the rest of the class arrived seemed wrong.

She hadn't been able to sleep since her last conversation with Granville, and only part of it was her nervous stomach at the realization that there really might be something building between them.

No, it was also something about Albin Pearson. The grief and anger she'd seen in him were real, but she just couldn't believe he was a killer. Dangerous, but not a killer.

"Miss Turner!"

Emily started.

"Hands up, please."

She raised her hands to the proper position, hesitated, dropped them. She looked at Miss Richards. "I'm sorry. I have the most unbearable headache and I'm afraid the influenza might be coming back."

Miss Richards frowned, then gave a brief nod.

Quickly gathering her things, Emily left the room, leaving an annoyed Miss Richards and a hum of gossip in her wake.

It didn't matter. She had to talk to Mary Pearson, and the train from Seattle should be pulling in shortly.

AT TWO-FIFTEEN THE Seattle train chuffed into the station, coming to a halt with a screeching of metal and a blast of smoke and grit. Emily was coughing and wiping her eyes, missing the moment when the doors opened and the porters let down the steps to each compartment.

When she could see again, a familiar figure was descending from the carriage one over from where she stood.

Walking briskly towards him, she called out. "Mr. Scott?"

"Miss Turner!" He looked surprised to see her.

She smiled at him. "I thought Miss Pearson might appreciate some female company. Mr. Granville agreed to accompany me."

And it would give her an opportunity to find out more about Albin Pearson. Surely Mary Pearson would be able to answer at least some of the questions that were troubling her.

Scott's eyes moved past her. "I don't see him."

"He has a carriage waiting."

He nodded, then quickly turned back to the train carriage when a soft voice called his name. Putting out a hand, he helped a young woman down the steps from one of the sleeping compartments.

Emily's eyes took in soft brown hair, slate blue eyes, a gentle smile and a very shapely figure. Mary Pearson met her look, then cast her eyes down and blushed slightly. Emily advanced towards her, hand outstretched.

"How do you do? I am Emily Turner."

"Mary Pearson. And it's very nice to meet you."

"She's had a long journey. We should get her home."

Emily's gaze flicked to Mr. Scott, narrowing as she saw the tenderness with which he regarded Mary's bent head. Was he smitten? And so quickly?

She held back a quick grin at the idea of the petite Mary and the very large Scott together.

In the carriage, Emily turned to Mary, seated beside her. "You had a safe journey?"

Another blush. "Yes, thanks to Mr. Scott," she said, casting a look at him from under her lashes.

Emily noted a second look cast in Granville's direction. Was she playing up to both of them? And after Granville had been introduced as her own fiancé?

Emily's gaze sharpened. "And he told you what has been occurring? Your uncle's arrest for the murders of Mr. Cole and Mr. Morgan?"

Mary's brow puckered and tears stood in her eyes. "Yes. I still can't believe it."

"You knew nothing of the events leading up to his arrest?"

"No. My uncle and I left for Seattle on the sixteenth, where he left me with relatives. I haven't heard from him since."

"I'm so sorry," Emily said, softening at the pain in the other woman's eyes. Perhaps she'd misjudged that glance at Granville. "It must be very hard."

A nod, a delicate half-sniff and Mary's lacy handkerchief came out.

Mr. Scott looked like he wanted to gather Mary close and protect her from everything, Emily noted, wishing she didn't need to ask her next questions. "Do you know why your uncle came back? He might never have been arrested if he'd stayed in Seattle."

"He has business dealings here. He and my father..." her voice broke, resumed. "They found gold in the Klondike. My father..."

She stopped and looked down, hiding her eyes. "My father was a dreamer. He put much of his money into a gold map, dreaming of even greater riches. It is why he partnered with Mr. Cole. And he died for it."

Her voice quivered. "My uncle invested in property here. And he too will die here."

"Only if he is found guilty," Emily said.

Mary raised her damp eyes, met Emily's look. "You think he might not be?"

Scott seemed about to protest, then glanced at Granville and sat back.

Emily said nothing for a moment, regarding Mary's pale face thoughtfully and casting a glance at Granville, who was watching them with no expression at all on his usually expressive face.

"I wonder if we know the full story of the deaths, especially that of Mr. Morgan," she said carefully. "He sounds a most unpleasant man. I gather you knew him?"

"Yes," Mary said, and hesitated.

"We're here," Mr. Scott broke in, as the carriage drew up in front of the shabby boarding house where the Pearsons lived.

He sounded relieved, Emily thought. Did he have the sense of things unsaid hovering in the air that she had? Or was she being fanciful?

"Will you stay for tea?" Mary asked with a wistful smile, gathering her dignity around her like a grand duchess entertaining the tenants.

Over china cups and the ham and cress sandwiches provided by the landlady, Emily found it hard to turn the conversation back to the topic of murder. Mary was playing the gracious hostess, making sure the cups were filled and that Granville and Scott had a surfeit of sandwiches, but she wouldn't meet Emily's eyes.

Emily watched Mary over her cup of tea. Was she as sweet as her expression and her cast down gaze suggested?

Emily caught the occasional sideways glance, quickly veiled, that suggested there was more to Mary than she wanted to show. And Emily was sure the other woman knew more about her uncle's situation than she was letting on. But how to win her confidence?

Emily cast a glance at Scott's bemused expression. He wasn't likely to interfere. Good. "Your father and your uncle must have been very close," she began.

Mary's lashes swept down. "Yes. They were always together."

"Were you equally close to your uncle?"

"I knew him well as a child, but not since. He and my father were always off chasing gold," Mary said.

"Yet he seems to be willing to do much for you."

Again the sideways glance, a slight frown. "You mean the gold."

She did? Emily didn't respond, just tried to make her expression encouraging. It seemed to work.

"He's told you then," Mary said. "Yes, he intends to give everything to me. The investments, all of it."

"That's very generous," Emily said. "He must love you very much."

Mary's smile was tinged with bitterness. "He loves my father's memory that much. And he doesn't expect to live. Nor does he want to, no matter what I say."

Mary's face crumpled, and Scott sat nervously on the edge of his chair, looking like he wanted to leap to her aid. Granville, for all his polish, looked uncomfortable.

Mary's pain and the depth of her distress seemed genuine. "I'm very sorry," Emily said.

Mary put her handkerchief to her lips and waved an acknowledgement as she fought to regain her composure. "Now I have gold of my own. I don't need his." Her voice broke.

Emily's gaze flicked to Scott. Had he told her about the map and the mine? He looked confused, so perhaps not. Then how had the woman known?

Emily's eyes narrowed slightly as a preposterous idea began to take shape. "Gold of your own?" she repeated.

Mary nodded. "The map that was my father's, as was the mine. More money than I ever dreamed of."

Emily's eyes moved to Granville. Was he asking the same question she was? His head was slightly tilted as he watched Mary, but his look was pitying.

How to ask the one thing she needed to know? "Were you able to spend much time with your father before he was killed?" Emily asked.

"No." A muffled sob. "He wanted to have enough money that we could live in style, first. I barely saw him when he returned from the Klondike—though he bought me this," and her fingers clenched around a slim gold locket at her throat. "Then he was off after more gold."

Mary's grief touched Emily, and she wished there were some way she could comfort her. Probably she'd been wrong to suspect her story. Feeling like an Inquisitor, she asked "Have you no-one else?"

Mary shook her head. "My mother died when I was very young. My father and my uncle raised me."

"And the relatives in Seattle?"

"Very distant—second cousins only. I'm afraid I wore out my welcome there. I was never so glad to see anyone as Mr. Scott when he arrived to escort me back." She gave Scott a little smile, and he beamed.

Ducking her head, Mary dabbed at her eyes. "I simply wish he hadn't come with such dreadful news."

Emily sipped her tea, hiding her thoughts behind the polite ritual of the afternoon call. Even if it was morning. "You didn't grow up here, then?"

"No, I was raised just outside Denver."

"Oh, before I forget," Emily said. "Mrs. Raynor sends her best regards."

A look of surprise, hastily veiled. "Thank you. She's a lovely woman," Mary said.

"And very fond of you. You worked for her for nearly four years, I believe? Was it your first position in the area?"

Mary nodded. "More tea?"

"Thank you."

Mary busied herself pouring tea for all of them, and passing out the tea biscuits that the landlady had brought them. "Yes, we left Denver when word of the Klondike rush got out. I came as far north as Vancouver and waited for them here."

Emily noted a sudden alertness in Granville's gaze. What had Mary said? "It must have been difficult, growing up without a mother, just you and two men."

"It is not very ladylike of me, but I adored it," Mary said.

"Did you not feel unsafe?"

Mary leaned closer, gave her a conspiratorial smile. "I dressed as a boy much of the time. And my uncle taught me to shoot."

"Oh, how very brave of you. I've never even held a gun."

"Living here? You should learn to shoot—every woman should," Mary said.

For a moment Emily was distracted. She'd never thought herself holding a gun, much less shooting one. But being a journalist could be dangerous, so… "Perhaps I'll ask you to give me lessons, then," she said, leaning forward a little.

"I'm not very good, I'm afraid," Mary said. "But just the sight of a woman brandishing a firearm is enough to put fear into most men." And she smiled directly at Emily, merriment dancing in her eyes.

Emily smiled back as laughter broke the tension in the small room. Granville and Scott relaxed and reached for biscuits as Mary poured more tea.

Which gave Emily time to remember her own purpose here.

Mary had played that well, Emily thought, watching the other woman's downcast face and capable hands. The distraction had almost worked, and the humor was a nice touch. Especially since it was genuine.

"I'll ask my fiancé to teach me to shoot, then," Emily said, with a nod and a smile to Granville.

"You don't need to learn," he said quickly.

Emily wondered if the masculine arrogance in his voice was

real, and hoped it wasn't. Giving a little shrug, she shook her head at him and exchanged a wry smile with Mary Pearson.

"When does Mr. Pearson go to trial?" she asked Granville.

"The indictment hearing is Thursday, the trial should be the following week," he said, ignoring Scott's instinctive protest.

Mary Pearson sucked in a quick breath. "So soon?"

"Yes."

"We know a good barrister," Scott said quickly. "Don't worry—Randall will defend your uncle."

"He should be able to get him a lighter sentence, since your uncle didn't actually shoot our client," Granville said. "There were others hired to do that, and none of them survived the avalanche."

She hadn't known that. Emily glanced at his face, but couldn't read his expression. His eyes met hers, and softened. She gave him a tiny nod. "You've been talking to the police from New Westminster?" she asked him.

"Yes. They haven't found the bodies, but they've confirmed four men are missing from Port Hammond," Granville said. "Two are brothers of your Mr. Riggs, the third is a nephew and the fourth often works for them."

"So that explains how Andy Riggs knew about the ambush," Emily said.

"Yes. Pearson hired them, but it could be argued that he only hired them to get the map back."

"Doesn't lessen the fact that we were shot at, nearly killed," Scott said.

"The hirelings got greedy," Granville said. "They thought to kill us so we couldn't talk, then steal the map and double cross their employer. Pearson."

Emily nodded, her brain connecting previously unrelated pieces. It *was* possible. "If he didn't order those murders, he won't be hung."

Mary's eyes were huge and filled with tears as they darted from one to the other. "But what about Mr. Morgan?"

"He wasn't a nice man," Emily said. "I believe him to be a blackmailer, and perhaps worse. Perhaps he was shot in self-defence?"

"Which is legal here," Scott put in.

A light had begun to glow behind Mary's eyes. "How good is your lawyer?" she asked.

"Josiah Randall is very good indeed," Granville said.

"I must speak with him," Mary said.

43

TUESDAY, JANUARY 30, 1900

"She's gone," Granville said as he joined her in the elaborate front room in her father's house.

Emily hadn't heard him come in. Her stomach tightened. She looked up from her study of the *World*. "Mary?"

"Yes. You knew she'd run, did you not?"

"I suspected it," she said. "Once I realized she had to be the one who killed Morgan, not her uncle."

And Emily was glad of it. She didn't want to see a woman hang, and she suspected having Mary Pearson in a Vancouver prison would be more trouble than any of them were ready for.

"How did you guess it was she who had hired Riggs and shot Morgan?" he asked.

"I didn't, not at first. But I liked her uncle, and something just felt wrong. Then she said he'd taught her to shoot.

"And that she'd been raised as a boy," Granville added.

"Yes," Emily said. "I began to see what could have happened. When did you suspect?"

"About the same time, though I'd felt all along that Pearson surrendered too easily. There was no reason for him to come back to Vancouver. We'd never have found him in the States."

"Will they find her?"

He shook his head. "They won't look. She's left a signed statement with Randall saying she shot Morgan in self-defence. Hiring Riggs and company to commit a robbery that failed isn't sufficient reason to send men after her."

"What about the death of your client?"

"Cole? She says she hired Riggs and company only to steal the map, which belonged to her in any case. That the men who shot at us and set off the avalanche went too far. And there is no-one left alive to dispute her claim."

"Do you believe her?"

One eyebrow lifted and the little laugh lines appeared beside his eyes. "Someone tried to kill us in Denver," he said. "An exceptional marksman—if I hadn't ducked, I'd be standing here dead."

Emily drew in a harsh breath. "That isn't funny. And you didn't tell me that!"

"I didn't want to worry you."

She shook her head at him. "I begin to think it a good thing I'm not really going to marry you."

"I think we should discuss the matter further."

She slid a glance at him. He was grinning at her.

"Perhaps," she said, and smiled back. "So tell me, which of them was it?"

"I would guess Mary," Granville said. "I think she was determined to avenge her father. He seems to be the only person she has ever loved."

It didn't surprise her that Granville was willing to believe a woman could be a crack shot, though Emily rather thought Mary's motive might have been rather more self-interested. "So what stopped her? I mean, it sounds as if she didn't keep shooting?"

"No, it was only the one incident, on our second day there. And I'm not sure what stopped her. It was either because she found out we meant to give her the map, or she found out we were looking for little Sarah. I'm inclined to believe the latter. She had just lost her father, and she seems softhearted enough to care about the plight of another fatherless child. It also seems to be what she told her uncle."

Again Emily wasn't so sure about the purity of Mary's motives, but she saw no need to tell Granville that. It was like him to believe the best of a woman.

"How is Mr. Scott taking it?" she asked instead.

"He's not talking much."

Emily nodded. It would take him time to get over it, though she doubted he'd really known Mary at all. The facade of the quiet, demure miss seemed to be something she could assume at will. It had probably stood her in good stead in her years with Mrs. Raynor, judging by that lady's high regard for her former maid.

Emily doubted Mrs. Raynor had ever seen the side of Mary that was a crack shot and comfortable hiring killers. "And what of the mine?"

"Scott and I discussed it. It's not right that Mary profit from Cole's murder, any more than Cole had the right to profit from Jim Pearson's."

"I begin to think the shaman was right," Emily said. "That mine is cursed, or at least unlucky."

He laughed. "Perhaps it is. There've been too many deaths already, and those are just the ones we know of."

"So what will you do about it?"

"It's done—we've burnt the map. The gold from the cache can be our payment—Cole owed us that."

"And you'll just forget about the mine?"

He shook his head. "No-one can just forget a mine that rich. But it rightfully belongs to Pearson's heir—Mary. Since she can't collect on it, the gold can stay in the ground for another thousand years until someone else discovers it."

"What if James Pearson stole it from someone else first?"

"It's possible, though his brother says James invested his own take from the Klondike. It doesn't change anything—without the map, Mary won't get near the mine."

"Can you really ignore all that gold?"

He shrugged. "The cache was a rich one—enough to set us up for some time."

"But you went to the Klondike to find your fortune. Now you have, and you're letting it go?"

"It isn't mine. And too much gold can create more problems than it solves. I learned that in the Klondike, if nothing else."

It was like him to value justice over gold. She studied his face. "What would you have done if you'd found gold there? In the Klondike, I mean."

"Gone back to England, bought land, flaunted my success in my brother's face." He grinned. "I prefer the life I've found here."

"Won't others still be after you, thinking you have the map?"

"That's why we burnt it, with Benton and Frances as witnesses."

"Brilliant. They'll get the word out, in order to protect both of you."

"Well, Frances to protect Scott, and Benton to please her. But enough of that—I think we should be discussing our own nuptials."

"Our supposed nuptials, do you mean?"

"Exactly. We need to determine a date," he said, and reached into the pocket of his waistcoat, drawing out a small velvet box. "And for veracity, you really should have one of these."

"Oh, Granville," Emily said, gazing at a beautifully set emerald, flanked with diamonds.

"It reminded me of you," he said, placing it gently on her finger. "Do you like it?"

"Indeed I do." Emily smiled up at him, and slid into his waiting embrace.

AUTHOR'S NOTES

In researching and writing this book, I've made every effort to respect the timeframe and keep the historical details as accurate as possible. I have used historic figures for a number of minor characters, and kept them as close to the historic records as possible, though in some cases I've created incidents and conversations specific to the plot of this book.

Slumach and his rumored lost mine existed, and the details of the murder of Louis Bee are as accurate as the historical record allows. Numerous gold seekers have lost their lives searching for Slumach's mine since his death in 1891. Slumach's nephew, Peter Pierre, is also an historic figure, and I've drawn on documented conversations with him for the flavor of his dialogue. Charles Hill-Tout is also an historic figure, a self-taught ethnologist who made local contributions to the ethnology of the native races of the west coast.

I hope you enjoyed reading as much as I've enjoyed writing it!

Many thanks to my first readers Carla Lewis, Sandy Constable, Roberta Rich, Bobbi Randall, Kayo Devcic and Linda Roggeveen for insightful comments on early drafts of the manuscript, and to my mother for her eagle eye for typos. Any errors or omissions are, of course, mine.

I am also indebted to the resources and helpful staff of the Vancouver Public Library Special Collections division and the University of BC Special Collections and History Divisions. A number of historical works have been very valuable to me in researching this book; many of them are listed on my website at www.sharonrowse.com.

THE SERIES CONTINUES...

THE MISSING HEIR MURDERS

A John Granville & Emily Turner Mystery

1
FRIDAY, APRIL 13, 1900

John Lansdowne Granville stared at the letter in his hands while the rain battered at his office window. A chill draft, smelling of manure and burning coal, crept in from the street below. "Beware the Ides," he muttered under his breath.

The quote felt apt, even if today was the Ides of April rather than March. And he was no laurel-wreathed Caesar. He grimaced at the thought.

"What's that? Something wrong, Granville?" Scott said, looking up from the ledger he'd been wrestling with. His business partner had a half-grin on his face, but his eyes were watchful.

Granville crumpled the heavy white paper in one fist and tossed it across the mahogany partner's desk the two of them shared. He watched as it landed on an unsteady stack of reports they'd both been ignoring. "Not a thing."

"'Cause I got to tell you, the way you look now, you'd scare off a Mama bear looking for her cubs."

Granville gave a crack of laughter. Truth was, he'd rather face a grizzly than deal with this letter. "We've been offered a job."

Scott eyed the crumpled page, written in a spiked, forceful hand. A challenging job would be welcome, but Granville's expression and the postmark signaled trouble. "In England?"

"No, here. In Vancouver," Granville said. "We need to find the Earl of Thanet's heir."

"How'd he lose him?"

"Quite deliberately, I assure you. Apparently Rupert Weston is a remittance man."

"I thought they only paid off the younger sons to disappear over here, not the heirs," Scott said.

Behind Granville the windowpanes rattled as the storm increased. "And until a most unfortunate boating accident a few months ago, you'd have been right. It seems Weston's two older brothers drowned in unexpectedly rough seas off the Isle of Wight. Hence the search for the new heir apparent."

"Huh," Scott said. "Wonder what young Weston did that got him sent to the colonies."

"Whatever it was, all will be forgiven now."

"He's unlikely to have reformed any, not from what I've seen of the remittance boys."

Scott was right, but the casual dismissal in his voice grated. Granville had refused to admit it at the time, but he hadn't been far from a remittance man himself, not so long ago.

It had been his father's money that took him to the Klondike, though he'd refused to accept another penny once he'd got there. Which proved to be a mistake, since he and Scott had never managed to strike it rich. Despite eighteen months of hard work in extremely trying conditions.

"True enough," Granville said with a wry grin.

"But now he's the heir none of that matters?"

Granville nodded, amused despite his own misgivings by the incredulous note in Scott's voice.

"I'll never understand you English." Scott tossed the crumpled letter back. "Where's this Earl send the money?"

"Post office here in town—care of General Delivery."

"I'm guessing their letters have been returned?" Scott said.

"You'd be right about that."

"So Weston might still be in Vancouver."

"Might be," Granville agreed. "If he is here, he's laying low."

"Gives us a place to start, though. Sounds easy enough," Scott said. "So what's the catch?"

Granville eyed Scott with affection, grinned. "The catch, as you so succinctly put it, is that Thanet isn't hiring us."

"Then who is?"

"Thanet's brother-in-law, the boy's uncle," Granville said. "And the request comes by way of my brother William."

"The Baron? That William?" Scott said.

"That's him."

"But the job's legit? No reason we can't take it, is there?"

Granville shook his head. "*Et tu, Brute*?" he said mournfully.

"Huh?" Scott said, face blank.

That earned him a half laugh, as it was undoubtedly meant to. "William has never done anything straightforward in his life, and most particularly not when it involves me."

"You don't trust him even on something as straightforward as this?" Scott asked. "Or is there some particular reason Thanet isn't the one hiring us to find his missing son?"

"I gather he's too mired in grief to take any action. But based on hard experience, I don't trust William on anything."

"So what's your dear brother up to, then?"

"Currying favor with the Earl of Thanet, I suspect. Or trying to, through the man's brother-in-law. Probably as close as William could get to the Earl."

Scott gave a bark of laughter. "Probably. So we find this Weston, it's easy money and Brother William's in your debt. Sounds like a no fail plan to me."

"Which means we're missing something. I wonder what happens to the estate if we don't find Weston, or if he's already dead."

Scott gave him a sharp look. "Why should we care?"

"Because William will have looked at every angle of this before involving himself. And the most obvious path is seldom the one he follows. He'll not concern himself if we're injured or killed in pursuit of whatever goal he has in mind—in fact it might sweeten it for him."

"Nice brother. But he's thousands of miles away. How dangerous could it be?"

Granville shrugged. "How dangerous was it up on the creeks when a fellow didn't know enough to provision for winter?"

Scott grunted. "Killed by what we don't know? At least it won't be boring."

"Getting tired of guarding nervous bankers are you? Fine, we'll take the job," Granville said, and flicked a disdainful finger toward the crumpled ball he'd made of the letter. It was probably time he stopped avoiding William and his schemes, anyway.

"That was quick." Scott eyed his partner. "And I've seen that look before, usually right before you get both of us into trouble. What're you planning?"

He was planning to outmaneuver whatever his unscrupulous older brother might have in mind for him. "There's nothing to stop us taking on this case and finding young Weston," Granville said. "Once we have all the facts, we can decide how we want to handle it."

"You planning on bamboozling Brother William, then?"

There was a reason he and Scott had remained friends after their return from the Klondike. "Exactly," Granville said, striding towards the door. "What do you say?"

The grating of wood chair on hardwood floor told him his partner was behind him.

"I'll probably regret this," Scott said. "But when do we start?"

By the time they'd made their way to the imposing granite-faced Main Post Office on Pender Street, the wind had lessened. Shaking the rain from his hat, Granville was amused to find himself standing in front of a long marble counter that could have been in any post office in London, being glared at by a dapper young man—nattily attired in black and white—who seemed to have hopes of being this century's Beau Brummell.

Granville wondered if anyone had told him how unlikely that was in Vancouver, of all places. As far as the English were concerned, the clerk's focus should be on making money, like all good Colonials.

"No Weston here."

Granville had met friendlier icicles. "But he does collect his mail here?"

"Can't give out that information."

"Fair enough. Can you tell me if you have uncollected mail for him?"

Granville watched the man's eyes dart to a section of wooden pigeonholes. Some were empty, some had a few letters, but one or two were stuffed with mail. Which one was Weston's?

"Sorry, that's classified," came the predictable answer.

"We just need to know when he's expected next," Scott put in.

"And how would I know that?"

"Can you perhaps tell us if he collects his mail regularly?" Granville smiled, put an extra hint of Oxford in his tone. "He's a friend—we lost touch with him in Skagway."

"Sorry."

"Come on, Granville," Scott said. "We're wasting our time here." Gripping his partner's elbow, he half dragged him outside.

"I wasn't done there."

"You were about to try bribing that clerk." Scott settled his hat more firmly in place, turned up his collar against the wind-driven rain and began walking north.

Granville buttoned his coat as he paced beside his partner. “I was indeed. And?”

“And I know the clerk’s brother,” Scott said. “Very officious family—and all of them hate Brits. No offense.”

“Seems to be a common sentiment in this part of the world,” Granville said. It was unsettling, and the fact that he found it so just annoyed him more.

Confining as he’d found being a member of the English gentry, he’d always taken the respect that came with it for granted. Now he couldn’t.

Scott chuckled, then sobered. “Yeah, well if you’d tried to bribe him, he’d have you arrested for tamperin’ with the mails or some fool thing.”

“That could have been embarrassing. Especially since the local constabulary are none too fond of us.”

“Getting some of them arrested will cause that,” Scott said with a straight face.

Granville recalled his first weeks in town with a grin. “True enough. But it saved you hanging for murder. I suppose it was worth it. So where are we headed in this downpour?”

“Newspaper office. I thought we’d advertise for Weston.”

“Hmm. News to his advantage or something of that sort? That makes sense.”

“Yeah, I thought so. The Province is around the corner. It has the biggest readership.”

“By all means.” Granville swiped absently at the rain dripping into his eyes, pulled his hat brim lower. “We’ll want replies to a post office box rather than our office.”

Scott thought about it for a second. “Keep this anonymous? Makes sense.”

“No point giving away our hand quite yet. What time does the afternoon mail get delivered?”

"Around four, but the earliest we can expect replies is tomorrow morning," Scott said. "The ad won't run until tonight."

"And meanwhile, we'll send a letter to Weston. That will get delivered this afternoon, am I right?"

"Yeah, so?"

"So we can see which box it gets delivered to."

"You're not thinking of robbing the post office?"

Granville hadn't been, but as a last resort, it had possibilities. "Why not?" he said with an inward grin as he watched Scott sputter.

"They'd recognize us."

"Calm down. I'm not thinking of robbing the post office. I just want to know how much mail is sitting in Weston's box, uncollected. If the box is full, Weston most likely left town in a hurry. And hasn't been back."

"Huh. That could work," Scott said.

"I thought so." Granville winked at his partner. "You post the ad. I'll write our letter to Weston. And tonight we'll visit a few poker spots, do a little listening. Weston was always a bit of a gambler."

Actually, Weston had been hopelessly enthralled by it, if even half the rumors were true.

"If we're not in jail by then," Scott said with a scowl that Granville didn't believe for a moment. "And I thought you gave up gambling—wait a minute. You know him? Weston? And you're just telling me now?"

Granville shrugged. "I know of him. The young idiot was part of a wild set at college. Got sent down from Oxford twice."

"Didn't you tell me you were sent down three times? Or was it four?" Scott said, poker-faced.

Granville ignored him.

With both Scott and their apprentice out of the office, it was quiet except for the steady pattering of rain and the scratching of

Granville's fountain pen as he dashed off a quick note to young Weston.

It was unlikely Weston would ever see it, but in case other eyes were checking the lad's mail, Granville kept the letter short. It simply asked Weston to contact them at his earliest convenience, for information to his advantage. Sealing it, he added the two-cent stamp, then clattered down the stairs and out to the post box on the corner.

That task complete, he sat down to the harder work of composing a letter to his eldest sister Louisa, now Lady Waybourne. He needed to know more about the Earl of Thanet, as well as the society gossip about the family and especially about the drowning of the previous heirs. Only one name had come to mind.

Louisa still thought very fondly of him, and her social connections were faultless. She would know all the latest *on dits* and family scandals. She was also his favorite sister, and could be counted on not to mention a word to Brother William.

It was well past noon by the time he'd finished the letter. With a little luck, Louisa's reply would come in time to do some good. In the meantime, he'd find out everything he could about Weston. Someone must know where he'd disappeared to.

Enjoyed this preview?
THE MISSING HEIR MURDERS
is available through retailers everywhere

Made in United States
North Haven, CT
12 July 2023

38841178R00193